DRAGON BLUES

OPHELIA BELL

Dragon Blues
Copyright © 2016 Ophelia Bell
Cover Art Designed by Dawné Dominique
Photograph Copyrights © Fotolio.com, DepositPhotos.com, CanStock.com

Published by Ophelia Bell
UNITED STATES

ISBN-13: 978-1540491480
ISBN-10: 154049148X

ALSO BY OPHELIA BELL

SLEEPING DRAGONS SERIES

Animus

Tabula Rasa

Gemini

Shadows

Nexus

Ascend

RISING DRAGONS SERIES

Night Fire

Breath of Destiny

Breath of Memory

Breath of Innocence

Breath of Desire

Breath of Love

Breath of Flame & Shadow

Breath of Fate

Sisters of Flame

IMMORTAL DRAGONS SERIES

Dragon Betrayed

Dragon Blues

Dragon Void

STANDALONE EROTIC TALES

After You
Out of the Cold

OPHELIA BELL TABOO

Burying His Desires

•

Blackmailing Benjamin
Betraying Benjamin
Belonging to Benjamin

•

Casey's Secrets
Casey's Discovery
Casey's Surrender

A bird in hand is worth two in the bush.

CHAPTER ONE

"You're no goddess. Goddesses don't let themselves get tied up, spread-eagle, and fucked into oblivion. Spread your pussy wider, little beast. If I can find heaven in that sweet place, maybe ... just maybe, you can be my goddess again."

Belah squirmed in her bed, her thighs clenching together while the too-real fingers in her dream teased between them. A moment later they spread her open, and the touch of a man she should hate sank into her. Nikhil's dream-touch drove her just to the edge, taunting her with crude words, reminding her with each syllable how she was his to do with as he pleased, how her orgasms were his to control.

She hovered between desire and disgust, hating herself for wanting him to find her worthy of his worship, for craving his touch and the dark freedom of the oblivion he offered.

Just when she was about to leap off that precipice into rapture, the music started. The same song had been haunting her slumber more and more frequently, and always began at the same moment in her dream of Nikhil. The beautiful notes called to her, lured her attention away until he was nothing but a mist of regret evaporating into the abyss his words had offered.

Instead of falling into the darkness with her old lover, her wings stretched wide and the music carried her higher. At the apex of her climb into the bluest sky, silken feathers caressed her skin, filling her mind with the music. In this dream, she soared and sang, the need for oblivion abandoned in favor of the attentive, winged caresses that now seemed to hold her aloft in spite of her own ability to fly.

She rarely found release in her dreams of Nikhil anymore, as though he withheld that gift from her until she submitted to him fully. She used to want what he offered, but over the years and with the knowledge of what he'd become, she was less and less inclined to take pleasure in her dreams of him.

The hands and wings that carried her into the sky in this new dream didn't ask for submission. All they seemed to care about was how to sing her to the heights of pleasure with every soft touch and urgent plunge into her. The mysterious lover in this dream never left her hanging, but ultimately, it was only a dream.

Belah woke, rising reluctantly to the surface of consciousness while clinging to the last, delicious vestiges of her new dream-lover's touch. Her body tingled and her shoulders ached pleasantly as though she'd just spent the night flying and not snuggled deep beneath the covers of her bed. She rolled over and hummed in pleasure when a similar ache twinged between her thighs. She replayed the dream in her head, working to piece together concrete images, but only able to recall impressions. Wings and music and bodies entwined. And an overwhelming sense that whoever was producing the music wanted nothing more than her happiness.

Once upon a time, Belah had wished for oblivion. Now she just wanted to go back to sleep so she could dream of flying.

"Did he come to you again, sister?" Aurum's suggestive tone reached her from across the Glade, conveying her sister's eagerness to share. Nightly visitations of the carnal variety had plagued them both ever since they'd completed the ritual with the Dragon Court to reassemble the Verdanith—the key that would allow Belah and her siblings to leave the Glade for the first time in thousands of years.

"I don't remember a man who ever made me feel so alive, so free," Belah answered, sighing at the memory.

"Did he show his face yet? Or any clue as to who he is? My dream lover is still a mystery. He smells of wild, ancient places, tastes of spring rain and flooding rivers, and he ruts like a beast, but I still have yet to see his face."

Belah flinched at the word "beast" and the pleasant sensations of her dream dissolved, replaced by the sting of old wounds, both physical and emotional. Even after three thousand years, she had trouble hearing that one, small word without being reminded of what it had once meant to her.

"I am sorry, sister," Aurum said, a wash of her guilt flooding into Belah. Belah closed her eyes and gritted her teeth. They all had their own regrets, she knew that. But Belah's was the only one that had created a monster that could destroy their race.

She forgave her sibling and rose, suddenly hating the softness of the bed. It served as a reminder of what her life had been like before she and her siblings retreated from the human world almost three thousand years ago. Most days the old mistakes were far from her mind, her old lover's atrocities becoming abstract acts of evil that bore little connection to the day-to-day reality in the Glade. Yet today she couldn't shake the memory of Nikhil's touch and the way it encroached on the more pleasant images from her second dream, reminding her how he still affected her life even after all this time.

Her life… such as it was. Days ceased to have much meaning beyond her occasional observations of the scenes that played out within the small reflecting pool in her private corner of the Glade. The world had moved on without her, but at least the dragon race still thrived despite their enemy growing ever stronger.

The Glade itself was the perfect idyllic retreat. Its deep, wide, lush valleys surrounded by cliffs were perfect for soaring through. With its temperate weather, clear skies, and steady breeze, nothing ever changed within the Glade, which made it easy for Belah to simply exist. Her old, dark cravings had all but disappeared, thanks to the reliable *sameness* in the sanctuary she shared with her siblings. Now her only urge was to eavesdrop on the human world from time to time, though the compulsion was, more often than not, related to her desire to seek out her old lover. Three thousand years should be enough to shed unwanted urges, but Belah was immortal and such deep desires weren't so easy to let go.

She left her room, heading to the reflecting pool in the garden outside, unable to stay away after the reminder of her past. Somehow she couldn't help but poke at the old wounds whenever they twinged.

Settling cross-legged on a cushion at the edge of the pool, she expelled a slow breath. The blue smoke swirled across the surface, ushering ripples toward the outer rim before settling into an opaque layer just above the water. Concentrating, she parted the smoke and peered beneath at the mirror-smooth surface and the small images that took shape.

The world moved so swiftly now that only a few minutes of watching exhausted her. Humans never stopped. But she found she could focus on the slower-moving auras of the higher races, and with a small effort, use her powers to tap into their thoughts and find links to their mutual enemy, the Ultiori.

After a few minutes, her head ached, and all she'd learned was that the higher races were finally aware of the latest dragon Ascension. The Ultiori were relatively quiet. She buried her head in her hands and groaned.

"You won't find him."

Belah's head shot up. She stared across the pool at her dark-haired brother, Ked, and scowled. "What makes you think I'm looking for him?"

"You always do. Whether it's because you still love him, or because you know he's the key to finding *them*, I don't know. I think it might be a little of both."

She stared at the pool again, her gaze unfocused while the old conflict twisted in her gut. Her old lover, Nikhil—now the leader of their race's most brutally powerful enemy—had somehow managed to locate a pair of treasures Belah herself had no access to. Treasures that were more dear to her than her own life. Her own son and daughter had been his prisoners for the last three thousand years and had yet to be located, in spite of constant searching.

"There has to be another way to find them. If I can just figure it out, we can kill him and be done with it."

Ked sat down on the other side of the small pool, resting his forearms atop his knees.

"I don't believe killing him is really what you want, either," he said.

Belah wanted to argue. She wanted to lash out the way she'd done countless times since that day three thousand years ago when their entire world had changed.

When she'd closed her eyes on her wedding night, Nikhil had been her lover, her husband. But upon waking, he was their enemy. His singular goal had shifted from her pleasure to capturing her kind, and any other higher-blooded creature who happened to get in the way of his search for her. At first he only killed, but for the last several centuries, he'd started taking captives and experimenting on them. Few ever escaped, but the ones that did always expressed how they wished for death while they were in his clutches.

As hard as it was for Belah to believe Nikhil had become that monster, she had seen enough evidence of his atrocities to break her heart ten times over. Since then, she'd spent hundreds of years alternately blaming her brother for taking her away and thanking him for the same. She had no blame left for anyone now, not even herself. What she wanted was to simply find her children.

"He fed the darkest parts of me. I know now that it was my own fault for allowing it—I indulged in him like he was a drug, and I fostered that darkness in him just as much. But after everything he has done, how can there be anything human left of him? I was a fool to think he could be empowered to survive being my mate…"

"We all wanted it to work," Ked said. "Otherwise none of us would have agreed to the wedding in the first place. None of the races are exempt from that burden—we all had a hand in making him. We all wanted our combined magic to mean we could have human mates strong enough to withstand the power of immortal love."

He was humoring her, she knew. He'd been doing it forever… validating her mistakes. She hated when he did that. None of the others treated her that way. She'd done this. She could own the consequences.

"And we made a monster who can't be stopped! For all we know, he's already picked up on the influx of magic into the world, now that the Verdanith is whole again. It could lead him straight to the Glade. If he shows up on our doorstep, I'll have no choice but to kill him, and you know this!"

Belah hated how frantic her tone had become. Only a few weeks had passed since they'd agreed with the Dragon Court to reassemble the Verdanith. The magical keystone that held open the door to the Glade had been in pieces for the last three thousand years. Breaking it had been required to protect their race, but it had effectively trapped Belah and her siblings inside their magic-infused sanctuary. Meanwhile, each piece of the Verdanith itself never stayed in one place for very long, a failsafe that ensured their enemy couldn't easily pinpoint the source of the dragons' power.

The recently ascended Dragon Court had argued that with the new generation, they needed to increase their numbers more than ever before, and the only way to do that would be to make the Verdanith whole again and let the magic flow freely. Belah and the others had agreed, knowing their enemy's focus had long ago shifted away from the hunt for the power source, but it was only a matter of time before the Ultiori caught wind that things had changed.

"We're connected to the world again for the first time in ages, Sister." Ked tapped at the surface of the reflecting pool, sending ripples across to her side and distorting the images from the human world. "And the power flows both ways now. You've had the dreams as well, haven't you?"

Belah shook her head, prepared to deny anything of the sort. The dreams were her private escape, her secret indulgence, and they harmed no one. She'd long ago given up on the idea that she would ever have another lover, much less a mate. The dreams were all she had left.

A shadow passed over the reflecting pool, and before her eyes the surface shimmered, then coalesced into an image. Her breath caught in her throat as her secret, unconscious wish took shape. The bodies weren't identifiable, but one was undeniably female and writhed in ecstasy surrounded by a shining blue aura. Glowing, feathered wings fluttered around and around the female shape in soundless rhythm. The image was silent, but Belah could hear the music that accompanied it in her mind, and though the image on the water failed to convey the erotic nature of the union, she felt it again deep in her core.

8

"Ked… this isn't fair."

"Just watch."

The image faded away and a new one took shape, similarly framed with feathered wings, but this time the central figure was male and shrouded in shadow, and the feathered shape was decidedly female.

Belah's gaze shot to her brother, but he was engrossed in watching the image play out. She let her eyes fall back to the water and she watched, enraptured by this secret her brother had chosen to show her. Had he been dreaming of a turul female all this time while Belah dreamed of a turul male?

"Do you hear music when you dream of her?" she asked softly. A turul's music was known to reveal the truth in anything. If the dream magic were real, they had to believe what the songs from their sister race of falcon shifters told them. The magic of the Four Winds the turul worshipped may be at work if she and her siblings were all having similar dreams.

"The sweetest thing I've ever heard," he said with a sad smile. "There's so much pain in her songs, though. I ache to comfort her."

The rough, deep rhythm of Belah's dreams sounded both anguished and deeply sexual, and resonated deep in her soul. She yearned for that male so strongly—if only he could be more than just a fantasy.

Belah caught movement in her periphery and watched as their other four siblings joined them and settled around the pool. After a moment, Ked's dream disappeared and Aurum's golden breath drifted over the surface. When the cloud parted, Belah observed a visual that closely resembled her sister's descriptions of her own dream. After that, the others shared their dreams one by one, and the true meaning of Belah's dream became clear to her.

Each of their dreams depicted one of their sister races as the lover—for herself and Ked, it had shown the feathered wings of turul lovers, and for the others, she'd observed the ursa and nymphaea. The revelation that they should interbreed with the other higher races went against everything Belah had believed, but could never wholly come to terms with. The four higher races each had different laws where breeding was concerned, but while they occasionally had sexual dalliances with one another, one law they all had in common was that they should not mate each other or produce offspring.

The dragons were the only race bound by their own law to only breed with humans. There had been only the six immortal siblings born, and so their Mother and Fate encouraged Belah and her brothers and sisters to take many mates among the primitive, yet plentiful mortal race that walked the earth at the beginning of time. They should not dally with each other. Mingling their magic would result in undesirable consequences. Specifically, an offspring conceived of two immortals would upset the fragile balance of magic in the world. Human genetics were simpler and would allow the dragon's magic to prevail, producing as pure-blooded a dragon as possible with the dragon parent's magic undiluted by any other magic.

Four of the six siblings had obeyed, knowing the risks were too great not to. But humans were too simple for Belah—too fragile for the blue dragon who wished for a mate strong enough to be her equal, not one that would be reduced to insanity the second she chose to mark him. She convinced her brother to disobey, and they had come together out of frustrated need to connect on a deeper level with someone less filthy and primitive, less prone to breaking. Belah would forever regret that mistake.

The son Belah had borne to her brother had been taken from her at birth and hidden away. Even though her old lover, Nikhil, had been human, her unorthodox marriage to him was similarly rejected by their Mother, and the daughter Belah had given birth to taken from her as well.

Any other dragon who risked breaking the laws would wind up standing trial before Belah and her siblings—together, they made up the long-feared Dragon Council—and if found guilty, would be compelled to submit and become the sexual playthings for one or more of the six immortal siblings until their sentence was complete. On the surface this sounded like a blessing, but in reality, the dragon forced to submit would be rendered incapable of finding pleasure with their mate and would complete their sentence with little sexual desire for some time.

When Belah or her siblings broke laws, they had an even greater power to answer to, and their Mother and Fate could be very unforgiving. Belah had let her dark cravings lead her astray, had wed a man who should not have been hers, and had allowed him to violate her body and shed her blood for the sake of her own pleasure, and his.

Her daughter had been taken while Belah lay unconscious after surviving Nikhil's brutal attention on their wedding night. It didn't matter to her Mother that she had begged him to do what he had done.

What mattered was what Nikhil had become. And now both Belah's children were at the mercy of their worst enemy.

Were these dreams Fate's message that those unions would finally be sanctioned by their gods? The Dragon Council itself had agreed to allow dragon pairs to mate each other without fear of punishment. There was ample magic in the world now that it would take more than a few creatures of their power interbreeding to upset things. If the higher races could now mate with each other as well, that changed every precedent.

When Belah's pool lay placid, the six siblings looked around at each other.

"We aren't going to find them sitting in here," Belah's red-haired brother, Gavra, said, stabbing his finger at the pool. "My true mate is somewhere out there, and for the first time in my entire life, I feel confident I won't drive her crazy by marking her."

"Any female who tolerates you is already insane," Aurum said, earning herself a splash of water that made her laugh.

"Why now?" Belah asked. "After all we've been through, why weren't we shown these visions *before* we locked ourselves away? Why couldn't we have interbred with the other races ages ago? So much pain could have been avoided!" She caught the slightest wince cross Ked's features and regretted her words, despite how true they were. If they'd had the freedom to couple with the turul at the beginning, rather than the dirty, primitive humans who walked the Earth, she and Ked would never have done what they did.

Aodh nodded his white-haired head. "True. And yet Fate allowed everything that came to pass. We are different creatures than we were three thousand years ago. The world is a different place, and our entire race has very different priorities now. Your faction was on the verge of civil war with Gavra's before your wedding ritual, sister. We were well on our way to killing each other."

"So we allowed our enemy to do it for us? How does that make any sense?"

Ever the most patient sibling among the six, Aodh, simply dipped his head. He exhaled, and his white smoke covered the pool for the second time. When it parted, Belah was shown a revolving view of the entire planet. At first, she recognized the concentration of dragon populations that she recalled from her height as Pharaoh of Egypt. Colorful, glowing clouds swirled around, highlighting each of their six Ascendancies. The clouds clashed and merged together, the sizes of each fluctuating wildly, then shrinking little by little until they were a fraction of what they'd been.

Abruptly, the clouds separated and remained static for several moments, as though time had stopped, yet the globe kept spinning. Soon the colored clouds shrunk by half in the blink of an eye, but every few revolutions of the globe, they'd double in size, then triple, before shrinking again, but never as much as they had grown. The cycle repeated over and over—grow, grow, shrink—and never again did the colored clouds clash.

"The enemy only succeeded in preventing us from growing our numbers, at first. But before the Ultiori existed, we were in true peril of rendering ourselves practically extinct. Without the threat of death from some force outside ourselves, we would not have grown so strong. Now it is finally our turn as the leaders of our race to ensure the race thrives. None of us had the freedom to truly love before, and now we finally do. We've been shown how to keep that love, too."

Belah met her brother's eyes, acutely aware of the excitement Aodh held in check. He had his own dark secrets and had long since been forgiven for them, but like the rest of the family, he still longed for lasting love.

Glancing around at them, Belah realized how much they had all given up—entire kingdoms left to the control of their descendants while the six of them locked themselves away, all to control the flow of magic to the rest of the race. Their sacrifice for the last three thousand years had ensured there was never a clear trail of magic that could lead the Ultiori to any of the six power centers of the dragon Ascendancies. They'd given up the love of their human subjects to hide in the Glade while their race took care of itself.

Now their dreams promised something even greater than what they'd had before. None of them had ever found lasting love, even in the thousands of years before Belah's tragic miscalculation of her own feelings. They'd only ever had each other, and Belah and Ked were the prime example of why that was never going to be enough.

"But we can't leave the Glade unprotected…" she protested. The newfound freedom they possessed was almost unfathomable. The very idea of leaving the comfort and security she'd come to rely on for so long was understandably terrifying. But it shouldn't border on paralyzing her… which was exactly what it was threatening to do.

"We won't," Ked said. "Only one of us will go at a time. The rest will remain behind until we're certain the Ultiori aren't seeking out the path to the entrance."

Belah breathed a slow sigh of relief, but the feeling was short-lived when she became aware of all her siblings' eyes on her. The back of her neck prickled with realization.

"No," she said, her voice quavering. "I can't be the first to go. It shouldn't be me!"

Ked gave her an understanding look. "It has to be you, Belah, and you know why."

Belah closed her eyes and grimaced. Her brother was right. If the Ultiori—if *Nikhil*—had discovered the shift in the flow of magic, only one thing would distract him from following it into the Glade itself. Over the centuries, he had never wavered in his craving for human women who resembled her, nor for female blue dragons. Her presence in the world would be the best deterrent to keep him away from the Glade and the source of their magic. But perhaps this was a blessing in disguise.

She opened her eyes again and fixed her gaze on Ked. "Fine, but if I do this, I am going to do whatever it takes to learn where Nikhil is keeping my babies. The turul mate I dreamed about won't mean a damn thing if I can't get our children back."

Deep in her belly, her old craving reared its head. The beast that slept inside her had lain dormant for centuries, but the prospect of contact with the one man who had fed that craving roused it from slumber. A wave of nausea overtook her and she buried her head in her hands. No, she couldn't let him have that kind of power over her again. If there was one thing her winged dream-lover had made her realize, it was that true love was coupled with joy, not oblivion.

She knew she would need to find *him*, too, if she were going to be able to endure a meeting with Nikhil. Because without the armor of the turul's love, she would be powerless to resist the lure of that old addiction.

CHAPTER TWO

"What's your type?" Erika asked.

The human woman stood on the other side of the bar counter Belah was seated at, chopping vegetables while her dragon mate stirred something aromatic in a pot. Geva's muscular forearms flexed as he tilted the pot for Erika to toss more ingredients into it. Then he set the pot back on the burner and adjusted the heat, covering it with a lid before he moved to the side and went to work, delicately filleting the fresh fish they'd picked up at the market earlier in the day.

Belah was mesmerized by the way he held the meat, the strength in his hands such a contradiction to how adeptly he handled the fragile flesh.

Erika laughed and waved a hand in front of Belah's face. "Yes, his hands are just as good at whatever you were imagining as they are at cooking, but they're mine."

Belah forced herself to focus on the woman's words rather than the novelty of the experience of watching a Court dragon cook for her. When she glanced up, she caught Geva and Erika sharing a secretive look, one she read easily as an agreement to make sure Belah was kept satisfied, regardless of how successful they were at tracking down a turul mate for her.

"My type? I don't know what you mean," Belah said.

"I mean, do you like your men clean-cut or rough around the edges? Conservative or adventurous? Tall or short? Dark-haired or blond?"

"Or redheads?" Geva offered, smirking as he placed the large, well-seasoned fish into a pan and slid it into the oven. His eyes twinkled and Belah was blessed with a flash of his thoughts—an image reminding her of the day when Geva and the First Shadow, Kol, attended her for a short time with their mouths and their glorious tongues, but there hadn't been time for much more than that.

"Babe, you are off-limits," Erika said, eyeing her mate. "I don't care how important she is. No offense, Bel."

Belah laughed at their banter. "None taken. But I don't think I can afford to be picky, can I? Turul are known for having mates they are fated for from birth. That means there is likely only one male out of all of them who is the one Fate intends for me to mate."

Erika frowned. "Is that so? I don't suppose there's a magical races matchmaking website you can sign up on, is there? 'Single Blue female seeks fated turul mate. Loves sunset flights over the beach, expensive gifts, and orgies in the park.'"

Belah raised both eyebrows. "What have you guys heard about my past?"

"The preferences of the immortals are legendary," Geva said. "You six set the precedent for the rest of us, which we followed for centuries. Taking multiple human mates was how we broadcast our wealth. It's only been the last two generations that scaled back. We do still love our orgies, though—that, at least, is not likely to change."

"I heard you had a harem before," Erika said, leaning on her elbows and looking at Belah expectantly. "What was that like?"

"It was a necessity," Belah said with a shrug and followed the pair of them to the dining table, where Geva began serving the salad. While it wasn't unusual for a lower-ranking dragon to serve an immortal in this fashion, she had expected one as high in rank as Geva to have human servants. Somehow the intimacy of the dinner was comforting, though, and she found herself relaxing and enjoying the company. It allowed her to feel normal for a change, as though she belonged in their world and the burdens of her former life were far, far behind her.

"Well, I know that," Erika said. "Geva enjoys reminding me when he's low on energy. But didn't you ever play with your pets for fun? Let yourself indulge every once in a while just because it felt good?"

Belah smiled to herself at the memories of how often she had done just that, though it had been a rare occurrence. She'd avoided creating bonds with the humans who were only intended as sources for the sexual energy she subsisted on. The times she had indulged for her own pleasure were the most memorable for both her and her pets, she was certain.

A darker memory seeped into her reverie—one that involved Nikhil directing her harem in an orgy that rivaled any other she'd experienced—and she shut down the thought before it could ruin her contentment.

"I haven't indulged purely for pleasure in so long, I'm not sure I remember how to," she finally said.

"I'm sure it's like riding a bike." Erika patted her arm. "If you need a little push, we can help."

Geva paused in the process of refilling their wine and stared down at his mate. Belah glanced between them, amused by the red dragon's surprise.

"What?" Erika asked, looking innocently up at him. "The poor woman hasn't gotten properly laid in... how long?" She looked at Belah for confirmation. "Three thousand years?"

Belah nodded.

Geva's brows creased as he returned to the kitchen to collect the main course and brought it back. "My love, you seemed determined a moment ago not to share even what my *hands* can do."

"Oh, I plan to keep you for myself. That doesn't mean Belah can't indulge with *me* if she wants. I'm definitely willing."

Geva sat with a somewhat playful scowl and began dishing food out onto their plates.

"See how infuriating it is to have a human mate with a mind of her own, Belah? You and the rest of the Council were lucky not to have to deal with mates at all for so long. Are you sure you want to try again now?"

A wave of sadness overtook Belah and she reached for her wine in an attempt to disguise her frown. After a hard swallow, she plastered on a smile, but Geva's look told her he'd seen through her already.

"My life isn't what you thought it was," she said, too weary from her journey to elaborate. She was hungry in too many ways and reached for her fork, digging into the fragrant meat on her plate. While she ate, she watched the pair across from her and regretted that she would have to refuse Erika's invitation. The young human's aura glowed with the vibrant energy of a pregnant female. Glancing between the couple, she doubted that they even realized it yet. Erika's status meant that Belah could give to them, but shouldn't take any of their offered energy for herself—not when there was an unborn child who needed it far more than she did.

Her mood lifted at the prospect, the idea of new motherhood for this young woman causing a sense of well-being to swell inside her. Smiling to herself, she let her worries go for the moment and dug into her food, choosing to imagine what color dragon the pair might produce, and what kind of wonders the child would discover in its life. Even though Belah's trip was the beginning of another chance for her to experience the same thing, it didn't hold the same sense of glorious possibility for her.

As long as two of her cherished children were being held captive by the Ultiori, she would never be fully content in her own life, even if she did find a new mate and conceive a child with him. It seemed ridiculous to even go through the motions of mating again without knowing where her son and daughter were. All she knew was that they'd been put into hibernation somewhere safe—yet the enemy had found them with the aid of a pair of Blessed twins who had been corrupted into becoming Ultiori Elites. That knowledge broke Belah's heart, because she knew those twins. She was the dragon who had bestowed their blessing when they were still inside their mother's womb. That day had been the day she'd agreed to wed Nikhil—which had become the biggest mistake of her life.

She forced her attention back to the table and her two hosts. The contentment and love that brightened Erika and Geva's auras was as cleansing as a cool breeze to her own state of mind, and she took a deep breath as though she could inhale their emotions. She should at least try to enjoy this experience while she could. Perhaps she really would find love again.

Quietly, she rose from her seat and began clearing dishes.

"Please, no. Let me take care of this!" Geva said, rising abruptly.

Belah waved a hand dismissively and he sat again, as though he'd been pushed by some invisible force. He let out a little "oof" sound and the chair creaked under his sturdy weight.

Belah grimaced. "I'm sorry. I haven't used my powers in such a long time, I'm out of practice. You two are my hosts while I'm here. It would make me feel better if you let me at least try being human. Don't coddle me, please."

Erika eyed Geva, who frowned but didn't move, and looked back at Belah. "Be my guest. The trash is under the sink and there's dish soap down there, too—it's in a green bottle. Geva thinks we need a housekeeper, but they just get in the way."

Erika cast her gaze playfully to her mate's, and Belah was amused to see Geva relax and a slight redness creep into his cheeks. A woman who could make a Red dragon blush was a very special being, indeed. She glanced around at the open layout of their high-rise apartment, imagining the pair of them entwined on every surface.

The images shifted in her mind as she rinsed and stacked the dishes, then began to load the washer. Instead of her hosts' bodies merged in lovemaking, the images from her dreams filled her mind. She worked mindlessly, allowing the feelings to wash through her as the hot water flowed over her hands in the sink and the music from her dreams flooded her memory.

She began humming along to the secret song when Erika's surprised laugh hit her ears and made her stop and look up.

"How in the world do you know this song?" Erika asked. Belah looked at her, confused for a second before she realized the music was no longer only in her head, but reverberated through the entire apartment, filling the air around her with enough potency to make the small hairs stand up on her arms.

"I dreamed of it," Belah answered.

She moved to stand in front of the small, black box that was the source of the music and closed her eyes. "Where did you find it?" she finally asked when the song ended and she opened her eyes to see both her hosts staring at her.

"Find it?" Erika asked. "I didn't find it… I know these guys. They're old friends I met when I was an undergrad. I'd always come to the city when classes weren't in session. After Dad died, I hated going back to that big, empty house in Massachusetts. At least in New York I knew I could be alone without *really* being alone."

Beside Erika, Geva had picked up an illustrated case that displayed an image of three pairs of wings spread out and arranged in a triangle. Looking over his shoulder, Belah could make out the words "Fate's Fools" written in the center.

"You say you know these musicians?" Geva asked, eyebrows raised.

Erika lifted one shoulder in a half-shrug and gave her mate a teasing smile. "I was groupie number one back in the day. They're phenomenal live. That's actually a bootleg one of their fans put together—they've never signed with a label, as far as I know, but they still play in the city regularly. If you guys like the music, we should go check them out. I bet they still play at the same bars. Guys like them hate change and tend to stick around."

Geva's shoulders shook with a low laugh. "My sweet love, I think you've given us the best clue to start our hunt for Belah's mate. These musicians are turul."

"What the fuck?" Erika grabbed the case from Geva's hands and stared at it.

"What is it?" Belah asked, reaching for the case. Erika let it go with an irritated sound and walked away.

"Holy fucking *Christ*, why can't anything I ever loved *not* be connected to you guys? Now my favorite band of all time has to be, too?"

"Your favorite band?" Belah asked. Before she could rein it in, her power pulled Erika back. She struggled for a second to release the woman from the snare of her mind, but Erika was already facing her when she finally let it go.

"Belah... you have something you want to share with us?" Erika said in a sultry tone, her breath brushing against Belah's cheek. Belah clenched her eyes shut.

"I'm sorry. I didn't mean to. I shouldn't have, especially not you."

"Especially not me? Oh, honey, Geva really doesn't mind if we get cozy. As long as you don't mind if he joins in when I need him. We're trying to have a baby, you know."

"That's why I can't," Belah said, forcing herself to restrain her powers and resting her hands on Erika's shoulders. She exhaled softly through her nose and met Erika's gaze. At the last second, she forced a smile on her face that she hoped would seem genuine.

"Congratulations, Erika. You're about to become a mother."

CHAPTER THREE

Erika dropped her hands to her belly and stared down at them, dumbfounded. Behind her, Geva slowly set down the music case and stared at Belah.

"A baby? She's really…" His words caught in his throat and he moved toward them.

"Yes," Belah said. "I can see it in her aura. There's no mistaking the fertile glow of a new mother. So as much as I appreciate the offer, you know I can't accept your Nirvana. Your baby needs it."

Erika turned and looked up at her mate. "It happened," she whispered, then grinned through burgeoning tears.

"It did," he said softly. "Oh, my love." His words cut off in his throat as he swept her up in his arms and squeezed her tight.

Belah beamed at them, happier than she'd been since ancient history. And even though she was hungry for magic now that she was outside of the Glade—with its perpetual source of power and the regular visits from the Catalyst to attend them— she knew she could wait a little longer.

Geva and Erika retreated to their bedroom. Only moments later, the energy of the entire apartment shimmered with the power of their lovemaking.

Belah examined the music player and finally worked out how to set the music to play on a continuous loop, then sat on her hosts' sofa and closed her eyes while the beautiful melodies washed over her.

She spent the night letting the music fill her and trying to picture the turul male who would soon become her mate. She still could only envision bits and pieces—the silken caress of feathers a contrast to the callused fingertips that brushed over her skin. Sometimes it seemed like he had an extra pair of hands that only managed to increase her desire for him.

If only she could let herself forget about the greater desire to seek out Nikhil now. She eventually opened her eyes and stared out the high windows into the twinkling lights of the city. How far away was he now? She could fly away and seek him out, but her energy was low and she had no idea where to look.

Over the last few centuries, Nikhil had been increasingly difficult to locate through her reflecting pool, to the point that he'd eventually gone entirely dark. Even though she knew almost every location of the numerous Ultiori compounds, she never caught a glimpse of his aura at any of them. And when she did see brief glimmers of him, they only lasted for fleeting moments before he disappeared again, as though some dark veil blotted out his existence.

A small part of her believed that she didn't need to seek him out, but perhaps that was only wishful thinking. He had loved her in his way, though at the end, the darkness must have taken over his mind. She'd loved that part of him—the sadistic nature that gave her so much pleasure leading up to their wedding night.

She still remembered his missive to her that night—that he would do that one thing for her, but to never ask it of him again. He would deliver her into that perfect oblivion just once in the manner she had asked for it, because he loved her and would have conquered the world for her glory. Had it been a cry for help that she'd ignored? She spent the last three thousand years asking herself that question. If she hadn't asked for that final gift from him, would the darkness have ever fully taken over? Could he have been redeemed at all?

Could he be redeemed now?

The question haunted her. She'd had no contact with him in all this time, but she'd seen the devastation he had wrought upon the dragons and the other higher races. He was as brutal and meticulous a foe to them as he'd ever been to her enemies when he was her commander. She only fleetingly craved his touch— the bite of his whip or the cut of his blade—now that their love had been revealed for what it really was.

Thanks to the clarity of hindsight, Belah had realized the truth was not as romantic as she'd believed. She had been broken when she found him, still longing for the lost child that had been taken from her. Nikhil had been physically destroyed and near death. The pair of them had filled a void in each other. Or maybe they had recognized a kindred emptiness they both possessed, and had reveled in the realization that they weren't alone in their cravings for oblivion and pain—his craving to give, and hers to receive.

It was love, to a point, but she knew now that it was built on a damaged foundation that would have inevitably crumbled. And it had, in the end. The atrocities he'd perpetuated on them since losing her were not acts of love.

In his absence, she had taken stock of her own role in making him what he was. But in the end, she had to admit to herself that it wasn't love that drove her desire to find him, but the knowledge that her children were out there somewhere. That he had found them meant they were within her grasp for the first time since losing them. Her craving for oblivion had all but disappeared the moment she learned of their presence, and even though she still had no idea where they were, for the first time since losing Zorion and Asha, she had hope of being reunited with them, and Nikhil was the key to that reunion.

If he had ever loved her, she believed he would find her. And so she would let Fate dictate her path yet again. Even though she cursed that timeless creature daily, she knew balance must be kept, and Fate never failed to make that clear.

At least she had her dreams, for now … and if the music was to be believed, she would have more than dreams soon enough.

⁓⋇⁓

Unable to fully sleep, Belah rose when the first glimmers of sunlight touched the walls of the apartment. She poked her head into the fridge and the cabinets, examining all the foodstuffs her hosts had in stock. One of the human pleasures she'd nearly forgotten about was the food—something she and her siblings hadn't required while living in the Glade. But her craving for it had come back with a vengeance, and along with it, the vivid memories of her favorite dishes.

Geva and Erika lacked a few key ingredients, but she could make do with what they had.

By the time her hosts came padding out of their bedroom, she had the table covered in food and fresh juice. They dug in amid murmured compliments and gratitude. Belah simply ate and enjoyed their company, letting the little pang of envy she felt for Erika's healthy maternal glow settle in her belly. If she succeeded with her goals while she was here, she would have an abundance of wealth at the end. She would have both her lost children back and a new one growing inside her, too.

"Geva," she finally said when the handsome Red sat back with a sated sigh. "You said you had a clue where to start looking for a turul mate. Was it the music that told you?"

"Sort of…" he began. "The band itself is turul, we know this much, but Erika isn't sure those males are good candidates for you."

Belah raised an eyebrow at Erika.

"They're musicians," Erika said with a shrug. "I mean … you're practically a goddess. I envision someone a little more … refined … for you. But what do I know? Maybe you like them rough around the edges like that."

Geva chuckled. "I tried to tell her that turul aren't exactly the most refined in general, and most of them are musicians as it is."

"They're phenomenal lovers, at least. Well, Ozzie is, anyway. I don't know about Iszak or Lukas."

"Ozzie?" Belah asked.

"Oszkar West. He's the drummer in the band. Iszak and Lukas North are the two sax players. Ozzie's their cousin, I think."

"I'd like to meet them," Belah said. "Even if neither of them are the right turul, they make beautiful music. Judging by their names, they're descended directly from the Winds."

"Well, that's where the clue comes in," Geva said. "Their grandmother is a turul seeress. She poses as a psychic and a matchmaker for the locals. The humans love her, but more importantly, she's been around forever."

"He just means she's older than him," Erika interjected. "How old did you say she was?"

"Sophia North's almost two thousand years old. I remember hearing about her before my hibernation. She knows everyone—I'm not even exaggerating. She's a little scary, though, as old as she is."

"I'm probably a little scarier, given my history," Belah said. The pair went silent for a beat and Belah regretted trying to make light of the truth.

"We all have regrets," Erika said. She set her hazel-eyed gaze directly on Belah, the force of it imbued with enough meaning that Belah couldn't help but wonder what the woman had experienced in her short life to have become so wise.

"Mine are somewhat epic, though, wouldn't you say?"

"This is your chance to change that. Tell us what you want, Belah," Geva said. "We are your servants."

"That's what I *don't* want. Being my servants is a risk. I'll accept your help, but please consider me an equal while I'm here."

"I guess that means you're doing the dishes again?" Erika said with a grin.

"It would be my pleasure," Belah replied.

⁓

A few hours after a short subway ride and then a trip on a ferry, they reached a quaint apartment that had a locked door and a buzzer outside. Several names were listed next to a row of buttons, but the word "North" stood out. The name glowed with an intriguing hint of old, lingering magic. It had been there for ages, yet hadn't faded.

Geva pressed the button and the speaker next to it crackled to life. He spoke a swift greeting in old draconic that surprised Belah, considering how young he was.

Geva caught her surprised look and shrugged. "My mother was the queen. I had to learn all that shit. Never knew why it was worth the bother at the time."

The door buzzed open and they entered, then walked several floors up a dark, narrow staircase. The door at the top landing was open, but they paused at the threshold. Geva peered through, then called out.

"Hello? Mrs. North?"

A smooth, feminine voice called out from somewhere inside over the faint rhythm of music. "Send in the beast herself. Alone. She's the one with the quest."

All Belah could see was a wall of high windows, the sunlight streaming through them. It illuminated a dense collection of objects that were painstakingly organized on shelves and small tables throughout a comfortably furnished room.

Layers of colorful rugs covered the floor so no wood was visible beneath, and the furniture was old and well-worn, yet still sturdy. It had the feeling of a large nest, the way the sofas were arranged, with a large hassock in the center and several books strewn about, as well as musical instruments leaning here and there—a guitar against the fireplace, a saxophone in the corner, an oboe on the mantelpiece. Beneath the high window, the sunbeams glinted off the polished ebony surface of a baby grand piano.

Steeling herself for a confrontation she shouldn't have been anxious about, Belah stepped into the apartment.

The air seemed to shift around her in a disconcerting way. She tried to ignore it, making her way into the living room and standing by the fireplace, taking in the myriad framed photos that were leaning here and there, and covering the walls on either side of the chimney.

Most photos featured a trio—two men and a woman who resembled each other so closely they must have been siblings. In several photos, there was a fourth figure—a handsome male who looked nothing like the others, but who often seemed joined at the hip to the female.

Something in the man's bearing struck a chord with her. A glimmer of his aura was visible in the photo, and its familiarity betrayed the fact that he was Blessed. But why would he be with a turul, if that was the case? Blessed humans were meant to be mated to dragons.

"Fate's a devious bitch," said a voice from behind her.

Belah spun around and stumbled back, shocked at the sight before her. Where the over-stuffed furniture and knickknack-laden shelves and tables had been was nothing but a bare cliff-top opening up to a wide, empty sky. At the edge stood a statuesque woman with dark, slanted eyes and jet black hair cascading over her shoulders. Her olive skin glowed with power.

Regaining her bearings, Belah said, "Sophia North… I've heard so many things…"

The woman waved her hand in the air. "I know why you're here, girl. I've been waiting for the moment to tell you what I really think of you." Sophia's gaze traveled down the length of Belah's body. After a moment, she simply sniffed dismissively. "I suppose you'll do. But I warn you: what you want must be earned. I'm not about to hand you the answer."

"What I want…?"

Sophia studied her for a moment, and Belah was sure the woman could see deep into her soul to every dark secret she held within. All her desires must have been on display, the way the woman's gaze seemed to strip her down to the bone. She'd never felt so naked before.

"Your dreams, girl. The children you desire won't come unless you work for it."

"What do I need to do?" Belah said, straightening her spine and meeting Sophia's hard stare.

"You need to stop accepting the hand Fate has dealt you, sister. Nothing worth treasuring ever came to us without a fight."

"I just want my babies back." Belah struggled to keep her voice steady, and even though she knew she was here for another reason, she felt compelled to share this desire with the woman who stood across from her.

Sophia's gaze softened. "Theirs is not the only love you want returned to you. But they are safe and will come to you in time. Focus on your dreams, but don't ignore the signs that you find in the darkness."

Frustrated by the woman's cryptic dialog, Belah crossed her arms. "Fine, but you're also supposed to help me find a turul mate. Can you at least do that?"

With a loud *pop* the open sky and cliff disappeared, and Belah found herself back in the over-decorated living room with the sweet strains of beautiful music filling her ears again.

"Oh, sure. Honey, what you want to do is go to this address at seven o'clock tonight. Tell the maître'd you're with the West party and he'll seat you." Sophia hurriedly scribbled something on a piece of paper and handed it to Belah. "You'll enjoy the food—it's dragon-style gourmet. Delicious, but a little too rich for my blood."

Belah stared down at the writing, almost dizzy from the abrupt shift in the turul woman's behavior. That was it?

"That's all I have for you," Sophia said. "Unless you want to tell your friends it's a girl, but I'll leave that up to you." She ushered Belah back toward the doorway where Geva and Erika were seated on the top step, with Erika leaning on one wall and Geva on the opposite. Erika's bare foot was in Geva's lap and he was slowly massaging her instep while her eyelids fluttered in contentment.

When Belah appeared, Erika opened her eyes and smiled up at her.

"If I'd known how much more attentive dragons were for their pregnant mates, I'd have made sure he knocked me up sooner."

CHAPTER FOUR

Going on a "date," as Erika called it, was quite a production. The other female fussed over Belah's attire, hair, and makeup, her attention reminding Belah of her time as Empress in Egypt and the way her slaves had flitted around her every day. Finally, with Erika's approval, they left the apartment and climbed into a sleek, black car that drove them to another part of the city.

The restaurant itself was barely noticeable, except for the strong aromas of delicious food wafting up from a grate in the sidewalk. She felt overdressed when they descended the steps to what seemed to be a basement beneath a tall building, but once inside, she understood why she was dressed the way she was.

A pair of Shadows flanked the entry, a subtle reminder of the pair of black dragons who were tasked with unobtrusively ensuring her safety, and who were somewhere nearby now, watching over her. Inside, the restaurant was decorated with the richest décor she'd seen since her own dining hall at her palace. The room was filled with members of the higher races—dragons and turul, mostly, but here and there she caught sight of an ursa or a nymph.

She followed Sophia North's instructions when she spoke to the maître'd. He nodded and instructed a hostess to lead her deeper into the restaurant while Erika and Geva requested a separate table.

Uncertain of what to expect, Belah sat silently at the table and stared at the empty chair across from her. At some point, a waitress set a goblet of red wine in front of her and another at the empty setting.

Would whoever sat there be the one? She heard the music in her head as clear as the melody that played over the restaurant's sound system, though it paled in comparison to what she'd heard from the turul band Erika shared with her.

A moment later, she heard footsteps from behind and turned to see a striking man with thick, blond hair that brushed his collar, and sky-blue eyes that settled on her intently.

He gave her a forced smile and paused at her seat. "You must be Belah. My grandmother said you were beautiful. I didn't expect a woman inspiring enough to stand in as a muse, though."

"Thank you," she said, trying to hide her confusion at his hidden disappointment. She could tell he had expected something different, but he was being polite in spite of it.

He covered his reaction with an appreciative sweep of his gaze down her body when she rose to greet him, then took her hands warmly in his and bent to kiss her knuckles. The slight breath he released made her skin tingle, and she couldn't suppress the shimmer of blue scales that erupted faintly beneath the surface. Her date's eyes widened and he smiled.

"Oszkar West, at your service," he said, straightening up with a twinkle in his eyes. "But you can call me Ozzie." A slight hint of rough, rumbling accent bled through what she sensed was a poor attempt at appearing more refined than he was. His appearance made similar surface pretenses—he wore a suit of fine fabric, but his golden hair was long and slightly unkempt, and his cheeks were covered with a day's growth of matching scruff that accented otherwise clean, sharp features.

"Belah," she said simply.

They both sat and regarded each other while she took a sip of her wine. Any trace of his disappointment was long gone—now the filmy cloud of his aura crackled with silvery bolts of light, signaling his excitement.

"I like that you don't bother with the formality of a surname. I always wondered why dragons took human names. Names like 'Smith' and 'Jones' never fit."

"Humans used to take their names from us, you know. How many human 'Wests' are out there, do you think? Yet here you are, one of the direct descendants of Zephyrus. I'm curious, Ozzie, how many generations removed *are* you?"

He gave her a secretive smile as he summoned the waitress.

"Have you ever eaten here before?"

"Never," Belah said. This restaurant hadn't even existed the last time she'd set foot outside the Glade. *Most* restaurants hadn't existed then.

"Then would you mind if I order for us both? If you're as hungry as you look—" He glanced down at the hand that had betrayed her need for energy. "—then you're going to need the full set of courses. Trust me, the food here is as close to replacing true Nirvana as you can get."

Belah shook her head, pleased that he would offer to cater to her needs.

He rattled off a long list of dishes to the waitress that were half-familiar and half-foreign to her, but all sounded delicious. Every few seconds he paused and asked her preference, until he finally realized that she truly was happy to be served whatever he chose.

"Thank you for that," he said when the waitress disappeared with a bewildered look. "Most women wouldn't let me get away with taking that much control over a meal. You'd be surprised how hard it is for us to spoil our lovers nowadays."

"I suppose I miss being spoiled a little," Belah said, smiling and forcing away the memory of kneeling at another man's feet while he hand-fed her morsels of food from his own plate.

Glancing around, she took in the rich décor and the joyful energy that permeated the place. The best part was that none of the patrons knew who she was or what she represented. She was beginning to enjoy this world more and more, now that she was essentially anonymous. Enough time had passed that her part in the Ultiori's creation was little more than a legend—and aside from the dragon Court, she and her siblings were close to being considered myths by all the higher races.

She would no longer have the stature of queen, empress, or goddess if she didn't want it, nor the burden. And though it was clear to her from Ozzie's initial reaction that he wasn't the male from her dreams, it wasn't beyond the realm of possibility for her to find another like him who might treat her as though he treasured her.

Or owned her. The words popped into her head unexpectedly and she shut her eyes to the spike of nausea that erupted in her stomach. That was *not* what Ozzie wanted—that much she had read in his solicitous behavior so far.

"What's wrong?" he asked, wrapping his hand around her wrist.

The heat of his palm seemed to sear her, the pressure of his fingertips on her pulse point just heavy enough to bring back an ancient memory she'd long buried. She jerked her hand away from him with a sharp cry and opened her eyes, staring—surprised both at his touch and her reaction to it.

He immediately held his hands up. "Whoa, I didn't mean to piss you off. You didn't look so hot there for a second."

Belah struggled to gather herself and plaster on a calmer face. "No... I'm sorry. It's just been a really long time since I've... replenished."

The tense rigidity of Ozzie's shoulders seeped away and he leaned back with a deep, soft chuckle that reminded Belah of the percussive rhythm in the music Erika had played for her. The sound immediately calmed her.

"I'm prepared to be the appetizer, if it would help," he said. He cleared his throat, toying with the stem of his wine glass. If it hadn't been for his steady gaze meeting hers, she'd have thought he was being shy.

Belah shook her head and sighed. "You don't have to do this. We both know I'm not your true mate. Don't deny you weren't happy once you figured that out. Why waste any more time with me?"

Ozzie frowned and sat forward in his chair. "No, you aren't my *One*. I've been looking for her forever, practically. When Nanyo Sophia told me she'd set me up on a date with a dragon hoping for a turul mate, do you have any idea how excited that made me? This is fucking reverse Cinderella. I'm only disappointed because I knew the second I saw you that I was one of the ugly stepsisters."

"You're far from ugly ... and definitely not a female," Belah began, but he stopped her.

"My point is that you are still Prince ... ess Dragon Charming, or whatever. It doesn't matter how many turul males you meet; we will *all* want you, even if it's just for a night. I was only offering to speed that up because you seem to need it."

"I'm not quite the catch you think I am," Belah said, taking a shaky sip of her wine and forcing a smile.

"You're a dragon, baby. That's enough for most of us. And I can promise you that if I'd gotten that true-mate spark that told me you were my *One*, we would not be sitting here waiting for food right now. If you really are meant for one of my kind, I envy the bastard who gets to have you."

She let out a soft sigh. *You wouldn't if you knew the truth, sweet son of Zephyrus.*

Ozzie's head twitched to the side as though he'd heard something. He blinked and focused inward, then closed his eyes and shook his head. Belah bit her lip, remembering that turul only needed a breath to catch you in a lie, and hoped he hadn't caught her errant thought on the air that escaped her lips.

"Whatever secrets you have that you think would be deal breakers don't matter to me. If you want me as part of your meal, I'm just putting that on the table. I'm offering as a willing partner to a female I believe deserves to be served whatever she desires. Take it or leave it."

Belah smiled. Before she could reply, a small plate was set in the center of the table and the unmistakable aroma of fresh fish hit her nostrils.

Across from her, Ozzie tapped his fingers on the tabletop in a familiar rhythm that made her heart beat in tandem. He eyed the food in front of them, licked his lips, and grinned at her.

Belah bet he'd be an enthusiastic lover. Perhaps she'd take him up on his offer, but if the first course was any indication for how the entire meal would be, he would have to wait for dessert.

She enjoyed the rest of the meal so much, she completely forgot she'd arrived with Erika and Geva, who'd been dining unseen nearby, or that her pair of Shadow dragons were stationed somewhere within mental reach of her. When the meal was over, the pair would continue shadowing her and her date and would remain with her for the rest of her trip.

When the dessert had been served and consumed and the meal finally paid for, she accepted Ozzie's suggestion for a walk in the park. The moon was rising, full and silver-bright when he led her through the streets, deftly navigating the traffic. The swiftness with which the human world moved defied logic. Still, she allowed him to direct her with one arm around her waist and his deep voice in her ear, telling her to watch for puddles.

After meandering along winding stone paths through the night among the well-kept park, they finally stopped. The sight before her took her breath away. They were in a large plaza that reminded her of her old courtyard in Alexandria. At the bottom of the staircase Ozzie led her down was a giant pool with a fountain. An angel stood atop a large pedestal in the center of the fountain, water cascading down from the surface of it and into another tier before hitting the pool below. Beyond the fountain on the other side, the light from the rising moon reflected off a small lake.

Belah stood, enraptured by the sight of the winged beauty cast in silhouette by the orb of light behind her. Magic thrummed through the place, making her itch with need for a taste of it.

She turned and laughed delightedly. "This is beautiful!"

Ozzie's grin widened as he came up beside her. "It's a favorite spot of ours. My family's been playing music in the park for as long as it's existed, and she's always been a bit of a muse to us."

Staring up at the angel, Belah said, "I bet it was the other way around … some enamored artist saw the truth through your music and made her in your image."

His hand slid up the low-cut back of her dress, skin against skin. He pressed a soft kiss to her shoulder that made her shiver. "You don't believe in angels?"

Belah sighed and leaned against him, enjoying the warm, intimate contact and the comfort of his arms as they wrapped around her. "Not in the sense most humans do. I believe in winged sons and daughters of gods and goddesses, because I know they exist. You are evidence enough of that."

"Do you believe in devils?" he asked, pulling her around to face him and leading her backward. A light shimmered deep in his eyes that Belah found deliciously wicked.

"Only the kind devious enough to seduce a dragon." He may not have been the man she sought, but he deserved a prize for entertaining her so well tonight.

She found herself beneath the arched entry of the lower level of the terrace, in the shadows of the corridor that ran beneath the staircase they'd come down. Cold stone met her back as Ozzie pushed her against the wall. His hot lips brushed against her jaw.

"Someone followed us," he whispered between kisses down the line of her throat. "I didn't want to say anything because I was afraid I'd ruin the mood."

"I know," she breathed. "They're my friends." If it wasn't Geva and Erika that Ozzie had sensed, it was probably the pair of Shadows who were trailing her.

"Do they mind watching?"

"Do you mind if I don't mind if they mind?" She tilted her hips into his, pleased at the hard bulge in his pants and the way his eyes fluttered shut when she rubbed against him.

"By the Winds, no."

He cupped the back of her head and lowered his mouth to hers, while his other hand slid down her torso to slowly ruck up the length of her long, velvet dress.

Just as his fingertips snaked along the juncture of her hip, a cold wind blew through carrying a scent she knew, but hadn't encountered in thousands of years. At first it didn't register outside the anticipation of Ozzie's touch between her thighs.

A rough grunt sounded in her ear and Ozzie's warmth disappeared an instant later.

Belah opened her eyes in time to see a man-sized shape fly through the air, hit the wall across from her with a crunch, and crumple to the floor.

The familiar scent washed over her again. Her mind tumbled through a tangling web of memories. Arousal and pain, deep love and raw need, and above all, that unmistakable craving for oblivion.

She fell to her knees, unconscious of everything but her need to feel the hard ground biting into her kneecaps. The pain had only ever been a prelude to the release that powerful presence soon gave her.

In the corner of her vision, she saw Ozzie's body move, sluggishly trying to rise before he fell to the ground again and groaned out a harsh curse. She couldn't move now, either. Not when *he* stood over her.

Before her, his dark, familiar shape loomed large, with three other shadowy figures behind him.

"Little beast," Nikhil said. "I've missed you."

CHAPTER FIVE

Belah forced herself to look up at Nikhil. Her throat didn't want to work, but she made herself speak. "I'm not the woman I was with you, Nikhil."

His mouth twisted in a wry, humorless smile as he regarded her kneeling form.

"Your body begs to differ. I can smell your need for what only I could ever give you. That you would greet me this way proves you still belong to me."

No. Something about him was all wrong—but what had she expected? A roiling wave of nausea overtook her and she doubled over, bracing her palms on the ground while she retched, her primal need for him at war with her knowledge of what he had become. She belonged to no one, and whatever need he claimed to scent on her wasn't because of him, but rather, because of her simple need for energy—energy that Ozzie had been about to provide before they were interrupted. She wouldn't let Nikhil have that honor again. Once he may have been worthy of it, but not now—not after all he'd done in her name and without her blessing.

She wiped a thin trail of saliva from her lower lip and forced herself to stand. Her knees shook and she clenched her fists to still the tremors that ran up her arms.

She raised her head and opened her eyes.

What she saw wasn't anything like the memory she had of him, and delving into his mind revealed secrets that he'd never kept before. The once fearless warrior chomping at the bit to conquer the world for her glory was now filled with a singular, twisted need. He craved power, pain, and death like never before, that darkness a nearly opaque coating on what had otherwise been a vibrant aura when he was young.

Belah ached to turn back time, to return to her chamber in her palace in Egypt that first night he took her to that place of eternal release. If only she could tell herself that all hope was not lost, that the key to finding her children was within her grasp. If only she had marked him then—made him a proper mate—he would not have become this abomination.

It was too late now. Fire burned in her belly, her need to destroy the monster she'd created rising. She quashed that, too, but not before a flicker of blue flame escaped her lips, shooting just far enough to tickle the side of his jaw.

Nikhil flinched, his hand shooting up to his cheek. He hissed and his eyes widened.

"What did you do?"

Belah was still fighting to hold back the urge to set him alight and watch him burn. He had her babies, and had to somehow be convinced to tell her where he kept them.

"What did you do?!" he cried and surged at her, his hand clamping around her throat as he pushed her hard against the cold stone wall.

"I should only feel pain when I am inflicting it on another, not when it is done to me. Being tortured doesn't faze me, yet when I torture captives, I feel everything I do to them. Did you know that's what they turned me into after our wedding night? For the first two centuries, I was a *god,* but before long all the blessings I was given seemed like curses. I feel every bite of the blade when I slice another woman's skin the way I did yours. Do you still love my hand around your throat, little beast? Because I can feel the light fading from my own eyes the more I squeeze."

He squeezed harder, and the familiar darkness she once wished for began to seep into her vision. Staring deep into his eyes, she could sense the same dark cloud creeping into his mind, and knew he hated feeling it as much as he loved inflicting it on her.

She forced a constricted breath through her lungs so she could speak.

"I can kill you with that fire, if I choose to." Reaching up to grip his wrist, she pulled his hand away from her throat, forced his fingers open in front of her mouth, and breathed a blue tongue of flame at the center of his palm. Nikhil let out an agonized cry, struggling to pull away from her. When his skin blistered, she closed her mouth and twisted his hand back into an unnatural position. That should have hurt him as much as her fire did, yet he showed not even a flicker of discomfort. He was much stronger than she remembered, and he fought her, but he was still no match for her physical strength.

"Then kill me," he bit out. "I know you must have wished for my death all this time. If you could have destroyed me all along, why didn't you?"

"You have something that belongs to me, and I want it back."

She released his arm and he gingerly held his wrist, inspecting the welt in the center of his palm. He flexed his hand as though he'd simply been arm-wrestling and not had his fingers nearly bent double the wrong way around and his elbow twisted far enough to break, though it hadn't. The burn had clearly hurt him far worse than the other abuse.

"So this is a negotiation," he said, flicking his eyes back up to hers and dropping his hand to his side. "Very well. What treasure do I hold that's so valuable it kept you from obliterating me for three thousand years? And why are you only coming to beg for it now?"

"My son. The one that was taken from me before I met you. We've tried to find him all this time, but you seem to have hidden him too well." She carefully avoided mention of her other child. She'd taken a risk that he never knew the true identity of the two hibernating dragons he'd stolen. If he knew one was his own daughter, she feared she would never get them back.

A chuckle rattled out of his throat, the rough, scratchy sound betraying the damage he'd done to himself by attempting to strangle her.

"You mean the bastard child your own brother gave you? I always wondered why that statue had been so well-hidden when I found it. What are you willing to do for me to get him back, little beast?"

"One night. You can have me for one night. That's what you want, isn't it?"

"You're going to kill me when it's over. Why should I settle for a single evening? Watching you bleed out for me again would be the pinnacle of my desires. If anything, I want it more now than I did the first time. But I won't be satisfied with one night. Not after wanting you for so long."

"Fine. Name your price, Nikhil. I'll come with you now, if you want, and we can get on with it."

One dark eyebrow rose, and she realized what was so different about him. He had barely aged, yet his face was pale and a little gaunt, as though from long-endured fatigue. He was still a powerful man—even more powerful now. And the allure of the Blessing he'd received before he was born still lingered under the surface of that dark aura, though the corrupted magic that filled him now hid it well. He was still Blessed—if she hadn't stolen him for herself, would he have ever found the dragon mate he was meant for?

"Not tonight, sweet little beast," he said, stepping close enough that his warm breath gusted over her forehead. "You owe me a lifetime, but I'll settle for one week. Seven days are all I need to break you again."

He bent and pressed his lips to her temple. They were warm and dry and the gesture was strangely comforting. A spark of old longing shot through her. Now that the nausea had passed, she could remember the pleasure he'd given her and how beautifully devoid of worry the oblivion that followed had been.

His lips drifted lower, over her cheek, and down to her mouth. As he kissed her, one hand slid down her bare arm and he gripped her wrist, his thumb idly caressing the pulse point and the tender skin just above her palm. He kissed her there softly, and with deft grace produced a blade. Before Belah could react, the sharp tip of the dagger pierced her skin and he drew a swift line down along the inside of her wrist.

The pain surprised her and mesmerized her, the old need to please him taking over again. With a hungry look, he bent his head and darted his tongue out, trailing it along the line of her blood.

"No!" she said, finally summoning the presence of mind to yank her hand out of his grasp and wrap her other hand around her wrist, staunching the flow. She stared at the dagger that rested in his grip—the blade she had once given him on their wedding day, and the only object on Earth that could make her bleed.

"Yes, my love." His eyes sparked with lust as he began to move away from her, still licking his lips. "You still crave what I can give you. I can feel the way your body quivers under my touch. Oh, will I make you earn what you seek."

When he reached the three figures that stood guard behind him, he said, "My Elites will come find you when I'm ready for you."

Three hands reached up and rested on Nikhil's shoulders, the three dark-clad Elites watching her solemnly from the shadows. She looked at each in turn, opening her mind to theirs to seek out what information she could glean. The first had wavy, silver-blond hair and sad, gray eyes. The second seemed somehow familiar, with his closely trimmed, russet hair and gentle brown eyes. All three Elites exuded familiar power that reminded her of her own brothers. But the third sparked a sudden memory.

A shimmering bubble surrounded them. Just before they flickered out of existence, she met the gaze of that tall, painfully beautiful man. The slightest glint of recognition reflected back at her from his dark eyes, and he nodded his head almost imperceptibly.

"Naaz," she whispered when they were gone. The child she'd blessed so long ago was still alive, but one of Nikhil's soldiers now. Not just any soldier, either—an Elite. But what of his twin sister, Neela? "Oh, sweet, Blessed children." She raised her hand and wiped tears from her eyes. "Is this what he made you? Sweet Mother, forgive me."

Movement caught her eye from the shadows beyond, and she focused on the shape. Ozzie sat with eyes wide and mouth agape, holding his crumpled jacket to a bleeding cut on his forehead.

Voices from somewhere nearby called her name, the Shadows rushing through in a flurry, but Belah brushed them off. "I'm fine, and I think you guys can take the night off—they won't be bothering me again."

"Mistress, Kol told us never to lose sight of you," the leader of her guard said. "Something strange happened. One second the two of you were kissing, and the next … well, the whole scene shifted and the turul was on the ground. I don't know what happened."

Belah looked into his eyes. "Nikhil is what happened. He's learned a thing or two from the nymphaea. There's nothing you could have done, but I am fine. He's still not strong enough to take me, at least. And if you're not going to leave me, at least go back to pretending you're not here, if you don't mind."

"Yes, Mistress," he said, and he and the other Shadow exited the corridor into the night, where they seemed to bleed back into the shadows like ghosts.

"You…" Ozzie croaked. "You exist. The old tales were true, then, weren't they? That our enemy was made by … by one of the Dragon Council. You're the Blue Beast they tell stories about to frighten our children. If we don't behave, you'll come and turn us into unfeeling, blood-thirsty monsters like the Ultiori."

He pushed himself unsteadily to his feet. Belah could only stand and silently witness the growing disgust and fear cross his face. She gave him a sad smile.

"This is what misplaced desire can do to you, if you let it. You're safer waiting for your true mate, Oszkar, and cherish her when you find her."

"By the Winds, I'm fucking glad you weren't my *One*."

A pair of silhouetted figures appeared in the entrance to the underground passage and Erika rushed toward her.

"Belah! Oh, thank God. Geva said he had a bad feeling when we were walking through the park … Ozzie? What the hell happened to you guys?" Erika looked between the two of them, taking in Belah's disheveled appearance and Ozzie's blood-streaked face.

"You guys are better off steering clear of her," Ozzie said. He spat at her feet and Geva moved like a flash, lifted him by his collar, and shook him.

"Show more respect to a daughter of Fate, you feathered bastard," Geva growled.

"So you know what she's done, then? What her part was in the existence of those fucking Ultiori bastards who hunt us? I'm fucking swearing off dragons. You guys can have each other."

"Let him go, Geva," Belah said. "He isn't wrong."

With a grumble, Geva released him. Ozzie's feet barely hit the ground again before he shifted. His finely tailored clothing fell in a heap and huge, feathered wings beat at the air, carrying him through the shadows out of the underground corridor. His winged turul shape came into view high in the sky, blocked out the light of the moon for a moment, and then he was gone.

Erika rushed to Belah and squeezed her upper arms, rubbing gently. "Are you all right? Come on." She slipped an arm around Belah's waist and led her out into the open again, to one of the benches that surrounded the courtyard. Belah sat with Erika beside her and Geva squatting in front of her.

"Did they hurt you?" he asked, scanning her up and down. He let out a growl when his gaze fell on the still unhealed cut on her wrist. He grabbed her hand. "How did this happen? You're immortal. If the Ultiori have ways to cut one of you…"

"It's my fault. Everything Ozzie said is true. I'm the dragon who made Nikhil what he is."

"Bullshit," Geva said. "I'm the son of a Queen. When my mother died, she left behind all the secrets a dragon queen is privy to. That includes the fact that you had help from the other races. What did that Ultiori bastard want from you?"

"It isn't what he wants from me that matters," she said with a sigh. "It's what I want from him. He has my son and daughter."

Her shoulders slumped in defeat as she gave in and told her hosts the truth, leaving no detail unmentioned, except for one. They didn't need to know that she'd had a child with their enemy. That detail was no one's business.

"His power has grown over the centuries. He carries nymphaea magic now and knows how to use it," she concluded. "That's the only way he and his Elites could have disappeared the way they did. I've seen it before, long ago. The satyrs were often the strongest and could create a bubble that allowed them to manipulate the fabric of space and time. He must be using the same magic to hide my babies. No wonder dragon magic hasn't been able to find them."

"At least you figured that out. Knowledge is half the battle," Erika said. "We can have these … nymphaea … help look for them. My team can help, too. You don't have to give yourself to him again, Belah."

Belah let out a humorless laugh. "The nymphaea are a capricious race. I doubt they would care enough to bother."

Geva nodded. "Not to mention the males are extinct. It's no wonder the Ultiori have use of their power—they hunted down the males and captured and killed them until none remained. The females refuse to conceive male children anymore because they won't give the Ultiori the satisfaction of holding anything over their heads. Every one of the races had to adapt in some fashion."

Belah gripped Geva's hand where it rested on her knee and squeezed. "The hibernations saved us. In some ways, having a common adversary was a blessing. I just wish it didn't have to come at such a price."

"It's important that you know I don't blame you, Belah. None of the Court does, now that we know the truth. The other races will come around."

"Yeah, honey. Forget what Ozzie said. Besides, if you were the one for him, he'd have loved you anyway." Erika rubbed a comforting hand in a circle between Belah's shoulder blades.

"The fact that 'the one for me' won't have a choice isn't exactly a consolation. I never gave Nikhil a choice, either—he would have gladly accepted my mark and become my mate, even though it meant he'd lose his free will. I planned to give him that, despite my desire to the contrary. Our hope was that the wedding blessings he was given would protect him from the strength of my magic."

Everything had gone exactly as she'd hoped on the night of her wedding to Nikhil, but Belah had no control over what would happen when too much of her blood had flowed from her body to remain fully conscious. She could never have predicted that her beloved brother would misinterpret Nikhil's gift to her and spirit her away, believing he was saving her from a madman. None of them could have predicted that consuming her blood would allow Nikhil to survive her brother's fire, nor could they predict his actions in the aftermath of losing her.

They had all suffered so much since. She didn't know whether finding a new mate and bearing a child with him would have any effect on the future. What she did know was that she had a chance to redeem herself now, and to find her lost children in the process.

She would submit to Nikhil one more time to find out how to get her son and daughter back. And then she would kill him.

"Belah?" Erika said in a strangely panicked tone. "Please let go of Geva now, okay?"

Geva let out a pained grunt that made her refocus her attention on him. His teeth were bared in a grimace of pain. "Yeah, if you don't mind, I'd like to keep that hand."

She stared down where her hand still gripped his tightly. Shining blue talons had manifested where her fingers had been and pierced cleanly through his palm. Blood dripped from the wounds and onto the bricks that paved the ground beneath.

With a cry of alarm, she released him and forced her clawed hand back to its human shape.

"Jesus! Baby, are you going to be okay?" Erika reached for Geva's mangled hand and he winced.

Cursing softly to herself, Belah let out a quick breath, directing the numbing blue smoke to wrap itself around his hand. Geva's shoulders sagged in relief when the anesthetic properties of her magic took effect.

"Your date didn't quite manage to top you off, I take it?" Geva asked. His aura flickered as he inhaled, summoning his magic into his lungs, then exhaled his own healing power over the surface of his palm. The wounds knit slowly and his blood stopped flowing. He surreptitiously bent and shot a quick blaze out of his mouth to burn away the blood that had fallen to the bricks beneath. It would be foolish to leave even a drop of dragon blood out in the open.

"We were interrupted. I suppose it's better they stepped in before he made the mistake of making love to me. Fewer regrets for him this way."

"Yeah, but that doesn't solve the immediate issue, does it?" Erika said. "You won't let us help, so the least I can do is get you laid tonight. Come on, you two." She reached out and grabbed both their hands, pulling them along toward the steps that led up out of the plaza. "I know just the place, and hotties, that'll work for you. And maybe we'll even find you that mate in the process. Kill two turul with one dragon, so to speak. Though I am kind of bummed Ozzie wasn't the one. That man is sex on a stick—you seriously don't know what you're missing. I was kind of hoping we could compare notes after."

Belah let Erika lead her through the park, too weary from her need for energy to argue. The meal had certainly taken the edge off, but was still nothing close to an adequate substitute for the magic she needed. She no longer cared who Erika had in mind for her, as long as she wasn't interrupted again once she had him alone for five minutes. Though at this point she probably needed more than a single night, or a single partner, to be fully replenished.

After walking for several minutes among the busy city streets, she heard the music from her dreams and smiled. The pleasant buzz that always seemed to accompany those images incited fresh yearning to find the male who would belong to her. The fact that Ozzie had been one of the musicians had given her hope that he might be the one. Now that she knew it wasn't him, she wondered if the music was simply a turul thing, and that any one of the thousands of male turul out there might be *him*. If the music was merely symbolic, it might take weeks to find her mate, but she was willing to keep searching.

In the meantime, she would let herself enjoy the music the turul made, and would happily let Erika be the choreographer of her trysts to replenish in between searching.

The world fell away when she entered the dimly lit club and let Erika lead her to an isolated booth along the back wall. The place was nearly full, the patrons listening raptly to the band on stage. Belah sat and closed her eyes for a moment, allowing the music to wash over her and acclimating herself to the environment. The myriad minds of the humans and other creatures in public places could be distracting, particularly when she was too low on energy to block out the psychic noise. The coaxing nature of the music helped her focus her attention on it alone, and she let out a sigh.

"What do you think?" Erika asked.

"Oh, it's more lovely in reality than the recorded version," Belah said.

"No, silly. I know you love the music, but what do you think of the *musician*? He's why I brought you here—or one of the reasons, anyway. That's Ozzie's cousin, Lukas, on sax. I wonder why his brother isn't up there with him—they were always a duo before."

Belah opened her eyes and focused on the stage. In the center on a stool sat a striking young man with wide shoulders and dark hair that hung straight almost to his shoulders. One lock had strayed over his brow, nearly concealing half his face. His eyes were closed, his brows drawn together in concentration, his lips wrapped around the mouthpiece of his instrument like he was making love to it. She recognized him from the pictures she'd seen resting on Sophia North's mantelpiece, but he barely resembled the joyful young man in that image. This version of him exuded longing and loss and deep, aching hope for love, and every nuance of those emotions was expressed through his music.

"Oh," Belah breathed. Magic permeated the room, clearly emanating from the turul's lungs and filtering through his shining instrument. She'd never felt turul magic so potent, but a Prince of the North Wind would have that kind of power. She barely heard Erika's amused commentary as she sat forward in her seat to watch and listen. If this was the man Erika had in mind for Belah to fill her well with, she would have a good night indeed.

Then he opened his eyes.

Lukas North's stormy gaze locked onto hers, and Belah knew without a doubt that the music he played was for her, and her alone.

CHAPTER SIX

Nikhil's head spun from the *drift* as much as from seeing Belah. Nothing could have prepared him for being in her presence again after so long, and the sudden rush of magic transporting him halfway around the world didn't help his mind process her promise.

He reoriented himself to his secret chamber—his study, as it were—and found his chair and sat, leaning back in the soft leather with a sigh.

"Sayid, she messed you up pretty good." Sterlyn bent down in front of him, examining what had to be angry, blistering welts on his face and palm by now. The fucking things stung as though flames still licked his skin. They should have healed on their own by now, but if what she said was true—that she could kill him—maybe that was why an errant flame from her lungs could cause such wounds. He still vividly remembered surviving her brother's angry torrent of fire—still felt the searing pain of being burned alive. Yet Ked's fire hadn't killed him.

He'd taken days to recover after that long-ago attack, barely regaining consciousness while Belah's trusted physician, Meri, tended him. To this day, he still didn't understand why the woman had remained by his side for so long after her mistress had disappeared, but he owed Meri dearly for his life— and his sanity—in the wake of losing the woman he loved.

Now that Belah's flames had tickled his skin for the first time, marking him with visible evidence of her power, for some reason the knowledge that she could be the end of him aroused him.

"Sayid … may I heal you?"

Nikhil shut his eyes, nodding curtly and wishing that the nausea that the *drift* always caused would hurry up and pass. He tilted his head to the side under Sterlyn's gentle touch and waited. His entire head tingled and his nostrils flared, taking in the odd scent that accompanied Sterlyn's magic. The aroma was like a language that he didn't understand, but wished he could. Each one of his Elites had the same effect on him, and it was maddening that he couldn't understand that part of his own trusted guards, much less the magic he possessed himself.

He had too many weaknesses, really. For the first few centuries after losing Belah, he'd been a god. Their wedding ritual granted him immeasurable abilities that he'd learned to use.

Somewhere along the way, things changed. The powers didn't leave him, but here and there, things seemed to sour, those powerful blessings becoming curses he was forced to adapt to. Feeling the pain he inflicted on others was the least of it.

At least now that he knew Belah's weakness, he knew how to get her back. All he needed was a week with her and he was certain he could convince her to bear him that child he'd wanted for so long.

Sterlyn made a dissatisfied sound and Nikhil was forced to glance toward his Elite, whose hands hovered over his open palm with magic steadily pouring from his fingertips.

"I'm sorry. It's taking longer than it should."

The golden-haired knight never flinched when Nikhil looked at him, and for that he earned credit, but Nikhil was impatient tonight.

"I have work to do."

"A few more minutes, Sayid."

Nikhil sat back with a nod.

In the centuries that Sterlyn had attended Nikhil and his army, Nikhil himself had never suffered an injury his own body didn't heal on its own within moments. He wasn't impervious to damage, but he was as immortal now as his beloved Belah.

His head went fuzzy with arousal when he recalled that first taste of her blood on their wedding night. He groaned involuntarily, making Sterlyn pull back.

"Don't stop," he said grimly, and his Elite leaned forward again. He hated how slowly it took them to do anything, but it shouldn't have been surprising, since theirs was appropriated magic. It would never be full-power.

Fuck, until tonight, he hadn't had a hard-on in years, and knew that if not for the goddamn curses he'd have one now. It took more than just a thought to make his cock stand at attention. Just like the pain he inflicted on others, he never felt pleasure anymore unless he was giving it.

The sting of the burns Belah had given him made him want to scream, but he endured the pain as lovely little bites of intimacy from her. Something that had made him *feel* again. He had touched her, kissed her, felt the warmth of her body and the power of having her kneel for him, her body responding to his presence like they had never been apart. He'd gotten hard in that brief moment before she'd regained control of her reactions. Something he never believed he would experience again, and every aspect of that moment he would have gladly endured any agony for, if it meant he'd be granted the glory of her presence—his *Tilahatan*—his goddess. Did he dare hope that she might let him have more?

He opened his eyes finally when the faint nausea dissipated and allowed his Elite to administer healing magic to his cheek. The other two soldiers stood on the opposite side of Nikhil's desk, awaiting instructions. He ignored them, instead resting his eyes on the ornate phylactery that dominated the heavy, carved-wood mantelpiece across the room. Within the gold-ornamented blue glass was what remained of the blood he'd taken from his lover all those years ago. Even though he had bargained with her brothers to return it so she could be awakened, he hadn't been able to part with every drop.

Situated around the phylactery were three others, filled with the blood her brothers had offered in exchange, and which had ultimately become the lifesblood of his Elites. Only a few drops were ever needed, but had to be re-administered every year, or their minds lost traction on reality and their power faded.

More precious than gold and hidden away inside this chamber with magic it had taken him years to master, the blood represented his life's work. The three men who attended him now were the pinnacle.

Still, he wanted more. Though his Elites were like sons to him, Naaz, Sterlyn, and the newest, Marcus, couldn't replace the real thing. The child he'd never been able to have with Belah.

He would have more Elites, if men and women like them weren't so rare. They were like him in one crucial aspect: they'd each been blessed by a dragon while inside their mothers' wombs. There was one other Elite who still lived—Naaz's twin sister, Neela. The pair had been the first to accept his gift of immortality with the few drops of Belah's blood Nikhil was willing to part with, back when he still possessed a shred of sentimentality over her love for the twins. It was with them that he understood the connection between the dragons' blessing and a Blessed human's ability to survive consuming immortal dragon blood, and achieve an almost super-human state as a result.

Neela was locked in a cell now, inside the fortress-like compound Nikhil had built in the Canadian Rockies nearly a century ago. It was the only way to keep her brother in line. That was the one shortcoming of his Elites: they required tight leashes and harsh discipline or they rebelled, but he needed their power to remain effective. While each of them could *drift* on his own from place to place, Nikhil could only reach his secret chambers when he merged his power with theirs. They needed him as much as he needed them, not only because he held women they loved hostage, but also for their sanity. Without their annual dose of the blood from those phylacteries, they would each go mad.

Without them, the treasures he'd hidden throughout the world in chambers such as this one—concealed within one of hundreds of bubbles in the waters of time—would be lost forever.

One such treasure was what Belah had bargained for, offering a week of her submission in exchange for this prize he'd never understood the significance of until now. Cursing himself, he wondered whether she'd have found him sooner if he hadn't hidden the treasure away. But now he knew. What if he had never needed to look for her at all?

If you hadn't been forced to hunt for your lost love, you would never have grown as powerful as you are now. It's her blood you need, not her love. Don't forget that.

He shook his head, irritated by the reminder of the little shadowy voice that crept into his thoughts from time to time. The voice wasn't wrong, yet being near Belah made him wonder what it would be like to feel loved by her again—to have that child he believed she would bear him if they had enough time together.

For several centuries, he had done nothing but work to understand every nuance of the magic the higher races possessed and how he could make it work for him. He'd believed that if he couldn't reach Belah and get her to agree to be his mate in every sense, he would make his own child somehow. Create it from the magic of all the creatures who had witnessed their union.

He would do whatever it took to have that child.

After centuries of trying, he was so close to the answer he could taste it. So far, only one female captive had become pregnant, but lost the child soon after. Soon, he would uncover the secret of creating his own child from the research he'd done.

And if his week with Belah went as hoped, he may not even need that research.

He no longer cared about any thread of magic in the world but the one leading him to her. Though the phylactery with her blood in it glowed with power, an even brighter strand connected him to her in Nikhil's mind. He could pinpoint her location within a few miles, now that she was in his world again.

He'd been tempted to accept her offer to come with him tonight, but though he itched for her company, he decided to wait. When he'd left her, she'd been primed for him, her demonstration of power the perfect prelude to her ultimate surrender. He wanted to make her dwell on her need for him for a few days, at least. Withhold that instant gratification of winning her prize until he was satisfied she'd earned it. And even though her threat of death had surprised him, it didn't frighten him. He didn't believe she could ever go through with it. Love like theirs transcended death, after all.

Brushing a finger over the now-healed scar on his cheek, he smiled. To be marked by her had been a wish of his for ages. This wasn't exactly the mark he had hoped for, but given time, he believed she would eventually gift him with her true dragon mark, and they could finally be together forever.

He could wait a few more days. In the meantime, he had to revisit the secret chamber where he'd hidden Belah's requested treasure almost three thousand years ago. He had to have another look at this son of hers.

"Sterlyn, with me," he said, standing and gesturing at the blond Elite who had healed him. Looking at the other two Elites, he said, "Marcus, you're to cloak yourself and watch her. Never let her leave your sight. Naaz, return to the Institute and wait."

"Where to, Sayid?" Sterlyn said, his shoulders squared and his expression attentive.

Nikhil appreciated Sterlyn's deference, which was devoid of any of the resentful undercurrents of his other two Elites. The man was no less under Nikhil's thumb—Nikhil held the love of Sterlyn's life in one of his facilities, and they were only allowed to speak on rare occasions through a small window in the door of the red dragon's cell. He sensed all three of his Elites were biding their time in some fashion, but Nikhil had an eternity, so they would be waiting in vain.

"To the Alexandria chambers."

Sterlyn blinked and cast a furtive glance at Naaz, whose expression darkened considerably. "Ah, right, sir. Twelfth century BCE. Wouldn't Naaz be the best to join you—it's within his timeframe ... I wasn't born until Charlemagne was in power."

"It's within mine, too. I just need your blood, Elite. Now!"

Nikhil held out his hand, and with the other produced his dagger, made a small slice across the center of his palm that quickly welled with crimson. Sterlyn merely pursed his lips and nodded. With an apologetic look at Naaz, he produced his own blade, made a similar cut into his own flesh, and placed his palm against Nikhil's.

Closing his eyes, Nikhil pictured the chamber that lay deep beneath the palace where he'd first enjoyed the submission of one of the most powerful creatures on Earth. The *drift* began with a tugging sensation at his navel, and the room disappeared in a blur as though a rushing river had suddenly burst through the walls, catching him and Sterlyn in its onslaught.

The familiar pounding of his pulse in his ears signaled they were near their destination. Nikhil always hated the cloying darkness and the sensation of being both pushed and pulled at the same time. It was as though the river itself were a cord that ran straight through him with a knot at his core, tying him tightly to its current. Finally, the rushing sound faded, and the sense of movement abruptly stopped. The knot in his belly would take longer to fade.

His ears popped painfully and he opened his eyes.

Sterlyn was doubled over, retching in a corner with his bloodied hand pressed against the pale soapstone wall. Torches flickered in sconces around the square chamber. At one end, a dark passage loomed, one that Nikhil knew led to a door barred from the outside. There was no leaving this chamber through that door—he knew nothing but ruins lay on the other side. His temporal manipulation only extended to creating these small pockets that existed out of time. He used the pockets to create magical hideaways such as this one and the fifteenth-century office he spent most of his time in. There were dozens of others throughout the world, and throughout his own history. Within the network of chambers hidden inside this bubble were stored countless treasures, including the one Belah was searching for.

Nikhil wished he could truly travel back in time, but had learned the hard way that manipulating more than these small bubbles in places and times he was familiar with took far too much energy. When he'd first learned to *drift*, he'd immediately tried to revisit his wedding night, to see Belah one last time before she was taken from him.

The very second he caught sight of her from the shadowy corner beyond the door to their room, he'd been violently thrust back to his own time and lay sputtering on the floor of the prison cell where he'd originated, feeling like he'd nearly drowned. Calder, the satyr prisoner who he'd coerced into teaching him to *drift*, stood over him with arms crossed and an unamused smirk on his face. "I told you it wouldn't be pleasant," Calder had said. "Don't fuck with the waters of time."

The time the Alexandria chambers existed in was well past his wedding night. His earlier self roamed the palace above somewhere, and had gradually been hoarding away the treasures from the palace into the empty chambers beneath, but there were more chambers than he would ever fill before being forced to adjust to a world changing more rapidly than his own regrets.

Nikhil turned away from that dark corridor and the door to his old life and headed down another to a heavy wooden door. After a sharp glance at Sterlyn, the Elite turned away while Nikhil adjusted the pattern in the elaborate metal puzzle embedded above the door's lock. Once the correct arrangement of pieces was set, the tumblers clicked into place and the door swung open. Nikhil swept his hand across the puzzle, obscuring the pattern and walked into the room, his attention freshly focused on one of the two sarcophagi resting inside.

Nikhil had come across the pair of treasures by happenstance. When Naaz and Neela were both still loyal to him, they'd been on a *drift* together. But instead of reaching Nikhil's desired destination, they'd wound up in an immense and completely sealed circular chamber he'd never seen before, with a vast, smooth, domed ceiling. Glowing lights were set into the wall at intervals, and in the center on a raised dais rested these two treasures.

The twins had gravitated toward the dais like moths to a flame. Mistrustful of their excitement, Nikhil had latched onto their minds with his power, forcing them to their knees in pain while he examined the pair of statues that stood on the dais. They were exquisitely rendered representations of a male and a female, apparently slumbering. The artistry was so beautiful he decided he would add them to the vast collection of artifacts he'd collected over the years.

After moving the pair of treasures to this chamber and encasing them in the protective golden coffins, he'd forbade the twins from visiting the chamber again. The twins had raged at being kept from these treasures, to the point that Nikhil no longer trusted them to carry out his orders. He couldn't allow them contact with each other, either, for fear they would use one another to *drift* into the chamber.

No matter how much he studied the two elaborately carved figures he'd retrieved from that mystical room, Nikhil couldn't discern what it was about them that had so bewitched the twins.

"Help me," he said to Sterlyn, moving to one end of one of the pair of sarcophagi and gripping the handles that protruded from the huge, golden effigy of Horus that rested atop the figure.

Recovered from his bout of nausea, Sterlyn nodded and moved to grip the handles at the figure's feet. Together, they lifted the heavy cover and placed it on the ground nearby.

What Nikhil had thought was merely a statue with mystical properties offered new meaning now. The carved stone figure was a man lying prone. Majestic and graceful, he was easily as large as his dragon father. Nikhil's nostrils flared with distaste at the reminder that this treasure Belah so wished to recover was none other than the child she'd borne to her terrifyingly powerful brother.

Still, Ked hadn't been able to destroy Nikhil, and he now knew why. Only Belah's flames could permanently damage him. What powers would this product of such an abominable union possess? How dangerous was this man?

He leaned over the figure's face. It was serene and smooth, seemingly carved from stone Nikhil had believed to be obsidian. But now that he looked closer, he spied an inner luminescence, as though the stone in fact had pulsing blue veins beneath the surface.

The man's arms rested by his side, his body entirely nude from head to toe, and his cock a thick and rigid length jutting at an angle up between his thighs.

If he could be awakened and convinced to join Nikhil's cause, he might be a formidable weapon against the dragons—one that might convince Belah to stay with him forever. Nikhil began working out the argument in his mind, in which he convinced this man that he'd been abandoned by his own kind and rescued by Nikhil himself.

He studied the pedestal the figure lay upon, searching for some kind of symbol—some clue as to how he might revive the man.

"Sayid, can I be of help?"

Nikhil glanced up and realized he'd been cursing under his breath at finding nothing useful.

"I'm trying to figure out how to wake the bastard up," Nikhil growled. "Do you have any ideas to share?"

Sterlyn's gaze wandered to the man's cock as though his eyes were a compass and the appendage represented true north. After a second, Sterlyn swallowed. "No, sir."

Nikhil narrowed his eyes, certain for a second that his Elite knew something, but was guarding his thoughts. He only caught the glimmer of a phrase, *"...wants a mate."* That meant little to Nikhil. Obviously, the man was ready to mate.

"I should have brought Marcus," Nikhil spat. "He knows better than to waste my time."

"Perhaps the female will have some clues," Sterlyn offered, nodding at the second sarcophagus in the room.

Nikhil stood up with a grunt, and with Sterlyn at the other end of the effigy of Bastet, they removed the protective covering of the female statue and let it *thunk* onto the stone floor.

"What do you know of dragons, Sterlyn? Does that lover of yours ever tell you secrets?" Asking leading questions usually bore fruit, simply because most individuals couldn't avoid thinking of exactly what they wished to keep a secret when asked. He'd tried it often enough with his Elites that they guarded their minds well when he was near, but occasionally, he could still break through.

"They are sent to hibernate when they come of age, and spend five centuries in a kind of petrified state. At least, that's what Zamirah has told me. Then they awaken and assume the roles their parents filled while they slept, and their parents sacrifice themselves to grant the next generation a legacy of strong power."

Sterlyn's instant verbal response distracted Nikhil from his nosing through the man's thoughts. He frowned.

"I've heard their hibernation story from every single dragon I've captured and tortured. None of them have shared a single clue about how they're woken up. Do you know how impossible it is to extract information from a creature who exists purely to pleasure itself and others? All the fucking beasts ever want is sex."

Not that he had anything against sex, himself. He just had no interest in having it with anyone but the woman he'd lost.

He stared at Sterlyn, hoping the man might display some kind of reaction, even if it were internalized, but Sterlyn only stared back impassively. Though the female between them was a perfect specimen—beautiful and ideally shaped—she was smaller than the male. Her figure was made from a pale lavender, and like her mate, she also sported a shimmering web of veins that glowed beneath the surface like multicolored fire.

Nikhil wondered if the duo were indeed a mated pair. Entranced by the female's profile, he reached a hand out and gently brushed it down the bridge of her long, straight nose. His finger tingled from the touch, but he gained no new insight.

If he could awaken the male and hold the female hostage, that might provide some incentive for the male to do his bidding. But the female's pedestal was similarly devoid of any kind of clue.

"Let's go," Nikhil said. His mood was foul and his head ached from the *drifting* they'd done. He just wanted to go back to his private chamber and make his plans for his week with Belah.

"Should we cover them back up?" Sterlyn asked when Nikhil reached out a freshly bloodied hand to him.

"No. I'll be back, and with luck, when I return it will be to wake them up once and for all."

Despite having no desire for sex for eons, Nikhil still reveled in his ability to affect women with his skills. He had no doubt that he would be able to extract the information he needed from Belah herself. She had always been forthcoming when he was torturing her with his cock. He hardened at the thought, and regretted yet again that he'd decided to make her wait.

CHAPTER SEVEN

Lukas had found Heaven.

It existed in every breath his lungs pushed through the mouthpiece of his saxophone, and in the sounds that came out the other end. The combined shift of the audience when the music started told him that he'd done well—that subtle lean or tilt of their heads, the rhythmic tap of a foot somewhere in the crowd. This particular club wasn't the type of place for dancing, unlike the blues club his brother played at. The patrons came for the atmosphere of a jazz scene, which Lukas supplied them with in spades, his low, sultry notes laced with the tiniest bit of the North Wind that lived in his lungs.

It helped having an immortal spirit infusing his very being to attract fans—and lovers.

He never hit a wrong note, and could seduce a woman merely by playing the right song for her. But the second half of Heaven still eluded him—finding the perfect woman. Simply being able to seduce any woman he wanted didn't make it easy to find the *right* one. And he should know, because he'd been looking for her for nearly two centuries.

Yet he kept trying, because Heaven wasn't *only* music. The other half of Heaven meant finding the *One*. Only one woman in the entire world could be his true mate, and according to his grandmother, he would know her when he saw her. That didn't mean he couldn't find a distraction or two while he searched, though.

Tonight, his target was a lovely blonde at the cocktail table near the stage. She was seated with a pair of girlfriends who chattered back and forth constantly during the first set, but this young woman seemed like she couldn't keep her eyes off him. He threw her a glance and a smile in between solos. He'd test her with a few songs, then if she held true, he'd give her the full Lukas North treatment with the last song of the night, after which he'd take her home and enjoy the rest of his evening, hoping the next night the girl he found would be his one true mate.

It was still early, however. The band was only a few songs in, so his seduction was merely beginning. He released the mouthpiece for a breath and a quick sip of water, then secured his lips around it again, fingertips resting on the brass keys, worn smooth from constant use.

His fingers nearly slipped when *she* walked in—a dark-haired beauty with skin so luminescent it couldn't belong to a human woman. His lips parted and left the mouthpiece when his head turned to follow her through the room, unable to let his gaze dwell elsewhere. The blonde's allure dimmed to insignificance.

Just in time, he gathered himself and hit his cue with the bassist's heavy note. That note vibrated through him when she paused at her table, and lingered as she sat and closed her eyes, clearly entranced by the music.

Suddenly the beat he played to had nothing at all to do with the band. Their rhythm still guided him, but his true music—the music that came from his soul—was meant to match the beat of *her* heart.

He very nearly missed a note when he saw the glimmer of light in her eyes, and in the eyes of her male companion. Lukas recognized the third member of their party. His lips quirked into a smile at the sight of Erika Rosencrans, and he thought he understood. If any human woman he knew could snag a dragon for a mate, it was her.

His eyes were drawn back to the female dragon on Erika's other side. Was his mesmerizing female part of a mated trio?

Fucking dragons, he thought, confused and trying to shake off the thought that this female he'd never seen in his life should be his. If he could entice a dragon female into hearing him play, he didn't care about anything else. All he cared about was making sure *she* noticed him. Dragons had particular sexual appetites, and were very picky who they chose to share them with. He was simply honored that she was here in the audience. That was all.

But by the Winds, to have a night with her.

He hazarded a glance at Erika and the other dragon, trying to keep his focus on the music. The male, a huge Red dragon, hid his nature well with a close shave and clean haircut. The male dragon paused while the two females settled into the booth, then slid in beside Erika and bent to kiss her and sling an arm around her.

Lukas raised an eyebrow as their kiss continued. They were definitely a closely mated pair, from the looks of things. He glanced at the other woman in time to see her gaze linger longingly on the couple. And then the large Red rested a hand on Erika's belly and whispered in her ear.

Their beautiful companion turned away and met Lukas's eyes.

Blue, was all he could think. Her eyes were the first introduction, a vivid indigo. Her dress a deep, midnight-blue velvet that hugged every curve. Her hair a cascade of blue-black over creamy white shoulders. A pair of sapphires dangled from her ears, catching the light. The colors were only superficial to her mood, however, and he altered the key of his song to try to pick up that impression, knowing his bandmates would catch on.

He managed to keep up with the composition, but was grateful for a break to catch the breath she'd stolen.

She's the One. Right here. Right now. Right the fuck in front of me. He would wager that his grandmother would agree, if she were here to witness how mesmerized he was.

But a Blue dragon? Fuck.

He'd been with a few dragons before. The higher races were allies, and he'd found a sense of camaraderie in their shared secrets, so it was always a relief when they found a friend in the crowd. Especially one he didn't need to hide their true nature from when they went home together.

But this one ... she was something else. He'd heard about how amazing Dragon Ascension season could be, but he hated what it meant for the rest of the higher races.

The Ultiori would be out in full force, hunting.

If these two were here, looking as young as they did, that meant it had begun. Maybe months ago, but this was his first clue. He wondered if his brother knew. Maybe there was another female dragon who was his brother's true mate.

He cursed the dragons' efficiency as much as he praised it. They were good at staying under the radar, if even his race didn't know their new generation was awake. But the turul were good at keeping secrets too, and he'd been out of touch for most of the year.

None of that mattered when she moved, though.

She raised a glass as he finished the song. She was looking right at him, toasting him, and he was enraptured by her fingers on her glass, the slope of her arm, and the way her sweet, pink lips grasped the lip of the glass and drank, the line of her throat rippling as she swallowed.

He shook his head to dispel the sudden, sure instinct that he had to have her tonight. And forever. She *was* the One.

Dragons were complicated. Not like his race. The turul were simpler. They lived to fly, and cared about little else besides the wind and their music. The fact that they'd gotten tied up in deeper political issues didn't sit well with him, even less so after his sister's death fifty years earlier. He and his brother had managed to forgive the dragons in general—they hadn't been the ones to kidnap and drain his sister's blood in some barbaric ritual sacrifice. The Dragon *Council,* however—they were the ones responsible for the Ultiori's existence. Those six immortal bastards could suck his cock.

No, the rest of the dragons he had no issue with. Far from it, if the look she was giving him was any indication. He'd dive bomb the Dragon Council if he could, but this pretty dragon woman … he'd save her from their constricting laws. Take her away to an Enclave. Make sure she never had to worry about their fucking laws again, or about the Ultiori who hunted them. The urge to save her, care for her, protect her, was so primal that his head throbbed with the compulsion as much as his dick throbbed with arousal at the very sight of her.

He played stronger at the understanding of that urge. The turul mated for life.

He'd been skeptical about the truth of it, despite seeing his brethren coupling with each other, or with humans. He'd been alive for a very long time without meeting *the One*, so long that he'd ceased believing in her. Maybe there was no one out there for him. Maybe Fate was playing a big joke on him, letting his friends have that connection, but never giving him the chance.

The heart wants what the heart wants, his best friend had told him on the day he'd wed his mate. But love at first sight was still a myth to Lukas, until now.

He had to finish the set before he could talk to her. Never had he wished so hard to not be playing his saxophone.

The instrument itself had been his only love for so long that even his bandmates joked about how he loved it more than sex. There was some truth to it. Lukas had never found as much pleasure in coupling as he'd found playing music on this instrument. He'd tried, with all of them. Humans were enticing, but ultimately too complicated and too shallow at the same time, oblivious to the reality of the world they lived in. Ursa were fun, and he tended to gravitate to them more often lately, mostly because they seemed to enjoy his brand of humor and loved being entertained. The nymphaea were a little too … *female* for him. Perhaps having no male aspect to speak of made them that way, after the satyrs had been hunted to extinction.

He loved women, but also loved men for their familiarity. And the women he was most attracted to were the ones with powerful personalities.

Like his blue lady's friend … Lukas knew Erika well. He had very fond memories of her from when she'd hung around his and his brother's band in the early days—though she'd spent most of that time in his cousin, Ozzie's, bed. Erika had never known his cousin's true nature. She wasn't the woman for him, after all. But now it thrilled him to know she'd found a true mate in a dragon.

Lukas had always loved dragons. Perhaps it was their shared bond to the wind. The nymphaea could fly when they chose, but their true form was waterbound. The ursa were so tied to the earth that the sky was only of passing interest to them. Dragons craved the wind just like the turul did. Thrived on it. Air meant life for every creature, but the wind meant even more to his race. The North Wind was their deity—the one who gave them life. And she'd had an alliance with the Mother of Dragons since the beginning of time. Their fates were intertwined.

If only the Dragon Council weren't total jackasses. If only one of them hadn't fucked it all up for everyone. At least, that had been the legend passed down since practically the dawn of time. One of them had made the mistake that had changed their entire world and created the monsters they were forced to hide from now.

He might forgive them entirely, if this newly ascended beauty could be his. He might forget that his race and many others had wound up the targets of the Ultiori after the dragons went to ground.

Lukas's mood had been dark for several weeks over the same old thoughts, but lifted now that this woman was listening to him play what he'd always considered his mating song.

CHAPTER EIGHT

B elah closed her eyes, a little terrified by the effect the turul musician had on her. The music calmed her as much as it excited her. The notes that came out of that shining, golden instrument were as beautiful and primal as an ancient dragon's song—music she and her siblings had made together at the beginning of time.

The eerie way it mimicked the rhythm from the song in her dreams surprised her. Now that she was hearing it in person, she was transported by it. It didn't matter that a key rhythm seemed to be missing, as though a second instrument and the lyrics were left out, though she couldn't place where they belonged— the song reached deep into her and wrapped around her soul, anyway.

She didn't expect the sudden, aching need to be with this musician she now watched on stage, and the urge alarmed her. She could have chosen any man in the club Erika and Geva brought her to, but the man on stage was the one who captured her attention. And he was playing for her now; she could tell by the way his gaze never left hers the entire time. The sultry sounds he produced tickled her ears, then went straight to her core.

The humans in this club were all just as charmed by the music. But as empowering as being here was—seeing her effect on the men around her, especially—the effect of the music on her did just the opposite. The turul's focus gave her that same weightless sensation of surrender she'd felt so long ago with Nikhil, before he'd been perverted by his darkness. It wasn't a sense of being revered—worshiped—like other lovers. The music sank soul-deep into her, possessing her the way the wind did when she flew. But unlike the sensation of her surrender to Nikhil, there was no underlying sense of twisted need from the man on stage. The message was simple: *I can carry you away, if you let me.*

She shook herself, hating that she'd compare any potential lover to the monster she'd seen earlier that night. Nothing of what she'd loved about Nikhil remained inside the psyche of the man who had found her. When she'd known him before, his craving to inflict pain was always balanced by his confidence in his abilities to give just as much pleasure. He'd been the perfect embodiment of both to her, but now nothing but hatred remained. She wasn't sure whether she would react the way he hoped when she gave him that week with her. As much as her need for submission still burned in her belly—and had been reawakened by the very act of kneeling in front of her former lover—the idea of being taken to those places by this new version of Nikhil made her sick.

Lukas's music promised release of a different sort. There was a shadow of sadness in the sounds, but they were always tempered by hope, and even joy. If all the turul made music like this, she couldn't wait to find the man who would finally see her as his true mate—the one whose song sounded complete when he played it for her. In the meantime, she would enjoy the search, particularly if it meant she could experience these sounds over and over again.

Belah barely noticed the rest of the club, or even the fresh drink the waitress set before her. She closed her eyes just to experience the music, to surrender to it for a moment and imagine letting Lukas do just what his music seemed to offer—to carry her away

She opened her eyes again after the sounds took on an almost conversational, questioning tune—like he was trying to speak to her through the notes he played. She smiled up at him and was rewarded with a pleased look in his eyes that she'd acknowledged his message.

She let out a satisfied sigh when the song ended.

"He's hot shit, isn't he?" Erika asked, pulling herself away from Geva long enough to draw Belah into conversation. "His band used to tour worldwide, but I always love hearing them on their own turf. Especially Lukas. The man sure knows his way around a saxophone. His brother's just as talented—they used to play here together."

Belah nodded and took a sip of the wine in front of her. She closed her eyes, savoring the flavor and thinking how well the lingering mood from the music was complemented by the richness of the drink.

"He is nothing like I've experienced. Everything is so new and wonderful now. I wish I hadn't had to wait so long to leave the Glade."

She caught Erika and Geva both eyeing her with amused expressions and realized she'd been staring at Lukas, pondering whether he'd mind being watched by her Shadows while they made love—if he even knew they were there. He had a lovely, blue-tinged aura unlike those of the other musicians on the stage. It had the look of a smoky, glowing cloud around him, fluctuating with each breath he pushed into the mouthpiece of his instrument. When he began playing a new song, it was as if his aura pulsed in time to the beat, and bits of it flowed out of the end of the horn to drift through the air directly toward her.

In truth, she had probably chosen the perfect time to leave the Glade, particularly if it meant she found this lovely creature in his prime. Any other century, and she may have never discovered him.

The music seemed to have a profound effect on her companions, as well. Halfway through the next song, they disappeared from the private booth and didn't return for some time. The band was well into another set when they finally slid back into their seats. Erika looked flushed and both of their auras glowed tellingly. Belah looked forward to the cravings of expectant motherhood, when she found the right mate.

"I'll introduce you after their last set," Erika said. "I think he already likes you, so maybe he's the one." She gave Belah a knowing smile. "You should know he's a bit of a wild child, though. He's never seemed the type to settle down, but he has other talents besides his music. At the very least, you could have some fun, and you never know—maybe you're his true love, after all."

Geva let out a low chuckle, making Belah raise her eyebrows and study the pair. Intrigued, she asked, "You two have both been with him?"

Geva quirked the corner of his mouth without looking at her, his eyes still on Lukas. "Erika has excellent taste in partners, but no, we haven't had the pleasure of him yet."

Erika laughed. "Back in the day, it was Ozzie who I spent time with, but I heard plenty about his cousins' conquests too. Iszak and Lukas had quite a reputation." She turned to her mate with a sly look and said, "Maybe we'll have to ask Belah if she'd be willing to share."

Geva only shook his head. "Maybe after the baby comes." And with that, the couple were back to their tender kisses and caresses.

Belah sighed and set her attention back on Lukas, but her thoughts lingered on her hosts a moment longer. They were an inspiration for the kind of bond she hoped for, and when the baby quickened and grew larger in Erika's womb, she intended to grant the child a Blessing for the hospitality they'd shown her.

Until then, she appreciated the subtle, enticing energy the Red exuded. Being near the two of them made her feel alive and eager to find a mate. If Lukas with the seductive music and smoldering eyes was the one, then that was all the better. She didn't want to waste time.

The couple's intensity was as seductive as the music, and Belah shifted her attention from Lukas, watching Erika and

Geva over the rim of her wine glass. When Erika noticed and raised an eyebrow, Belah took a sip and set her glass down, smiling. "You two are refreshing companions, after spending so long away."

Erika reached for her own drink and took a sip while studying her. She licked her lips, her gaze flicking back to Geva, and then to Lukas up on stage. "You know, I heard a bit about what happened during the ritual with Rowan. I admit I'm a little envious that Geva got to spend time with you before. And that I missed it."

Belah's skin tingled under the growing heat in Erika's gaze. She recognized the fresh surge of aura that signaled an unborn baby's craving for power beyond what the mother could provide on her own. Erika probably didn't even realize herself that the impulse wasn't entirely within her control.

Geva's hand rested casually on his mate's thigh, but he stayed silent, watching. Erika leaned in, her aura flickering with excited curiosity. The thoughts that accompanied the impression were playful, but beneath them, Belah sensed Erika's own need to experience some of what her mate had. The music changed as Erika shifted closer, the tune becoming even more sultry and expectant—the drummer nearly missed a beat, but the bassist managed to pick up the slack. They must be quite accustomed to their sax player's improvisations.

When Erika's lips were close to Belah's ear, she whispered, "One thing I heard drives Lukas mad is being forced to watch when he can't touch." She slid her fingers through Belah's hair at the back of her head. The other woman's breath was warm and sweet from her cocktail, her lips soft and supple when they pressed against Belah's.

Erika's tongue darted out tentatively at first, the warmth of it oddly shocking to Belah's senses. She hadn't been this intimate with another female in so long, she'd nearly forgotten how sweet this kind of contact could be.

With that one sweep of Erika's tongue, Belah suddenly craved more and parted her lips, surrendering to the intensity of the kiss, giving herself up to it slowly. Erika deepened the kiss, her body shifting close enough that their hips and thighs touched. Belah clutched at her friend's arm for balance. So decisive a woman she'd never known outside of her own race, and it felt good to let go after the very rude interruption she'd experienced with Ozzie earlier.

Through the haze of arousal that one kiss incited, the music changed again, matching the shift in Erika's demeanor and the thoughts that clamored through her mind, all of them as plain to Belah as though she'd spoken. *God, I can't believe she's letting me do this. Will she let me in more? I have to try. Geva said none of them would lay back and accept me so easily. Too overbearing, my ass. I'll show him. She might not accept my Nirvana, but at least I can have a taste of hers.*

Beyond Erika, Geva's emotions only signaled pleasant amusement and intrigue, but not surprise. No, the surprise was reserved for Belah when Erika's fingertips traced a line along the slit in Belah's long gown and teased beneath across the sensitive skin of her inner thigh.

Erika pulled away from the kiss and pressed lips to the side of her throat, tracing a line with her tongue up to tease at her earlobe. "Can I?" she whispered, her voice husky, her aura crackling against Belah's skin like static.

Erika's fingertips lightly brushed against the edge of the lacy thong panties Belah had conjured, based on a description of what a potential lover might like. Her gaze drifted to the stage and locked onto Lukas. He was still a stranger, yet somehow she felt she was asking for his approval. He gave it with the slightest nod, the corners of his occupied mouth pulling back ever so slightly as though he were smiling around his mouthpiece. He couldn't have seen beyond their covered table to know precisely what was going on beneath, but Erika's position no doubt gave it away.

Without removing her eyes from his, Belah spread her thighs and sighed when Erika's deft fingers found her aching core and began to tease.

CHAPTER NINE

Lukas knew the moment Erika went for broke with her fingers between his pretty Blue dragon's legs. The woman's raven hair slid over her shoulders as her head tilted back, the sapphires in her ears sparkling at him almost as brightly as her eyes beneath half-lowered lids. Her lips parted and a sound only he could hear reached his ears—the softest moan of pleasure, so sweet and hungry it made his dick swell inside the leathers he wore. With a clever shift of his fingers on his sax, he changed the key and tempo of the tune to match her breathing.

Every woman had their own rhythm, but they were almost never in sync with his. Hers, however, meshed perfectly. His band fell into the beat like always, and the entire audience ceased to exist except for her.

He knew Erika was doing it to goad him. Being forced to watch without the option to touch made him edgy and irritable. Or it would have, on any other day. Today, the simple conviction that she was here just for him made him amenable to playing along. And it appeared Erika's Red mate was happy to go along with it, too—he'd slid up close to Erika's other side, and his arm was positioned so that there was no doubt Erika was receiving a similar treatment to what she was giving.

Sweet Jesus, he loved dragons. Wait until his brother, Iszak, found out Lukas had found *her*, and that she was one of the creatures they'd always secretly desired.

Having her put on a show just for him while he played for her was the perfect introduction, too. It let them simply see each other; it let her understand what he could do with his music. The music was a gift many of his kind had. He and his brother were what the humans might have called musical prodigies, but their command of the Winds and the powers they possessed were revered by his own race's standards—their musical talent was the least of it.

He wished he could draw this moment out longer, but it wasn't his touch inciting her to breathe heavier and bite her lip in an effort to suppress her sounds of ecstasy.

Moan for me, baby, he thought, even as he coaxed from his sax a sensual note that mimicked the sound he was sure she'd make. He'd only heard the first sound she made before she'd stifled the rest, but she seemed to appreciate the tune. Her chest heaved quicker, her hand tangled in the waves at the back of Erika's neck while Erika spoke into her ear. Erika urged her on with breathy words, hitching and rough from her own pleasure.

"Come so he can see—it'll drive him so wild, he won't be able to resist."

No, he wouldn't be able to resist. He'd been lost the second she walked through the door. Erika only needed to take credit for bringing her here.

As though it were his own fingertips playing her, the music's climax hit at the exact same moment her head fell back against the seat and a ripple of pure pleasure coursed down her body. Erika grinned for a second, waiting and teasing until his blue lady's pleasure finally ebbed. Then Erika turned, pulling her dragon mate into a deep kiss while the male carried her to her own obviously satisfying end, his ministrations still artfully obscured by the tablecloth.

The woman's breathing began to slow at the same pace as his song, and she never once let her gaze wander from him. Then the set was over and Lukas pulled his lips away from the mouthpiece. Reluctant to turn away from her for any reason, but needing to cool off, he winked at her, then stood up from his stool and bowed to the cheering crowd.

"You look a little shaky, man. Everything cool? You good for another set?" Dan, his bassist, murmured from behind him.

"Yeah. Take five. I need a drink."

He unclipped his sax and rested it on its stand, then turned and made his way down from the stage, past the expect-ant-looking blonde from earlier, only dimly aware of her excite-ment and subsequent disappointment when he walked past her table. He bee-lined straight to the booth in the back where his blue lady still sat, sipping a fresh glass of red wine and watching him come toward her as though she were expecting him. And shouldn't she be, after that?

For the first time in Lukas's life, words escaped him. He just stopped and looked at her, unable to articulate any kind of introduction. His fingers itched for his sax so he could play her another song, connect with her in the same way they had while he was on stage.

Erika's sultry chuckle rang in his ears. "Lukas, I'd like you to meet my friend, Belah. Belah, this is Lukas North. Fantastic show, as always."

"Thank you," Lukas said, tearing his eyes away from Belah just long enough to politely nod at Erika. He had the craziest urge to bow, but instead only held out his hand. *Belah, Belah, Belah,* he said over and over in his mind. What a fucking beautiful name. *Belah Blue.*

He did bow when she placed her smooth, pale hand in his. He bent low over it and pressed his lips to the silken skin, enjoying the little intake of breath he heard when he darted his tongue out to fleetingly taste her. He resisted the urge to pull her up and into his arms, instead raising his head and nodding again at Erika and her mate.

"I don't believe I've had the pleasure?"

Erika grinned, her cheeks growing even rosier as she introduced the Red. "Gavin Hayden," she said, but stumbled a bit over the name. It hit him that she may not have been clued in by her mate that Lukas was a turul, otherwise she'd have used her lover's real name. He glanced at the Red and raised an eyebrow.

"My friends call me Geva. You're the first turul Erika's met … that she knew of, anyway," he said, reaching out and grasping Lukas's hand with his, dwarfing it in the process. Lukas was abstractly grateful that the females of the race weren't quite so large, but then the dragons did get to choose their human forms, unlike his race. He wholeheartedly approved of Belah's shapely curves.

Erika's eyes widened and she turned to whisper a question in her lover's ear. Lukas would let them deal with the miscommunication on their own. Shifting his attention back to Belah, he smiled.

"May I?" he asked, gesturing to the seat beside her.

"Yes," she said, scooting farther into the booth to make room for him.

One of the club's waitresses promptly set his preferred drink down in front of him, and he thanked her before turning back to Belah.

She regarded him with an interested look that barely concealed a deeper hunger. If he didn't know how dragons worked, she would have given him the distinct impression that he would be her dinner. Clearing his throat, he tore his gaze from hers and focused on the ice in his glass.

"Ah, how are you enjoying the show?" he asked lamely.

"More enthralling than my sweetest dreams," she replied, her voice smooth and cool, with a hint of a deeper resonance that set his musician's instincts vibrating. His cock definitely knew that song.

From the other side of the booth, Erika leaned forward. "Why isn't your brother up there with you tonight?" she asked. Turning to Belah, she added, "The pair of them together are even better. Of course, Ozzie's the glue. Their trio's what I played for you last night."

The mention of his brother and cousin made Lukas itch uncomfortably. Family meant everything to him, but ever since his sister died, their relationships had gradually degenerated. Erika had met them during one of their reunion phases about a decade past. They'd tried to be a family again—for their late sister's sake—but that never went well. Evie had been their front-woman, before the Ultiori took her. She was the one with the voice. Adding Ozzie to the mix was supposed to revive them, but hadn't really helped. Their music had improved somewhat over the years, but their relationship was still shit.

Erika didn't know that about him, though. At the time, she'd been attached to Ozzie's hip. She'd only known that he and his brother were broody musicians with short attention spans where lovers were concerned. Lukas loved his brother, but they'd established over and over that they simply couldn't work together for extended periods or they'd both self-destruct.

"Iszak has his own solo gig now. Fate's Fools still play at the Gatormouth once a month."

The truth was, they couldn't *not* make music together on a regular basis. He and Iszak still lived together, which was just about the maximum amount of contact he could handle with his brother—but necessary, according to their grandmother. So they compromised. Ozzie hated the band's schedule, but he was young, and drummers never had a problem finding gigs.

Turning back to Belah, he said, "You should come. The show's two weeks from tonight."

"You play with your brother, and … cousin?"

Her accented voice was so light and hesitant, as though she weren't a native speaker of the language. Even though she spoke perfect English, he had to remind himself that it was Dragon Ascension season and she might have been born in another country. Fuck, another *century*.

"Right," he said, nodding. "My brother plays tenor sax or guitar, depending on his mood, and our cousin plays drums." He beat out a soft rhythm on the table to emphasize.

"Your cousin … Ozzie…?"

By the Winds, was she adorable, working over the words in that sweet tone of hers. He wondered if she could sing.

"Well, his given name is Oszkar, but that's what we call him, yeah … Erika must have mentioned him. He's the best percussionist in the world, really. Kicks a beat like no other." He snorted slightly, thinking about how well he'd heard Ozzie kicking a beat with Erika back in her groupie days, but elected not to share that detail in front of Erika's intimidating mate.

"Does he come to your shows when you don't play together?" she asked, looking around.

Now Lukas was worried. "Never, actually … I mean, we have our regular gig, but we try to stay out of each other's hair in between. It's not like we need to practice. My bandmates hate that I never show up for that, but they know me."

"Oh." She seemed to visibly relax.

Before he could ask her about it, the telltale riffs from his bassist sounded, letting him know his guys were ready to start the next set.

"That's my cue," he said. He stood up and kissed her cheek, hating that he had to leave her now, but he was committed to all his gigs. Even though they were part of his human cover, he needed to play music like he needed to breathe. He wouldn't cut a gig short for a woman he'd just met, even if it physically hurt him to walk away from her.

And fuck, did it hurt when he walked away.

She's the One.

Lukas took his spot on stage again, with his sax in hand and his butt on his stool. When he locked eyes with Belah again, the ache in his soul disappeared.

And he played, their gazes never straying for the rest of the night.

By the end of the evening, he had no memory of what he'd played, only that the entire audience stood up and applauded and the guys were patting his back saying things like, "Holy shit, dude, where the fuck did that come from?"

Her ... it came from her. As he looked down at Belah's smiling face, he shook his head in wonder. "It's you," he mouthed to her, not even caring whether she knew what he meant.

Her head tilted, and she whispered back the word, "Maybe."

How could she not know? His gut clenched with worry, but she stayed, at least, smiling and waiting for him to pack up for the night. He watched her say farewell to her friends, and for the first time in forever, he was actually happy ... scratch that, fucking *ecstatic* ... to be going home for the night.

CHAPTER TEN

"I hope you like the wind," Lukas said with a grin as he led Belah through a dimly lit corridor to a doorway in the back of the club. Outside, he made a fancy show of handing her an object she had no idea what to make of.

He turned away while she studied the smooth, shining helmet. It was unlike any battle gear she'd ever seen, with its round shape and soft cloth on the inside, but hard and sturdy like a shiny black egg on the outside. The magic from his music still thrummed in her mind, and she smiled at him giddily while he secured the black case that held his instrument onto the back of his steed.

"You ever ride before?" he asked, shoving a helmet onto his head and securing the strap under his chin. "Put it on, baby. Don't want your pretty head messed up if we take a spill on the way home. I promise I won't—the wind will carry us—but it's against the law not to wear one."

"All right," she said, shaking her head at her own sense of being swept away. *Oh, Mother, I don't ever remember it being like this.*

Even with … She didn't finish the thought, refusing to sully the evening with memories of her past mistakes.

Lukas came toward her, shrugging out of his leather jacket. "Put this on," he said. "It'll keep you warm."

Cool air wouldn't be an issue for her, but she agreed with a nod, turning to let him slip the jacket over her shoulders. It dwarfed her slender frame, but smelled like clouds and rain and sky. She took a deep breath, reveling in the scent of him that surrounded her now, so utterly different from the dark, dangerous aroma of her old lover.

He eyed her long dress as she was about to climb on. "That might be a problem. Can you do something about it?"

The dress itself was conjured—everything Belah wore was, aside from the jacket he'd just given her. She nodded and gathered the skirt up, baring her long legs to him, and wrapped the length around her hips, tucking the fabric into itself like a sarong.

"Will this do?" she asked. Impulsively, she also kicked off her shoes and picked them up.

Lukas gave her an odd look, but nodded. "Climb on behind me and hold on tight."

He wasn't kidding about the wind, either. The name for his machine finally came to her just as she wrapped her arms around his waist and the engine came to life beneath them.

Motorcycle, she thought. *It's like a car, but better because it's between your legs and makes you feel like you're flying.*

The thought made her grin like an idiot, but it was true. She found it tricky not to stretch her wings as he sped down the streets of the city with her clinging to him. The need to fly made her shoulder blades itch, but suppressing it caused her need for magic to swell to bursting inside her. Once they reached their destination, she hoped he wouldn't waste time making love to her. To combat the urge, she clung tighter to him, letting her hands press against his belly, her face against the taut strength of his wide shoulders.

The sheer, vibrant life of him thrilled her. He was the first man in more than three thousand years whose contact made her insides melt with anticipation. During that ride, Belah nearly cried at how beautiful those sensations were, the warmth of his abdomen sinking into her palms where she pressed against him. She longed to touch him more, but knew it was better to wait.

She avoided reading his emotions, aside from the few bits that made her core grow warm. He wanted her. Of course he did, or else he wouldn't have extended his invitation. She wondered if those words he'd whispered from across the room at the club meant what she hoped they did. His reaction to her was certainly more optimistic than Ozzie's had been at dinner—not to mention after he had learned her secret.

She squeezed her arms tighter around Lukas and inhaled his scent, her heartbeat syncing with his in a way that made the confusion of her meeting with Nikhil fade away. Everything about Lukas felt like a puzzle piece shifting into place—even though a piece still seemed like it was missing, what was here undoubtedly fit.

And she absolutely wanted him. Her hand strayed lower down his belly, her need urging her to touch him. His aura grew warmer the lower her fingers moved, and that smoky cloud she'd seen around him earlier puffed out of him and filtered around her like no other aura she'd ever witnessed. The scent of the wind at high altitudes pervaded her senses, making her feel even more like flying. He gripped her hand at a stoplight and pulled it lower, pressing it against his hard length beneath his leathers.

"You want this, baby? Take it easy on me for about ten more minutes and you'll get it, all right?"

Ten minutes felt like ten million. But soon enough, Lukas pulled into a darkened street by a massive brick building. Belah heard nothing around them besides the lap of water nearby and turned to see the waters of a bay. He dismounted and lifted her into his arms, then set her barefoot on the ground. He walked to a huge door and lifted it. Inside was an almost empty room, brightly lit, with a shining gray floor like the garage on the bottom level of Erika and Geva's building. There was nothing inside but a long, waist-high bench along one wall, and a collection of cabinets, neatly closed.

Lukas came back to stand before her, tugged at the clip of her helmet, and pulled it off. For a split second he looked like he might speak, but he startled her with his lips suddenly pressed against hers.

The depth of his need pervaded her senses. He'd been about to tell her to come inside, she knew that much. But he was hard to read, which lent an air of mystery to him that only made her want him more.

She didn't care much, though. He tasted good, and if a Prince of the North Wind were such an enigma, it only betrayed the strength of his magic. If she were his true mate, she would finally have a lover she could mark without worrying he would lose his will to her magic.

As he kissed her, Lukas pushed his jacket off her shoulders and let his hands roam down her arms. She loved how decisive he was. How much he seemed to know precisely what he wanted and what might please her. Her old craving for surrender swelled within her and she let it come, knowing that with this man there was no hidden darkness threatening to take over. She leaned into him, threading her fingers through his hair and letting him devour her.

With a low growl, he pulled away. "Fuck, Belah. Can I take my bike in before you destroy me entirely?"

"Yes," she whispered, reluctantly releasing him. She let the hem of her dress cascade back to her ankles and followed him inside, dazed by the kiss and wondering how the hell her kind hadn't been secretly mating turul for centuries already.

She leaned against the tool-covered bench and enjoyed his steady, comfortable movements as he closed the garage door and worked on his bike for a few moments. He removed the case with his instrument first and set it beside her, kissing her again slowly before grabbing a cloth and walking back to the bike to wipe it down.

"She gets cranky if I don't clean her up after a ride," he explained.

Belah glanced down at the dark case he'd set beside her, resting her hand on it. "What about *her*? She did more work tonight, by my estimation."

Lukas grinned. "You're right, but she gets to sleep in a velvet bed, and she understands I have other priorities tonight. This lady …" He gestured to the bike. "She's more temperamental."

"Do you love all your women so well?" Belah asked, enthralled by this man who so perfectly embodied her ideal.

"No," he said, wiping down the shining silver pipes of his machine.

Blinking at him, she nearly asked why until he looked at her, his storm-gray eyes intense enough to burn through her soul.

"The ones who almost make me too shaky to finish a gig get extra attention." His movements slowed, his hand pausing on the seat of the bike, regarding her with parted lips. His gaze raked over her. "Fuck it, the bike can wait."

Suddenly he was before her, tearing his dirty shirt off over his head and flinging it into a corner. He lifted Belah up, set her on the rough wooden bench, and crushed her lips with his in a fast, hungry kiss that left her breathless.

He tore himself away with a gasp, as though trying not to drown. They gazed into each other's eyes, Lukas's heaving chest making it apparent to her that she had the same effect on him. It had been so long since a man had affected her this way, with every action more surprising and wonderful than the last, and all of it before they'd made love even once. He fascinated her in a way that was tough to articulate. And never had a man filled her with such hopeful anticipation.

As though sensing she wanted to speak, his eyebrows rose in inquiry. With one broad thumb, he traced the curve of her lower lip, a silent enticement to let her words come free.

"I like watching you," she said with a slight shrug.

"Oh? Did you enjoy watching me as much as I enjoyed watching Erika take care of you earlier?"

She flushed in response to the slow smile that tugged at his lips, and her magic fluctuated dangerously, her skin shimmering into pale blue scales under the harsh lights of his garage.

"Maybe not quite so much. I'd like to see how you look in that moment—then perhaps we'll be even."

"*That moment*," he repeated in a rough voice, so laden with desire it seemed to drip with it. "That moment might come quicker than you think, but I plan for us to have many more. Tell me how long it's been for you so I know how much I ought to pace myself. I want to give you as many orgasms as you give me."

He tugged her hips to the edge of the bench and pressed between her thighs, forcing her to wrap her legs around him. His erection throbbed hot and hard through their clothes, and she tilted her hips to rub against him.

"Too long," she said against his lips.

Please, let's start now.

She wasn't quite sure whether it was his thought or hers, but she was in no mood to hesitate once it became clear that was exactly what he intended to do. His hands bracketed her jaw and his lips were on hers again, the nips and tugs speaking a language to her that she'd forgotten she knew fluently. She answered with her own urgent, hungry bites, grazing her teeth over his jaw and neck, just rough enough to cause a little pain, but not to break his skin.

He pulled back, grabbing her hands in his when she reached for him again, and she hated even the short distance he'd put between them. The determined expression in his eyes betrayed the hint of a plan.

"Hold still, right here," he whispered, pressing her hands to the edge of the bench.

She nodded, thrilled by the command, and dug her fingers into the wood, determined to let him have control, even though the urge to touch him back was almost too strong to bear.

It gave her a moment to observe him in the light. She'd experienced Lukas's contact just enough to know he was a well-built man, but seeing gave her a different perspective than touching. He had the solid build of a dragon, but without their massive stature. He was still large by human standards, however, with broad shoulders and the form of a man comfortable using his body frequently. The dusting of dark hair across his chest made her fingers tingle again with the urge to touch him. Her moment would come soon enough. For now, she would simply enjoy giving in to his whims.

She tilted her head into his hand when he lifted it to her cheek in a soft caress. Her eyelids fluttered closed as she imagined the sounds of his music filling her mind earlier, the rhythm matching her every breath.

"Look at me," he said. "I want your baby blues to see what you do to me."

She did, opening her eyes to meet his gaze, so filled with need it made her core ache to have him, but waiting was part of the pleasure. Something deeper lingered in his eyes, too, and she tentatively reached out with her mind, hoping it might be the spark of something truly beautiful; a reflection of what had lit inside her when she'd first heard his music in person earlier that night. Hoping it meant that he saw her as more than a fleeting tryst and that his instincts were driving him toward her because she was his true mate.

His caress moved down her neck, fingers teasing at her throat. He bent and pressed hot, silky lips against her collarbone and trailed them further south, the path preceded by his fingertips tugging at the strap of her dress, pushing her bodice down until one breast was bared to him.

Belah tilted her head back with a moan when he wrapped his lips around her nipple. One hand strayed to his head to hold him there, but he chuckled and clutched it, putting it back down beside her thigh on the bench.

"You make me so hungry for you, baby. Watching you come to the sound of my music tonight was the best introduction I've ever had to a woman. Now you get to sit back and watch me play your body like an instrument, and I get to hear the music you make."

He moved his mouth to her other breast, the straps of her dress falling down to her elbows. One of his hands slid under her dress, pushing the velvet fabric higher until his fingertips reached the thin lace where her panties crossed her hip.

She let out a sharp gasp when he twisted the delicate fabric in his fingers and tugged hard. The cloth stretched and snapped.

"That's right, let me hear you," he said, glancing down at her exposed skin, her creamy breasts rising and falling, nipples hard and tingling, aching for his mouth again.

He tugged the remnant of her panties from under her and let them dangle from his fingers for a second before draping them over a small hook on the wall behind her. She didn't have the heart to tell him they'd fade away after she left him, but perhaps she'd never leave.

Then he was on his knees, his face a breath from the slick, sensitive skin between her open thighs.

All he did was blow, the soft breath gusting against her folds in a cool caress. Despite the fact that it was only air, it did something to her. The sharpest pleasure she'd ever experienced began with that sensation against her most sensitive flesh. It was subtle at first, but grew exponentially when his fingers parted her and he blew again, a targeted breath aimed right at her clit.

She moaned and tilted her hips toward him, wishing for more. And he repeated the process, moving his head in a slow circle, the current teasing her in a spiral, closer and tighter until his lips were against her, sucking gently.

The shuddering moan that escaped her then resonated through the room, deep and filled with primal hunger.

He didn't seem in a hurry to stop, taking his time with his tongue and lips teasing her and urging her to vocalize her pleasure.

"That's right, baby," he murmured. "Tell me how it feels with my tongue deep in your pussy. Tell me what you like."

"I want your hands on me, too," she managed to stutter out, and he immediately complied, reaching up and clutching both her breasts.

He pinched her nipples, making her gasp at the thrill the pain sent through her. As if understanding exactly how much pleasure it gave her, he did it again. When she let out a fresh moan, Lukas slowed the pace of his tongue on her clit and looked up at her.

"Like that?" he asked. He rose in front of her, his eyes wide and excited at the discovery, as though she'd revealed the best kind of secret. "How 'bout this?" He bent and took one taut, pink tip gently between his teeth, then bearing down little by little until the pain grew to a bright, hot point that made her cry out and clutch at his head.

"Oh! Lukas, no. I can't …" Sweet Mother, did she need more, but the craving for surrender was already frighteningly close to her ancient addiction to oblivion. The pain might send her spiraling into a dangerous pit she wasn't sure she was equipped to pull herself out of again.

"Baby, I may not be able to see your aura the way you can see mine, but the Wind tells me all your secrets if I want it to. It's nothing to be afraid of if you like a little pain. I just want to make you feel good, that's all."

Unable to help herself, she let out a breath of magic that filtered into his lungs and deep inside his mind. Instantaneously, she saw the raw truth of his words. All he cared about was her pleasure—he had no agenda of his own—no darker need for pain and destruction—just the desire to make her happy. Belah shuddered and arched her breasts up for him to take, clutching at his head to pull him back down.

"That's a good girl. But remember—no hands yet," he said, and she immediately slapped her hands back down against the bench.

Lukas stood up straight again, eyes never leaving hers as he unfastened his pants and released his erection. "I need to be inside you when I make you come," he said, and Belah only nodded, beyond ready to have him.

His thick length parted her slick folds and he sank deep. The first stroke only managed to make her aching core crave more, and the renewed spark of pain his teeth inspired in her breast only made that need crescendo. He pulled his hips back and thrust deep with a swift, violent surge, biting her harder at the same time.

Belah struggled not to reach out and cling to him, instead crying out her affirmation. "Yes! Ohh, yes, don't stop!"

The blue velvet of her dress slipped down, tangling around her thigh. Lukas cursed and gripped it hard in his fingers, ripping the front of it with a fierce pull that rent the fabric like gauze. The velvet parted and fell away around her hips, leaving her naked.

"Sorry," he muttered with a slight grimace, but thankfully, he did not cease his steady fucking.

Belah clung to him, needing Lukas close against her now that she was fully naked. The dress was the last thing she cared about.

"Oh, Belah," he moaned, pulling back to look down at her again. "You're the most beautiful thing I've ever seen. I can't … can't hold back, baby."

"Don't!" she gasped, digging her nails into his shoulders and pulling him back down into a desperate kiss. His steady thrusting hit her at the precise angle to set her entire body aflame with ecstasy. She closed her eyes then and opened up her senses to feel him fully. All his thoughts and emotions became clear as day to her, wrapped up in the beautiful, puffy cloud of his aura. But when she opened her eyes and saw the reverence in his gaze, she knew without a doubt that he believed she was more than just a quick lay.

The awareness made her clutch him tighter. She cried out his name, letting her true voice out, the roar vibrating the room as his power rushed into her with his climax.

The power of the Wind surging through them both was too strong for her to resist, too strong to deny the pull of her true form seeking its own release. She suppressed most of it, but her wings refused to stay hidden and came forth with a loud snap and quivering stretch when she came.

Lukas's own harsh cry sang out, and she opened her eyes just in time to see a pair of huge, feathered wings erupt from his back, shimmering with variegated gold and russet tones.

He grinned at her, panting and breathless. "Beautiful Blue Belah," he said. "Your wings are amazing."

"So are yours." She stared, wide-eyed, at the wings that almost perfectly matched the feathered version from her dreams. Then she laughed out loud at the understanding, shaking her head at her idiocy.

"What is it?" he asked, one eyebrow twitching as he looked down at her, perplexed by her reaction.

"I never knew how wonderful making love to a Prince of the North Wind could be."

She reached up a hand to his rough cheek, caressing him in wonder. Fate was having fun with her tonight, teasing her with one of Zephyrus's line, only to finally send her a child of Boreas who couldn't stop looking at her like he'd discovered heaven.

Lukas cringed. "No prince here. Those days are long past." He shook his head, his wings folding back in and fading into nothingness again as he separated himself from her.

"I've been out of touch for a while," she said.

"Ah, right … the Ascension was recent, wasn't it? We don't always get a memo, you know. It would be nice if you guys let the other high races know when you're waking up. Five hundred years is an awfully long nap. We tend to forget." He kissed her as though he were welcoming her home for the first time, even though she'd never been in hibernation. She had been as good as hibernating, however, and for a lot longer than five hundred years.

With a swift tug, he pulled her off the bench and lifted her up, cradling her in his arms and carrying her across the room.

"Where are we going?" she asked, disconcerted by the elation in his eyes. His smile infected her with mirth and she laughed out loud, his recent words nearly forgotten.

"I'm carrying you across my threshold. Because you are my *One,* and I'm never letting you go."

"Oh?" she asked, delighted at his confidence. "And how are you going to keep me?"

"By making you so happy you forget there's a world out there that dragons have to fear. There are no Ultiori in my bedroom, and no laws but love, baby. And I'm going to love you forever."

"You expect to bind me with words, then?" She gave him an amused look and he laughed, his face splitting into a wide grin.

Belah was secretly thrilled with his pronouncement. A turul would never use the word "forever" lightly.

"I have other means to make you behave, trust me," he said.

After a swift ascent up a dark, narrow staircase, Lukas brought her into a vast apartment that fascinated her with its modernity, just like everything else she'd seen since returning to the world. He didn't give her a chance to enjoy the architecture of the interior before he carried her into a room that only featured the barest hint of walls. They didn't even extend to the ceiling, which was lined with bars and pipes that extended to the brick walls on the sides. She made a mental note to ask Erika about it later. Then all thoughts left her mind as he laid her down on his bed and settled over her.

"So tell me what it's like," he said. "Ascending, I mean."

"Oh. Ah …" Belah tried to come up with an adequate response, and probably could have if he hadn't been busy with his mouth on her. His talented tongue was making slow, soft circuits over her sore nipples, and he kept blowing on them in between. She realized suddenly that the Wind was what had driven her so mad before. And now he was using it again to ease the soreness he'd caused. She sighed under his ministrations.

"No answer?" he asked between breaths.

"You just made me forget. Does it even matter?" she asked.

His dark brows drew together with his frown. "You're the first dragon I've met from the new brood. It's new to you, so I want to know what it was like. How you felt … how you were received …" He sighed and rolled away, sliding up beside her and propping himself on an elbow. "Fine, I need dirt, all right?

I need to know what the fuck the Council is doing. I've only heard rumors that laws have changed, but no word on what the fuck those bastards are actually going to do about the shit they caused."

Belah's skin prickled in response to his vehement need to hear about what she and her siblings had done. Her body still craved his touch, but he was just lying there looking at her—expecting—what? A condemnation? Yet the look in his eyes told her he desperately needed to know something.

"Why do the turul care about three-thousand-year-old dragon laws?" she asked, wishing she was really as ignorant as she sounded. A new broodling wouldn't know the first thing about the politics. She did know about the politics, but the turul were allies and had rarely expressed an interest in dragon law. That any of them would hold such animosity toward herself and her siblings—toward the laws they'd made to preserve their race or the reasons why they existed—was news to her.

"Most don't." His eyes darkened with emotion, and Belah couldn't resist a look into his mind to find out why. He glanced away just as she was hit with a poignant combination of pain and loss, buried deep in anger for something that had happened very recently.

"Lukas," she said softly, rolling over and reaching up to brush her fingers down his temple and urge him to face her again. "Who did you lose? Tell me what happened."

He swallowed thickly and gazed back at her, his eyes glassy from emotion. "I forgot what a Blue could do—you can see right through me, can't you?"

She nodded. "Only if you're open enough, and I can tell you're hurting now. Let me know why—maybe I can help. I'm good at other things besides reading you. I can ease the pain at least."

Lukas shook his head. "It doesn't matter what happened anymore because there's not a damn thing I can do about it. She's gone—my sister, Evie, is gone—taken and bled dry by those Ultiori bastards. I used to wish I could find the Council bitch who started it all. The Blue Beast, we call her. You know there are rumors among my people about how it all started? Do you even know what your leaders have covered up?"

A deep chill sank into Belah's gut at his words. *The Council bitch who started it all.* She pressed tighter against his warm body, hoping that the closeness might obliterate her shame, but the squeeze of his arm around her torso only made it worse.

"I know they're trying to fix it," she said softly, though she feared it may be too little, too late if someone he loved had been lost already. And how many others had been lost in the intervening centuries? Too many. And no matter what she and her siblings or the Court did, they wouldn't be able to undo those deaths.

Lukas turned onto his side with a heartbreaking sigh and pressed his face into her neck. "I'm just happy I found you," he said. "Because believe me, I needed something good to happen. And baby, you're even better than I imagined."

"I'm nothing special," she said.

"Oh, I disagree." Lukas brushed his hand down her side and gripped her hip, kneading his fingers into her flesh in a way that set her alight again. He pressed her back against the mattress, moving to hover over her. "You're perfect, Belah. I knew the second you came into the club tonight that you were for me."

To illustrate his point, he grabbed both her hands and raised them up over her head, pinning them there. He rose onto his knees, straddling her torso. Something soft slipped around her wrists and she craned her neck back to see what he was doing. Her pulse quickened when the rope bindings he'd wrapped around her wrists grew snug as he tied them to the sturdy iron headboard of his bed.

"This turns you on, doesn't it? Even more than me telling you not to touch me. And the little bit of pain I gave you—that drove you even wilder. I've never met a dragon like you before. Usually your kind are disappointingly assertive. How did you wind up so pliant? So fucking perfect?"

"Don't …" she started, but didn't finish when he regarded her with a raised eyebrow.

"Don't what? Don't pleasure you?"

She swallowed, unsure how to express her fears of going too far with him. She could easily break the flimsy bindings he had her in, but it felt too good to hover on that edge of giving up control, and once the ropes were tied, she didn't think she'd *want* to break them.

"Do you take pleasure in it? In taking away my control … causing me pain?"

He sat back, regarding her quietly. "Not as such, no. There was a time when I needed it just to feel like I had some control over a life that was otherwise under Fate's thumb. It was never about the pain unless my partner asked for it, though. Now it's always about her pleasure, and my magic lets me know all the little secrets of a woman's darkest fantasies. I think yours used to be darker than they are now, just like mine, but you're scared of who you are, aren't you? It's nothing to be afraid of—that need for submission. And I'm not some kind of crazed sadist who gets off on hurting people. If you don't like it, just say no."

Lukas slipped away from her without waiting for a response, and a moment later returned with a lit candle. The flame flickered as he settled back over her, his thick muscles offset by the shadows cast from the candlelight. His magnificent erection rested hot against her belly when he straddled her hips again, holding the candle above her breasts.

She knew exactly what the candle meant, but more than that, the sweet sensation of his skin against hers was already enough to make her core ache with need again. To be so utterly at his mercy now, anticipating the things he was about to do to her, she couldn't help but let out a soft moan even before the first drop of wax hit her chest.

He started slowly, tilting the candle and letting a small trickle of hot wax trail down between her breasts. He paused and waited, watching her intently.

"Yes or no?" he asked in a low voice.

Belah's breathing quickened as the wax cooled and hardened on her chest. Wet heat pooled between her legs and her core ached anew for everything this man could give her. Did she dare go down this well-trodden path and risk falling off that cliff again? Oh, but he had said the perfect things. He promised pleasure and nothing more, and she so wanted what he was about to give her.

"Yes."

"Remember, eyes open," he said in a voice thick with desire. She was dimly aware of his hips shifting ever so slowly back and forth against her, his soft sac sliding against her mound and his cock leaving its own hot trail just beneath her navel.

She couldn't stop watching him. Those deep gray eyes gazed down at her with such unrepentant emotion, obscured on one side by that errant lock of his straight, dark hair. His lips parted as though he were hungry to taste her skin, but he held off. The candlelight moved, and a searing drop of molten wax hit the tip of her breast, making her cry out with the pleasure of it. She pressed her thighs together and tilted her hips up against him, wishing like mad that he'd move his hips lower.

"Is this good?" he asked. "Or do you want more?"

She panted her answer. "More, please. Hotter."

His eyebrows twitched. "Hotter, hmm? That's right, you are more tolerant of extremes, aren't you? I'll have to see what I can do."

With a soft breath from his pursed lips, the flame flickered and grew even brighter. The next drip of wax hit her other nipple and trailed down beneath her breast. The heat was even more exquisite, sinking into her sensitive skin, and sending a blazing rift straight between her thighs.

"Let me hear you, baby," he murmured. "Tell me what you want."

"Lukas," she said, unable to bring any thought to mind but the syllables of his name, as focused as she was on the pleasure he gave her. "More, please. Don't stop."

CHAPTER ELEVEN

Lukas paused with the candle held over her belly. He could paint her with the molten fluid for hours and never get tired of her enthralling reactions. Her back was arched, her hands gripping the frame of his bed. He hadn't needed to bind her, but the presence of the ropes around her wrists had pleased her as he thought they might. And the red trails of the wax stood out starkly against the creamy perfection of her skin.

Again, he was astounded at how readily she'd given herself to him, at how perfectly she'd melded with him when they made love, and how his entire body still hummed from the orgasm they'd shared. She'd lit him on fire from the inside out, and the Wind in his soul made him burn even hotter for her, just as the candle flame flared from the tiny breath he let curl around it.

Her body, more than her words, signaled how much she needed the pain he was giving her. That a dragon female could give up her power so easily amazed him. They weren't generally submissive to anyone but their own kind. That she'd chosen to submit to *him* was an even greater gift. Her trust made it even more apparent that she must be the One—then again, he'd known that from the moment he'd set eyes on her.

Belah's hips tilted up against his ass again, her soft skin brushing against the underside of his balls, causing his cock to throb ever harder. Her skin seemed to soak in the heat from the wax, her body growing warmer by the second. No wonder she needed it hotter. He blew lightly again on the candle's flame, just enough to feed it, to make the wax hotter. He could only take it so far without it burning up entirely, though. He was nearly finished. At least he was nearing his own breaking point of need to be inside her again.

"Lukas," she whispered. "Please. I need you."

"One more second, baby," he said, shifting down past her hips and gently pushing her legs apart.

She was skittish despite her obvious craving for pain. Some deeper demons kept her from letting herself go. He had to be careful, or he might scare her away. He'd heard enough stories of turul finding human mates, only to have them run because they were spooked by the instant adoration.

He slid a palm over her warm thigh and she obligingly shifted, spreading herself for him.

The way her pussy opened for him was mesmerizing. He wanted to taste her, but held back. She needed something different.

He tilted the candle over her stomach and let a continuous stream of wax run in a long line down the center. With a spark of creativity, he altered the path to make a full circle, then continued in a tightening spiral. It pooled in her navel and she cried out a breathy moan, her belly tightening and quivering. He continued lower still, using his knees now to push her legs even further apart and urging her to bend her legs to spread her pussy wider.

Belah was panting hard now, her breasts rising and falling rapidly. He held the candle upright for a second to let more hot wax collect in the caldera around the wick. Keeping it poised there, he bent his head between her spread thighs and captured her swollen clit between his lips, unable to resist a taste before he gave her the final gift. Her velvet flesh was hot and slick, and it was all he could do to release her instead of delving in with his tongue. He pulled back just far enough to give himself room and tilted the candle over her flesh.

The red stream trickled across the top of her cleft first, and she jerked against her bindings.

Lukas paused. "Too much?"

"No. Sweet Mother, I love it."

The brief taste of her had already made it clear how much she loved it. Her sweet snatch was dripping with her arousal, her clit hot and swollen with need.

Lukas's head pounded with the unmistakably deep connection he already had with her after their earlier lovemaking. Everything after was a treat.

With a slight turn of his wrist, he let the rest of the wax pour out, right on target.

Belah bucked her hips, as though inviting more of the molten fluid to flow between her legs. With his free hand, Lukas gripped the back of one knee and pushed it up and wide, then sent another hot stream of wax against her sensitive flesh, this time letting it trickle further down between the cheeks of her ass.

She let out a resonant cry that included his name repeated over and over, the sweetest sound he'd ever heard.

He blew out the candle and tossed it to the floor, then bent and blew on the still cooling wax. It instantly hardened, and he kept blowing until it froze entirely, cracking from the shock of the quick temperature change.

"Please, please, I need you," she cried as her flesh trembled beneath his breath.

"You got me, baby." Lukas brushed the fragments of frozen wax away from her pink folds and released her leg, moving close between her thighs, his cock in hand where the candle had been moments earlier. This time, he'd fill her with his own molten fluid.

He thrust hard into her, reveling in the way her muscles immediately clamped down around him, as though she never wanted to let him go.

She struggled against the bindings and he reached up to swiftly untie her, but didn't let her move her hands down. Instead he twined his fingers through hers, holding them above her head while he pistoned into her with hard, urgent strokes.

"That's right," he said in response to the look of utter worship she gave him. "You're all mine now, aren't you? Let me feel that sweet magic when you come for me, baby. Give it to me, Belah. My love."

She answered with her body's silken curves undulating beneath him, rising to meet each of his steady thrusts. Her legs wrapped tightly around him and her muscles gripped his cock so perfectly he struggled not to let go too soon.

She didn't speak again, only lifting her head to capture his mouth with hers. He sank down atop her, devouring her lips and tongue with his and simply letting their shared orgasm carry them both away like the current of a strong breeze beneath their wings.

"I never want to stop," Lukas whispered once his climax subsided and he could gaze into her eyes again with a somewhat clear head. "How in the world do I stop after finding you?"

"Hmm, maybe we just take a breath and enjoy the moment?" Belah suggested. She made no movements to dislodge his cock from her body, nor did she remove her legs from around his hips, though she relaxed a tiny bit. She'd closed her eyes and seemed to be listening to something, with her head tilted and her mouth a soft curve of a smile that he wanted to kiss, but was too curious about its origin to destroy it just yet.

"Why are you smiling?"

"You're inside me, and I love it."

Lukas raised an eyebrow and glanced down between them to where his cock was still solidly entrenched inside her, steadily growing hard again. Belah laughed.

"No, that isn't what I mean. Your magic is in my blood now, and it makes me hear music."

"What kind of music?" he asked, a little worried.

"*Your* music. I hear every note. I *feel* every note in my soul now. I am yours, aren't I?"

Lukas studied her face, trying to grasp the enormity of the moment and suddenly having trouble even believing that he'd found her. *Her.* Part of him almost rejected the idea that he could be so fucking lucky that she'd walked into his life. That she felt his music in her blood, in her soul … he could barely believe it, but he saw it in her eyes, and knew the truth passed from her lips when the Wind didn't contradict it.

"You're my *One*, Belah Blue. About fucking time I found you."

He sank into her deep and buried his head against her neck. She sighed and rose to meet him.

Their bodies merged again and again, chests pressed together and hips rocking in tandem. He took them both over the edge repeatedly, rejoicing every time she cried his name.

They eventually parted, sticky from sweat and exhaustion. He pointed her toward the bathroom that adjoined his brother's room, hoping Iszak hadn't returned from his gig yet. Blues shows tended to run later.

She returned, carrying a warm cloth that she wrapped around his limp cock, cleaning him gently. The motions of her hand stroking him with the damp terrycloth made him hard again. He groaned.

"I don't know if I have more in me, baby."

She cupped his balls and bent down, kissing each one gently. Somehow he was sure the act was intended for more than just to turn him on. When she ran her tongue along the length of his cock, he knew he wasn't getting to sleep until she was good and ready.

"You taste like you've got more," she said, and kissed the very tip of his cock. Her tongue flicked out and he saw the forked tips for the first time. More than that, he *felt* what they could do, teasing around his head like there were two.

Thankfully, she only tormented him for a few moments before taking him entirely in her mouth. Even after his previous orgasms, he didn't last long. It was all he could do not to grab her head and ram her down onto him to get more depth, but the second he clutched at her silken hair, she took him all the way until he was sure she couldn't breathe. He lost all sense with the sudden, slick heat of her throat around him and came harder than he had before, surprised at the volume he produced after making love with her for hours already.

"Fuuuck!"

Belah sat back and licked her lips. Her entire body glowed and Lukas could only stare through half-lidded eyes at the beauty who'd just blown his mind. Dragons… who knew? They glowed after sex.

He lifted a hand to reach for her and paused to stare at his own hand, which also seemed to be glowing. He waved it experimentally in front of his face.

"Shit …" The word sounded odd in his ears. "Did you roofie me?"

Belah snuggled down beside him, every inch of his body coming alight with her touch. He had the strongest sense of his every cell reaching out for hers and turned to wrap himself around her.

"I don't know what that means," she said. "I've been out of touch, remember?"

He chuckled. "Sorry. I feel high. You know what that means, right? Drugged. Loopy. Loaded. Stoned. Flying while still on earth. You missed the seventies, or you'd know all this. I fucking *loved* the seventies. At least after 'Nam was good and done and I was still alive. I did all the drugs, and baby, yours is the best."

He shouldn't have mentioned Vietnam, because that brought to mind all kinds of horrors, but her steady stroking touch made all that go away again, until all he cared about was her soft skin and the gradual sinking of his consciousness into sleep. His last thought before darkness took him was: *Thank you for her.*

CHAPTER TWELVE

B elah stirred from her dreams, hazy, yet sated and content. Lukas breathed slow and steady beside her, deep in exhausted slumber. The strains of music from her dream still drifted through her ears and she hummed along softly with her eyes closed.

Her hums faltered after a moment when she realized she was only hearing one half of the composition that had filled her dreams. This time, however, it was the half that she had yet to hear while awake—the half that had been missing from Lukas's song. She stopped humming and opened her eyes, turning her focus to the ambient sounds in the dark room, and then what was unmistakably actual music playing from somewhere very close by.

Her heart sped up. It wasn't the tune that Lukas had played, but the counterpoint that should have accompanied it—that *had* accompanied it in her dreams. The rhythm matched perfectly, but the notes were different—rougher and deeper in pitch, but no less beautiful.

Glancing down at Lukas's sleeping face, Belah brushed a kiss across his forehead and silently slipped from the bed.

The music came from above, filtering through the ceiling and the roof beyond. Navigating her way through the moonlit shadows of the apartment, she located a stairwell and stole naked into the darkness. The music grew louder as she approached and she carefully let herself out a door and into the damp night air on the roof.

Rough gravel bit into her bare feet, but she cared little for the discomfort, or for the cool breeze that drifted over her naked skin. Across the roof from where she exited, a solo figure sat, silhouetted by the moon. Silvery light glinted off an instrument in his hands that resembled the one Lukas played, only much larger.

She hesitated to move, lest she disrupt the man's playing, but Sweet Mother—if Lukas were the one, how could this man's music fit so perfectly into the missing gaps of her dream? Who was he?

Slowly, she took a few steps to the side, hoping to get a better look at him. Once in profile, she blinked, confused. *Lukas?* No, it couldn't be him. She'd left him sound asleep below. Upon further inspection, she saw that this man was slightly larger and thicker around chest and shoulders, his hair cropped close to his head where Lukas's had been long. But he had the same angular cut to his cheeks and jaw, and from the way he played, the same beautiful, talented mouth.

The music transfixed her. With chest heaving, she began mouthing words that seemed to fit the sounds that carried through her memory and through the air across the roof to her ears. In a voice she hadn't used for eons in such a manner, she sang, the song pouring from her soul in accompaniment to the music that came from the man's saxophone.

His aura flickered around him, the shimmering cloud that reflected a turul's connection with the winds signaling his awareness of her, though his playing never faltered. His head shifted in the direction of her voice and his dark eyes rose until they were locked onto hers.

The moment was charged with energy, his eyes widening with unexpected recognition. Belah kept singing, both elated and confused by this need to match the notes of his song with her own voice, all the while in her mind she replayed the notes of Lukas's song along with it. Together, it all felt right. Whoever this man was, with his shadow of dark emotion—sadness that filtered into the sounds coming from his instrument— he was meant for her, and she had to have him.

Her voice rose to a crescendo, along with the notes of the music he played. Around her a light breeze picked up, flowing across her body and twisting in the long strands of her hair. The sounds of their songs merged together and the breeze became a cool wind swirling around her.

When he played the last note, it seemed to go on forever, and she sensed he didn't wish to end the song. A din of emotions reached her from his mind—the strongest was his belief that somehow, he'd conjured her with his music and that she wasn't really there. He wanted her so badly, but feared that she would fade away the moment that last note faded into the heavens.

Tears began to well in his eyes as he continued to force the note to persist, but even his magically imbued lungs were running out of air, and so were Belah's.

They trailed off at the same moment, their gazes still locked. She took a tentative step closer. He removed the strap from his instrument and set it on the ground, leaning it gently against his seat, never once turning away from her. Slowly he stood, his gaze roaming over her, flitting up and down her body in disbelief.

Yes, I am still here, she wanted to say, but held the conviction that anything but a song would disrupt their connection.

They stood a few feet from each other, his mind still a blur of confusion and wonder at her very existence. Finally, he made an incoherent noise of impatience and rushed to her.

His large body loomed, then his arms were around her, lifting her up while he gripped the back of her head and tilted it back for his mouth to find hers. His fingers twined in her hair and she let him devour her, tongue lashing between her lips while her own answered with equal fervor. His momentum kept them moving until she felt cold brick against her back and was vaguely aware that he had her pressed against the wall beside the door she'd come out of.

One large hand cupped her breast, and his hungry lips trailed down to take her nipple fully into his mouth. Belah raked her fingers through his short hair, clawing at the back of his neck while his suckling mouth pulled and teased at her, soon switching to the other breast.

His hips tilted up, pressing hard against hers, his erection straining at his jeans. She ran her hands down his hard chest, pulled his shirt up and off, then went for the button of his jeans. Heavy breaths gusted against her ear as she unfastened his pants and reached inside.

She stroked him, coaxing his massive length out of his pants and rejoicing at the velvet heat of his skin against her aching core. With one hand bracing himself against the wall beside her head, he wrapped the other around her thigh and lifted her up higher.

Belah wrapped both legs around him, leveraging herself up his body with one hand on his shoulder. She sank down onto him, taking him entirely in a single stroke and crying out as he stretched her slick channel, fitting as perfectly as Lukas had. He pulled out slowly and rammed hard into her with a harsh grunt, nailing her hips into the wall. It would have been painfully uncomfortable, if Belah didn't love it so much.

His dark eyes remained fixed on hers, focused intently on her face as though committing her features to memory. She still sensed the lingering disbelief in his mind, even though he was buried deep inside her. She couldn't speak through the unbearable pleasure of his touch, dared not destroy the primal connection they had in this moment. Unlike Lukas, this man's love was raw and unrestrained, wild and unapologetic.

He fucked her rough, almost desperately, driven by the belief that this might just be the only taste he ever got of her. She found herself pinned against the wall, his fingers twined in hers, holding her arms above her head. Only their joined hips and her legs around his waist kept her aloft.

Gravity didn't matter when they could both fly, and soon she gave into the buffeting winds that surrounded them, letting her wings unfurl. Her new lover moaned, his soft nips and licks turning into harder bites along her throat the more frantic his fucking became.

His hands tightened around hers and he reared back, staring down into her eyes as his face constricted in pleasure. With another violent thrust, he spilled his orgasm into her and his own wings snapped wide, feathers fluttering in the harsh wind.

The door beside them banged open. Belah's gaze shot to the side, then down, surprised to realize that the pair of them were hovering together several feet off the rooftop. Beneath her stood Lukas, his eyes wide with confusion, then wild with fury.

"Iszak! Let her go, you son-of-a-bitch! She's mine!"

Iszak North. Sweet Mother, one brother couldn't have been enough, could it?

She tried to extract herself from Iszak's embrace, but he held tight. The wind picked up speed as he finally pulled away from her. She pulled in her wings and they almost fell, but Iszak caught them both at the last second and lowered her slowly.

Iszak's hands still lightly gripped her hips as he regarded his brother. "I beg to differ. The Winds sent her to this very rooftop—they finally answered my mating call after all these years."

"Bullshit. She answered *my* call tonight and she came up here from *my* bed. Belah, tell him you're mine."

Lukas's face was grim and frightening. The winds howled around them, chilling her. Beside her, Iszak pulled away and advanced on his brother, jerking up and refastening his jeans before shoving his finger in his brother's face.

"I don't give a fuck where she came from. My music called to her. No one else could have answered but *her*."

The wind howled around Belah, whipping her hair across her face so it was difficult to see. The night darkened, clouds blotted out the moon, and thunder rumbled around them, sending tremors through the rooftop.

Her skin prickled from the chill, the wind so loud and violent she shouldn't have been able to hear their voices. Icy drops of rain pelted her skin, and a sudden gale slammed into her, pushing her hard against the wall. Her head flew back, cracking painfully against the bricks, but the brothers seemed not to notice. They were singularly focused on their anger.

The raindrops cascaded sideways one way, and then the other while Iszak and Lukas stepped around each other, eyes wild. They were yelling now, but the noise of the growing storm was too loud, the wind too strong. Their auras had grown as volatile as the clouds above, lightning cracking overhead while they pointed and yelled.

The truth was plain as day to Belah, but neither man could see through their confusion and anger to get it. They were both hers. Why couldn't they accept the fact?

Not even magic as strong as hers could convince a turul of a blatant truth he chose to deny, and she would be a fool to get in between the pair until they worked it out. But every dragon knew better than to test Fate by flying into a storm like this.

Backing away from them both with a sigh of resignation, she turned, launching herself off the roof while simultaneously shifting. She beat her wings as hard as she could to clear the storm, which continued to blind her and tear violently at her wings for a mile or more before it abated.

She turned back once, hovering in the air for a moment and observing the massive cyclone that had formed around the two Princes of the North Wind.

She spoke under her breath, hoping they would hear across the distance, despite their disquiet. "You both know what is true. Come and find me when you wake up to it."

CHAPTER THIRTEEN

szak's rage dissipated, and the elation of finding *her* dimmed when he realized she'd flown away. *Belah*. His brother knew her name, and as much as he rejected the idea that Lukas had found her, there had to be a good reason for that.

"She must have been confused—thought you were me," Iszak said, though he didn't believe that, either.

"You've become an expert at lying to yourself, brother," Lukas said. "Give it up. I saw her first. She came to the show tonight with Erika. I played for her, and she couldn't keep her eyes off me. It was like I tranced out. The music flowed like it never had before."

"No!" Iszak yelled, rounding on his brother and pushing him hard into the wall where he'd just had Belah pressed as he desperately made love to her. "It's been so long since we started searching. I won't let her go."

Lukas's scowl became a smirk. "Sorry, man. Nanyo always promised me I'd know the second I laid eyes on her. It was like all the air left the room, except for our own breaths."

Frantic though his conviction faltered, Iszak gripped his brother's shoulders and slammed him into the wall again. Lukas grunted and winced, pushing back against Iszak's heavy grip, but he wasn't letting go.

"She sang for me," Iszak said. "She fucking *sang*. We haven't had a vocalist for that piece since ... *fuck*!"

Lukas's eyes widened and he stopped fighting Iszak's grip on him. "What?"

"Yeah. I couldn't believe it. I always thought that without Evie to fill out our trio, we were doomed to be alone. Like it was our music—all three of us together—that would bring our true mates to us."

"She sang Evie's part?" Lukas said.

Iszak nodded grimly and let go of his brother, who just stood there, dumbstruck. Neither of them had spoken of their sister since before they enlisted and shipped out to Vietnam decades ago, shortly after they'd learned of her death at the hands of their enemy. They had opted to go take out their grief and impotent need for revenge on someone else's enemy. The entire experience had left them damaged beyond repair. Now that old song was all they had, but they hadn't been able to play the original composition together since.

"I don't fucking believe it," Lukas said. "What did she say to you?"

Iszak shrugged and bent to retrieve his shirt, then walked across the roof to pick up his sax. The instrument had fallen onto the pebbled rooftop and he gritted his teeth. "Scratched the finish on one side—fuck," he muttered. "I don't think I've ever held a note that long. She held it, too. Fucking lungs on that woman—I don't think Evie could even hold that kind of a note. Her voice was ... nothing like I've ever heard. Like ..."

"A dragon's trumpet."

"She didn't *say* a damn word to me. But the song … she knew all the words. I'd almost forgotten them."

"Evie made up the lyrics to it. Nobody's sung it since her, either. I don't think she ever even wrote them down on paper—I sure didn't. But she knew?"

"Every fucking word," Iszak said, turning back to his brother and heading for the door.

"Jesus," Lukas breathed and followed Iszak down the stairwell. "I don't even know what to say, man."

Iszak stomped into his room and set the saxophone in its case.

"Just admit you fucking believe me," he said, scowling at his brother.

Lukas leaned in the doorway and raked both hands through his hair, grabbed handfuls, and let out a frustrated snarl. "God*damn*it. It couldn't have been easy, could it? What do you think it means? I mean … this changes everything."

"Doesn't mean a fucking thing, dude. I'm exhausted. Do you mind?"

But Lukas wasn't budging from the doorway. "No. We found her. I never thought we'd have to share, but for fuck's sake, Iszak, *we found her*! How the fuck can you sleep?"

Iszak gave his brother a weary look as he slipped out of his clothes and climbed into bed naked, for the first time in his life hating that he was sleeping alone.

"In case you didn't notice, she's not here, and I don't have a goddamn clue how to find her, do you? I got the impression she wasn't exactly happy with us when she left."

Lukas stood silent for a moment, worrying at a callus on his fingertip. His gaze was distant for a time. Then he refocused. "I might. Remember Erika Rosencrans?"

Iszak chuckled. "There's a blast from the past. Didn't she always love it when you watched Ozzie fuck her? You don't think Belah was doing the same thing, do you? Teasing you?"

"No, dude. Erika's friends with her. The woman's mated to this huge Red now. It suits her … she's still likes a huge tease, though." He laughed and shook his head. "I love how some things never change."

"And I suppose you know how to find Erika? If she's mated to a dragon, she'll be protected. The Wind is good at helping us find things, but dragon magic's been tight as a drum for centuries. I doubt they've loosened up any. She may be the *One*, but until we're properly mated, that radar shit doesn't work."

"She's somewhere in the fucking city, I know that much. We've gotta do our Fate's Fools gig next Saturday. Together. If we're playing our mating call together, it'll be powerful enough for her to find us."

"Man, I can't even stand to look at you right now, much less spend two hours on stage with you. Ozzie's lousy at playing interference between us—he just likes to escalate the issue to see us at each other's throats."

Lukas's throat worked and Iszak could almost hear the unspoken curses his brother held back. Finally, Lukas threw up his hands in frustration.

"Suit yourself, man. I have no fucking idea how to get through to you." With that, he turned on his heel and left, slamming the bedroom door behind him.

Iszak turned out the lamp beside his bed and lay there, hating the way his chest ached like a heavy stone had settled against his sternum. He'd had Belah in his arms tonight and everything had felt right. More than that, she'd felt fucking *perfect*. How was it remotely fair that she belonged to his brother, too?

What he wouldn't give right now to have her back in his embrace. To be able to actually *say* what he'd felt the entire time he'd been inside her.

He'd been so overwhelmed by the sight of her he could barely even believe she was real. She'd just appeared on the rooftop and started singing, her beautiful, naked curves swaying to the tempo of the plaintive tune he always played. The one his sister had promised would call *her* someday. He'd never believed Evie's crazy composition would attract the love of his life, but he still played his part of it every night after a gig, in Evie's memory. His brother had reworked his own part into a new version that he'd turned into a regular show. The audience never knew that there were two parts missing … Evie's and Iszak's parts. The vocals and the bass. The alternate arrangement Lukas had written for his band didn't come close to the truth.

Iszak was glad of that, at least. Lukas also hadn't ever tried to replace Evie's vocals with either singer or instrument. Their sister's voice was irreplaceable.

At least, he'd thought so. Until tonight.

He relived those few moments in his mind, from the first sight of Belah and the way her voice sank into his bones, singing all the words of the song his dead sister had written years ago, to his semi-trance that kept him playing, needing to complete the song, and then wishing he could never stop because he was afraid she would disappear if he lost breath enough to keep going.

But she hadn't disappeared. She'd held onto him just as tightly and desperately as he'd held onto her once they'd come together.

And holy fuck, they'd been flying at the end. Actually fucking *flying* while they fucked. He'd never felt anything remotely close to that sensation of losing his mind with pleasure while the Wind held him buoyed and weightless.

He tossed and turned for an hour, replaying every moment until his brother had appeared and everything had gone to shit. His elation turning to anger at Lukas's assertion that she was his. Iszak had lost track of her in the middle of their argument, not even aware of the mini-hurricane raging around them.

"Fuck!" he yelled, throwing the covers off and turning on the light again. He started to head back up to the roof naked, thinking he'd fly, but the weight in his chest told him otherwise. Until he found her again, he was probably grounded. It wasn't a good feeling.

Iszak grabbed his jeans and pulled them on, then headed to the kitchen. From the freezer, he pulled out the frosty blue bottle of turul vodka. The label taunted him with what he really wanted as much as the color of the bottle did, but he'd settle for the contents and the oblivion it offered. He didn't want any of it, really. The vodka was a substitute and an escape. Flying would be the same.

He wanted her. Now that he'd found her, he wanted *her*. He wanted the feel of her thighs around him again, the sound of her voice singing for him. She didn't sing like his sister had—nobody could match Evie's voice—but Belah had her own raw cadence that betrayed a past as dark as Iszak's. She'd lost something, or been hurt in some way that still stuck. And fuck if the memory of her voice didn't haunt him now.

He made his way up to the roof again and settled in the plastic patio chair he'd sat on earlier, took a biting swig of the vodka, and stared up at the glowering moon. Oblivion would be better than wishing for a thing he couldn't have. She was a dragon … that much had been clear when her wings had come out. He didn't know what his brother was smoking, but turul and dragons never mated. None of the higher races interbred. It was a rule.

A rule that's been broken, and you know it.

As if he wouldn't break every fucking rule to be with her, if he even knew where to find her.

A soft scuffling came from behind him, and he turned to see Lukas juggling furniture with his saxophone hanging from the strap around his neck. His brother cursed when the small table he held balanced on one arm nearly toppled to the ground before he caught it mid-air and acrobatically tossed it up, bounced it off his heel, caught it adeptly on his head, and retrieved it with his free hand. After a few steps, Lukas ceremoniously set the table down beside Iszak's stool and set another bottle of turul liquor on it, followed by a bag of chips and Iszak's favorite bean dip.

"What time is it?" Lukas asked.

"Fuck if I know. Late."

"You're an asshole."

Iszak glared at his brother, but his grumbling stomach detracted from the menace he felt.

Chips. Dip.

"Fuck you," he said with little venom. "Are you going to open those?"

"Hold your horses," Lukas said, walking across the roof to find another chair. He came back with another well-worn plastic patio chair and set it down. He opened the bag and handed it to Iszak.

"Thanks."

"Don't thank me. Listen to me." Lukas opened the bean dip and handed it to Iszak. Then he reached for the liquor that Iszak still held in the crook of his elbow.

Iszak glanced between the food and the alcohol. Finally, he nodded and Lukas snatched the liquor, taking a long swallow.

Iszak dug into the chips, savoring the salty crunch. Fuck, did food taste good just now. When he shoved a bean-dip-laden chip into his mouth, he groaned.

"So, it's Sunday today," Lukas said, wiping his mouth and tapping a rhythm on the side of the blue glass of the bottle.

Iszak nodded.

"Nanyo's expecting us."

Iszak's hand slowed as he reached into the bag for another chip. He blinked, trying to clear his head of the fatigue and alcohol. But this wasn't a trick question.

"Right. We're having breakfast with Nanyo, like every Sunday." *So what?*

"I think we should have a battle plan."

Iszak's hand faltered on its way to his mouth with a fresh chip coated in delicious, cheesy, spicy dip. Fuck.

"Drinking's my battle plan," he said around his mouthful of chip. He reached out. Lukas handed him the bottle. "Armor against the harpy."

He took a swig, relishing the burn and the smooth tang of the icy liquor as it slid down his throat washing the salt and bean flavor with it.

"Jesus, dude. I know she's terrifying, but if Nanyo knew that's how you felt, she'd disown you."

Iszak glared at his brother. "It's not about her. What's she going to say about our little issue? We fucked up somehow. How else would we wind up with the same woman as our true mate?"

"I don't fucking know, dude! I just know that it's a problem, and Nanyo's good at fixing shit like this. So my plan is to just lay it out for her and wait for her answer. Nothing good ever came from keeping shit from Nanyo."

Iszak eyeballed his brother. "We're in the same family, right? You're talking about the same grandmother who had the three of us singing in every tavern, busking on every corner of every city, from the time we were old enough to sprout pubes. You don't think she had a hand in pushing Evie away? Our own sister would just as soon latch onto a man she *knew* wasn't the One, rather than stay."

Lukas shrugged and reached for the bottle. "Marcus did find her while she was singing."

"Not *our* song, though. She was singing a fucking Beatles tune that day they met. Not even a good one."

Lukas chuckled. "She always had to make all the covers we did gender appropriate. And I liked Marcus at first. Even started to believe we could *make* it happen if we wanted it bad enough, after she started getting hot and heavy with him."

"So you believe that we're in the same fucking pickle now."

Lukas raised an eyebrow, produced his sax, and put it to his lips. He set a jaunty rhythm with it, playing a song Iszak knew from way back during the war.

He couldn't help but laugh and start singing about pickles and motorcycles. But when he reached the lyrics that dealt with dying, they both trailed off before finishing. The Vietnam War was long over, but the scars it had left on them both remained.

"Nanyo never fucking stopped us from nearly destroying ourselves," Iszak said bitterly. "She had to know the shit show we'd be flying into."

Lukas tapped a soundless rhythm on the keys of his sax, and Iszak could hear the notes even though his brother wasn't blowing through the mouthpiece. "She knew there wasn't a goddamn thing we could do for Evie. Fighting over there as pilots meant we'd live. The Wind was always on our side. Fighting the Ultiori would have gotten us killed."

"The fucker dodged," Iszak said, also dodging his brother's suggestion that they'd avoided a bigger risk by going to fucking *war* for a cause that wasn't their own. "You know that's what happened. We always knew he was lying about something. Where'd he take her, do you think? Mexico? Canada? Would she have convinced him to go back to Budapest? Not that it fucking matters now."

Without being asked, Lukas passed the bottle back and Iszak took it. "Do you think she loved him, even though he wasn't the One?" Lukas asked.

"You mean even though he's the rotten bastard who got our sister killed? Why the fuck should I care if she fucking *loved* him? It wasn't enough."

"Because now that I've met Belah, I know there's *one* mate for me. That means there had to be *one* for Evie, too. After Evie left, Nanyo kept going on about how nothing that really mattered was simple to find, and that Evie's path might be rough, but that didn't make it the wrong path. I just wonder if someone's out there wondering, like we both were until tonight, if they're ever going to find her. What if she isn't really dead?"

"You know she's dead. There's no other way she'd have given up a feather covered in her own fucking blood."

Iszak struggled to hold back the bile that rose to his throat, tossing back more liquor to force it down. The day they'd received that macabre package filled with mementos of their sister's had been the day he and Lukas had enlisted in the human army. The blood-stained feather had been the worst of it, and no matter how long he cursed at the Wind, it never contradicted what the message had implied: their sister was dead at the hands of their enemy. And that fucking human bastard, Marcus Calais, had led her to her death.

"She'd have wanted this for us," Lukas said. "Maybe Marcus wasn't the One for her, but she wasn't afraid of taking a chance on him. She could have been right about him—she always had great instincts about people."

"She was wrong, though."

"But *we* aren't wrong!" Lukas yelled, tilting his head at the sky. He followed up the outburst with a frustrated howl, then turned to glare at Iszak. "Our fucking *hearts* aren't wrong, dude. Belah sang for you. She sang *our song*—the song no other woman but our dead sister knew the lyrics to. We've got to figure out how this works, with the two of us. For Evie. She'd have …"

Iszak cut him off. "Wanted this for us. Would she really, though? Would she have wanted us at each other's throats? Belah didn't exactly hang around, you'll notice. And fuck, what if she doesn't even fucking *want* the both of us?"

He left his deepest fear unspoken: *What if she doesn't really want me?* Iszak knew he could be a dark, surly bastard, and Belah hadn't even seen him at his worst. One quick, hard fuck against the wall wasn't a good representation of what kind of sick things really got him off. Jesus, what if his lack of preamble was what had really scared her off? Had he been too rough with her?

Gradually, he became aware of Lukas staring at him and turned his head to behold a look of utter incomprehension.

"You fucking moron," Lukas said. "She's a *dragon*. If we had another brother who'd gotten stars in his eyes when he saw her, she'd still want the three of us. I'm not sure if dragons even *have* a limit. Didn't you wonder why I let it go so easily? I'd do anything to have her, even share her with your pathetic ass." Lukas paused and frowned as a fresh thought seemed to occur to him. "Fuck, I hope we're the only ones."

CHAPTER FOURTEEN

The scent of breakfast set Iszak's stomach on full rumble mode, as though he contained a monster that wanted to escape.

Lukas groaned beside him as they made their way up the stairwell in the Brooklyn rowhouse to their grandmother's top-floor apartment. "Oh, fuck, she's laying it on today. I smell everything." He paused to inhale and swallowed as though he were eating the air. "Fuck … palacsinta with raspberry syrup …" His nostrils flared again. "Pogača, too, and fresh sausages, eggs … You think she knows already? She probably fucking already knows. That'll save us some trouble."

Iszak snorted. All the aromas he loved most came from that apartment, but he couldn't get the sweet, winter rain smell of Belah out of his head.

"She'll still make us squirm until we get it all out," he said.

"I don't know how the fuck Ozzie's lasted as long as he has, living with her."

"Better him than us," Iszak said, reaching the front door to his grandmother's apartment and putting on a smile before they walked in.

"Nanyo! You beautiful woman!" he bellowed upon entry. "I could smell the food from a mile away. You're torturing me!"

The diminutive, elderly woman by the stove wiped her hands and bounced a little on her heels before rushing to him and wrapping him in a vise-like embrace. Jesus, he was always surprised by how strong she was.

"Iszak! Lukas! It's a good day, a *grand* day for us. I thought we'd celebrate."

Lukas took Iszak's place in their grandmother's arms, and Iszak made his way through the foyer around to the living area. He took a deep breath, letting himself be comforted by the familiar space he once called home, and still did, in some fashion. His grandmother could be a harpy, sure. "Soft" wasn't in her repertoire, but wherever she lived would always be home to him.

A strong hand clapped down on his shoulder, and he turned to see his cousin grinning at him.

"The woman's on fire today," Ozzie said. "It always fucking terrifies me when she's like this." His grin didn't falter, but Iszak caught the undercurrent of desperation in Ozzie's voice.

"Yet you stay," Iszak said, raising an eyebrow. He eyed the dark bruise that graced his cousin's forehead with the half-healed cut through the middle, but didn't ask. His cousin had always been a troublemaker. Whatever had earned him that knot, he'd probably had it coming.

"She gets me laid, man. And you've tasted her cooking."

Iszak's other eyebrow went up. "She's your grandmother."

"Jesus, that's not what I meant," Ozzie said. "She discovered the fucking Internet. I know you guys had it hard when you were under her thumb, but she's all about dating websites now, so I just let her have fun with it. She set up my profile with my photo. She sets up the dates, and I go where she says, when she says. Makes her happy and gets me closer to the One."

A bubble of mirth swelled in Iszak. His grandmother had always been the matchmaker for everyone, and not just her own family. Every human who lived around them for as long as Iszak remembered had come to her to find their mates, and had never been dissatisfied with the results. Babies were named after his grandmother. Many were named after Iszak and his siblings for the little tasks they pulled off to help complete a human love affair his grandmother had orchestrated.

Now she was dead-set on doing it for Ozzie, too. More power to her, he supposed.

"So this little celebration … does that mean you found the One?" Iszak asked, hopeful.

Ozzie's face fell a little and he snorted. "Fuck no. So fucking close, though. Last night's date … I wish." His cousin's face darkened further.

"Does the doozy on your skull have anything to do with it? Who'd she set you up with, anyway?"

Ozzie grimaced. "Dodged a bullet, that's all."

Lies weren't a turul thing, but Iszak knew his cousin was obscuring the truth, and the plaintive glance Ozzie gave him told him his cousin knew he knew.

"Don't tell her," Ozzie said. "I don't want her to obsess over a fuckup. She's still learning how things work."

Iszak nodded, but when Ozzie turned away to answer their grandmother's request, he watched the older woman intently.

Sophia North didn't obsess. She didn't fuck up. And she sure as shit had a reason for everything she did. Even if it led to the death of one of her own family.

He followed his cousin to the open dining area, accepted the stack of plates from Lukas, and helped set the table while his grandmother and brother began fanning out the spread.

After the four of them sat, they clasped hands and sang their thanks to the Winds like always. And, like always, his grandmother added her thanks to the sun and moon and earth for their bounty. Most turul didn't acknowledge the other powers in the universe, but his Nanyo had always insisted they were all beholden to each other. That they shared responsibility for all their bounties and all their strife. Even though he knew his true mate was a dragon, Iszak still wasn't convinced, but this time he listened and gave his grandmother's hand a squeeze when she finished.

They dug in with gusto, devouring the meal until there were little but scraps left. If Iszak didn't know better, he'd have looked at the destruction of the dishes and thought a cyclone had come through, sucking everything but the plates and cutlery into the heavens.

His eyelids fluttered as he sat back in his seat, his grandmother's cooking lulling him into complacency. He was ready for a nap now, and the overstuffed sofa in her living room was calling to him. He was fantasizing about falling asleep on the old, familiar cushions when his grandmother's sharp voice shattered his lethargic, food-induced fugue.

"When am I going to meet your mate? You should have brought her today."

Iszak looked at Lukas, who sat across the table from him. His brother gave him a bemused smile and shrugged as if to say, "Who knows?" Their grandmother had always seemed to find out their secrets, sometimes long before they knew the truth themselves.

"She's busy, Nanyo," Iszak said.

"'Busy' is a useless word. It means as much as 'fine.' I ask you how you're doing, you say 'fine.' You're never fine. I ask you if you can come help an old woman, you say you're 'busy,' but you're never busy. Why is this woman so busy? If she's yours, she should be here."

"She's a dragon, Nanyo," Lukas offered. Iszak scowled at him.

"Fuck," Ozzie said. "You landed a dragon? No wonder she was cooking so madly. You're the man, Iszak."

Iszak glared at his brother, hating the confrontation he knew was imminent. Lukas stared back, his gaze resolute. Their grandmother would know, no matter what. And whatever she said would determine their lives

"Dragon or not, she's yours. Busy or not, she should be here. Your demons are at it again, Iszak. She should be here."

"My ... demons?"

"The stone in your belly that won't let you fly." She pressed a gnarled hand against his midsection.

Ozzie shook his head and stood to begin clearing dishes. "Jesus, man. You found your mate—who is a fucking dragon— and you're not out there fucking on Cloud Nine right now? Lukas, can you talk some sense into your brother? You guys live together. Did you get to meet her, at least?"

Lukas's expression darkened as he continued staring down Iszak. Ozzie stood in the archway to the kitchen, his gaze flitting back and forth between them. Finally, he set down the stack of dishes and cursed. "You guys going to let me in on the fucking secret here?"

Lukas raised an eyebrow at Iszak as if to say, "Are you?"

"I wasn't the only one who found my true mate last night. Lukas did, too. In fact, I probably have him to thank for bringing her home with him." He gave his brother a sad smile before turning to his grandmother and Ozzie. "The problem is we seem to have scared her off and we have no idea where to find her."

Ozzie gawked at them. "Wait a sec … you're not saying what I think you're saying, are you? The same female? Can that even happen? I mean, who gets to have her? Are you even allowed to share? Jesus, I'd be willing to share just to know I'd found her, not the goddamn *anti*-mate I got set up with last night. I'm telling you, I think I'm done with Internet dating. No offense, Nanyo, but it's a bit too dangerous."

Ozzie turned back to his chores with an over-affected shiver and a shake of his head.

"Stepping stones," Nanyo said to Ozzie. "You will never find the start of the path if you don't commit to the journey, and you can't expect to reach your destination after a single step."

Iszak sighed, weary of his grandmother's repeated philosophy that the journey wasn't meant to be easy. She still maintained that Evie's choices were the right choices and that their sister might still be alive, despite all evidence to the contrary.

Lukas finally spoke up. "Well, we found her for a night, but how the hell do we get her back?"

"Are you willing to compromise? To let go of your demons and be patient? Open yourselves up to love, because that is what it will take to keep her. It may take more strength than you believe you have. Your mate is a very special female."

Iszak narrowed his eyes. "You sound like you know her already. What aren't you telling us?"

The older woman's eye's twinkled. "I know that to love both my handsome grandsons, she must be incredibly special. Believe in her, call to her, and she will come."

With that, Sophia North rose from the table, her departure signaling she had nothing more to say on the matter.

Iszak rose, following Lukas to the kitchen with the remaining dishes. The pair worked silently, while their cousin's compulsive need to beat a rhythm on every dish filled the house with music. Their grandmother sat at the piano in the other room and played an old tune Iszak recognized as a variation on his own song. Supposedly, it was the song that had brought his parents together.

Was the song all it would take?

"What are you doing on Saturday, Ozzie?" he asked.

Ozzie shrugged and tossed a couple of towels to Iszak and Lukas, who began drying and putting away the dishes. "Trying to avoid getting in the way of the fucking Ultiori again," he muttered.

Iszak stopped cold and stared at his cousin. On the opposite side, Lukas was a mirror image to his rigid posture, mouth hanging open.

"What did you just say?" Iszak asked in a slow, even tone.

"What the fuck do you mean 'again'?" Lukas asked. He pointed at Ozzie's bruised brow. "Want to tell us what really happened last night?"

Ozzie wrung out his dishrag and tossed it over the faucet, then turned to face them, shoulders sagging. He took a breath and tilted his head, peering into the other room to locate their grandmother. Under his breath, he said, "Serves me right for getting my hopes up, that's all. Remember the old tales about the Blue Beast who created those blood-hungry bastards? Well, she's real, and she's a fucking Ultiori magnet. They're in the city. All of them. Elites, even the big guy—and boy, is he a fucking nightmare."

"I thought you said Nanyo's been setting you up on dates. She wouldn't …"

"Don't tell her. It'd crush her if she thought she put me in danger."

Lukas snorted and shot Iszak a glance. Their grandmother wouldn't hesitate to put one of them in danger, if it meant they somehow stayed on the path she believed they belonged on.

"Where did you see them?" Iszak asked.

"Central Park, but it doesn't fucking matter, does it? They can be anywhere. Motherfuckers disappeared into thin air right in front of me."

"Fuck," Iszak said, the gravity of his cousin's revelation hitting him. One thing they all knew about the Ultiori leader was that he had a particular taste for unmated, female Blue dragons, and his victims rarely survived.

"We *have* to play sooner than Saturday," Lukas said. "Oz, we need to find our mate before the Ultiori find her. Nanyo seems to think if we play, she'll come to us."

"Shit," Ozzie said, looking between them both in horror. "Yeah, man, I'm there. I'm wherever you need me to be."

CHAPTER FIFTEEN

Belah couldn't get the music out of her head, or the memory of their touch. Lukas's intuitive desire to bring her pleasure through pain both thrilled and terrified her. She didn't want to want that so much, not again—it just reminded her of *him*. Iszak's rough, primal treatment was also a reminder. He hadn't spoken a word, but they'd understood each other perfectly.

There was one crucial difference between the brothers and Nikhil, however—*they* didn't look at her as an all-powerful, immortal goddess. Their worship of her was innate, from man to woman. All they sought from her was pleasure, and at the very core of that pleasure was the sweetest, purest emotion she'd ever sensed: love.

She and Nikhil may have loved each other, but what bound them together in the past had been power—his need to possess it, and her need to relinquish it. She could claim plenty of power now, but it was a tool best used where it made sense—and it didn't make sense to bring it out with either of the North brothers. Not unless she gave up all her power for them, whether they wanted it or not.

The power would still serve her when she gave herself to Nikhil again, though. At least, she hoped she'd be able to endure giving it up to him. Even when she'd done so in the past, she still maintained a level of control over him that he never realized she kept. And wasn't that what had ultimately ruined everything? The power she had over him had corrupted him as much as her blood. She'd created that monster as much as he'd created himself. She'd have to be the one to un-make him, too, and with luck, she would have her chance soon.

Belah had no idea when he would call in her offer to have her again. She'd sensed his devious desire to make her wait and dwell on her old cravings for the oblivion that he knew he could offer her. Only now that she'd had thousands of years to reflect on those desires, she understood how wrong she'd been.

Now she wanted her children back. Now she wanted to explore the promise of love and joy that Iszak and Lukas represented.

She knew the music for what it was now. It was a mating call, and she had answered. She had answered them both, but despite the conviction that they both belonged to her, something wasn't right. They weren't happy with it, that much she had sensed when Lukas had discovered her and Iszak together on the roof. Being battered by the hurricane winds their conflict had produced had left her physically bruised, but the barbed thoughts that had shot between the two men made her heart hurt. Neither one wanted to admit that the other had seen her for what she was—his one true mate. She had no idea how to make them understand that it was the truth, and that it could be wonderful if they'd only come around.

Belah had spent another sleepless night basking in the rhythm of the recorded music and now stared out at the rising sun, trying to decide what she should do. Nikhil would be coming for her soon enough, and she *had* to find out where her babies were hidden.

But she'd found Iszak and Lukas, and she couldn't stand the thought of letting them slip through her fingers even more.

Rustling noises came from behind her, and a rumpled-looking Erika came into the room, barefoot and smiling.

"Morning," Erika said brightly, then stopped. "Hang on." She rubbed her eyes. "You shouldn't be here. Don't tell me Lukas kicked you out of bed. After the show last night, I was sure you had him hooked."

Behind her, Geva appeared, kissed his mate on the cheek, and headed to the kitchen. "Definitely caught the man's eye," the Red dragon said over his bare shoulder. "He had that look of a man who just knows he's met the woman of his dreams." He shot Erika an affectionate smile and his gaze lingered on her face. "Mother of his babies."

Erika rolled her eyes and parked herself on the sofa next to Belah's blanket-covered feet. She reached out and rubbed one of Belah's soles.

"Tell me what happened. Did he fuck and run? Do I need to go knock some turul heads?"

Geva snorted, then tilted a jug of orange juice to his lips and swallowed. "She'd do it, too," he said when he lowered the jug.

Erika shot her mate a withering glare. "We own glasses for a reason, hun."

Returning her attention to Belah, she said, "Talk or I'm putting a boot up that bastard's ass."

"Nothing's wrong with Lukas," Belah said, and offered a helpless shrug and a half-smile to her friend. "He's perfect. And so is his brother. Together, they're perfect, but they don't want to be … together, I mean."

Erika's mouth dropped open. "Did I just hear you right? You met Iszak, too? I think I need you to back up and tell me everything."

Belah recounted the events of the evening, her skin growing flushed and her core aching at the memories. But the ache settled deeper in her soul when she got to the part where Lukas discovered her with his brother, the pair of them hovering in mid-air while Iszak made love to her.

"They were so angry, so hurt. The winds that blew around them were too much for me. If that's the way they feel about me being their mate, I'm better off staying away from them both. Besides, something happened … someone they love dearly was taken by the Ultiori. They still hold deep anger for my part in the Ultiori's existence, and they don't even know it was me. I can't lie to them if I'm to mate them. It's bad enough that they hate each other right now. I couldn't bear it if they hated me, too."

She also couldn't bear the looks of pity on her hosts' faces, and the glimmer of a tear in Erika's eye when she looked at Geva in appeal.

The Red dragon frowned. "They'll tear themselves apart over this. Once a turul's found his true mate, that's it for him. If they can't be with you, it'll destroy them both. Let's just hope they care about each other enough to work out their own differences. They know well enough how dragons work—multiple mates are by no means unusual for us."

"They're good guys," Erika said. "I can't believe they wouldn't come around, all things considered. I mean, you're the *One*. Give them another chance, for their sake, Belah."

Belah smiled sadly. "I think I need to give them space." And just hope that her week with Nikhil was over and done with by the time she sought the brothers out again. Because if there was one sure way to prove she wasn't the monster they believed she was, it would be giving them the ashes of their enemy.

CHAPTER SIXTEEN

L ukas was wired from worry over Belah's safety. Even though he knew his brother's perpetual scowl meant Iszak was just as worked up over the situation, he hated the silent treatment. In spite of the liquor-soaked talk they'd had earlier that morning, and the revelation of the danger their mate might be in, he still resented the fact that she'd wanted Iszak in addition to himself. She'd responded to Iszak's music so instinctively that she'd sung the words to a song she couldn't have possibly heard before. The lyrics hadn't been uttered in five decades, and the latest brood of dragons had only just ascended within the last year.

But that was evidence enough that the song his sister had written had served its purpose of luring their true mate to them. And what if Evie had been here to sing it? Would it have called another dragon for her?

He and his brother hadn't played the song together in just as long. Even though they had a standing date at the Gatormouth, they stuck to the popular blues songs of other artists when they played together, only occasionally filling in the set list with their own arrangements. Their band hadn't been anything special in many years, so he hoped the club's manager would be willing to move up the date for their show.

The alley door that led the back way into the club was locked. Iszak leaned on the buzzer while Lukas paced impatiently.

"He'll do it," Ozzie said, trying to calm them down. "Davis owes us."

But when the door opened and Davis, the bleary-eyed old blues man who owned the club, stood frowning at them, Lukas wasn't so sure.

Davis ushered them in and they made their case anyway, sitting in the dim interior of the club around one of the tables, surrounded by the scent of stale beer and sweat.

Davis continued to frown while he listened, arms crossed across his thick midsection. His expression didn't bode well, but Lukas couldn't get a bead on any kind of reaction from him. Finally, Davis nodded and uncrossed his arms, hooking his thumbs into his suspenders.

"Best I can offer is to move you three to Tuesday. That'll mean giving that night's headliner Saturday, along with Saturday's take—you'll be losing money, but if it's that important to you to play sooner, it's that or nothing. Tonight's off the table. Mind if I ask why the fuck you guys want to make such a boneheaded switch? You pull in more than most of the other acts. More single women come for your shows, and that means a bigger audience all around. If I didn't know you guys better, I'd think you were doing this for a lady."

All it took was Lukas and Iszak's glance at each other and Davis let out a thunderous guffaw.

"Well, I'll be. Which of you landed a bird finally? After all these years of you nailing whatever pretty girl had the guts to sneak backstage …" He shook his head and then tilted his chin at their cousin. "Does this have something to do with Ozzie's messed up face? It's an improvement, if you ask me."

Ozzie reached up to test the cut on his forehead and shrugged.

"Doesn't matter which of us it is, does it?" Lukas said. "We're just hoping she'll show."

Davis shook his head. "Boys, you know my ad budget doesn't reach that far. Even if folks knew it was you guys playing on Tuesday, it's too short notice. I sure hope your girl has wicked ears on her, if you think she'll come just because you're playing."

"We're willing to take the risk," Iszak said, finally entering the conversation. He reached his hand out to Davis and the pair shook. Lukas and Ozzie followed suit.

Lukas's stomach churned as they said farewell to their friend. Davis had been a fixture for them for longer than the old man knew, but the Wind had the uncanny ability to convince humans that their memories were faulty. And humans were nothing if not adaptable. Davis loved to tell them that they reminded him of an old, unknown band he'd played with in his youth. Lukas regretted never reaching for the limelight, but they knew better. Less public presence meant less opportunity for their enemy to find them.

Now they needed to be found, and despite several hours flying over the city after leaving their grandmother's, they'd caught no glimmer of the other end to the blurred thread that connected them to Belah. She was hidden well, which should have comforted Lukas, but he still vibrated with the need to be close to her again. Even though he'd found her—his true mate—they hadn't sealed the deal.

For a turul, that meant the very intimate process of sharing breath, because the Wind was everything to them. The air in their lungs was sacred. The dragons knew how much it meant, even though their power resided elsewhere.

Lukas's own lungs ached now with the need to sing to her, to share that breath, first calling to the heavens before letting himself breathe for her.

Boreas breathes for us, we breathe for each other. It was a simple wedding mantra, but the one they held to as members of the houses of the four Winds.

He had no idea how it would work with Iszak in the mix, but if Iszak's story could be believed, Belah had lungs on her enough to accommodate them both.

They exited the club into the alley again, and a rough hand gripped Lukas's shoulder as he reached for the helmet dangling off his bike's handlebar. He turned to see his brother, lips firm amidst a rough visage that made Lukas wonder if he looked as rough himself.

"We're finding her. We're making her ours, brother. Both of us. Right?" Iszak's fingers dug into his shoulder painfully. His brother wasn't fucking around.

"We'll find her somehow. But I think the rest is up to her. Dragons are possessive and controlling as fuck. You gonna be okay with it if she wants to boss us around?"

Iszak's frown deepened, and Lukas wondered if he should let his brother off the hook and tell him he was joking. He decided he enjoyed Iszak's discomfort too much. Both of them enjoyed seeking solace in dark places after their sister's disappearance. It had started with Vietnam, but letting themselves sink into violence only highlighted their need for better balance for their dark cravings. A desire for bondage and discipline in the bedroom was yet another thing he and his brother had in common, but where Lukas could at least be more reasonable outside of his kinks, Iszak had gotten used to being an alpha asshole. He wasn't about to tell his brother that their mate had loved being tied up—it would spoil the fun of watching Iszak discover it for himself.

But now that Lukas had uttered the words, he decided if Belah wanted to turn the tables and boss him around, he'd kneel for her. He'd do anything for her.

Surprisingly, Iszak smiled. "I'd do whatever the fuck she wanted, if I could have her right now. We need to get her back, brother. Evie'd want it."

"Do you guys feel the chill? I think Hell just froze over," Ozzie said, drawing their attention to him. He stood, leaning against the leather seat of his bike, slowly shaking his head. "I can't wait to meet the girl that did this to you guys. I've seen you around women my whole life, and never once did you actually agree on anything so easily."

Lukas tilted his head toward the street. "C'mon and follow us back to our place, man. If you want to find your own mate, we've gotta teach you the song."

Ozzie's eyes lit up. "*The* actual song … not the alternate arrangement we used to play?"

"The one and only."

Beside him, Iszak slung a leg over his bike, already humming the tune. Two more days and they'd play it again together for the first time in ages. They'd play it like their lives depended on it, and she would come back to them.

She had to.

CHAPTER SEVENTEEN

Waiting was torture, but Belah couldn't do anything else. She would've retreated to the Glade, but was too close to everything she'd ever wanted that she didn't dare leave. The revelation that true happiness might be within her grasp made her restless. She wanted to do something, anything, to move the process along.

After three thousand years of simply existing, this impatience was foreign. The dread of fulfilling her promise to Nikhil tangled with her hope that Iszak and Lukas would be receptive to sharing her, once she'd given them time to work things out.

The only thing that helped distract her in the meantime was flying, which was tricky enough to do among the monolithic towers of the City. Her breath could cloak her somewhat, turning her scales reflective so that if anyone chose to gaze up at the sky, she was effectively transparent—but for the sake of complete concealment, she chose to have two Shadows accompany her when she went out. Nikhil would probably still be able to find her when he chose to call in her promise to him, but she could avoid betraying her true nature to the humans in the city while she flew.

Humanity itself was more fascinating up close than she could have imagined, even after watching the race's progress through her reflecting pool. When she wasn't flying, she let Erika and Geva be her tour guides, showing her around the city and introducing her to all its wonders. If she hadn't found Iszak and Lukas so quickly, she would have enjoyed living in this world while she searched, simply existing as one of the billions of humans who had spread across the Earth in her absence.

A few nights after flying away from Lukas and Iszak's anger-induced storm, Belah launched herself off the roof of Erika and Geva's building and spread her wings wide to catch the thermal currents that constantly blew between the tall buildings. Her two guards followed close behind, their breath concealing them all so they looked like nothing more than wisps of fog drifting through the night. She'd promised herself she would wait until after she'd dealt with Nikhil to seek out the brothers again at their home near the water. But with each passing night, she could feel the link to them both tug at her. The bond was a strong one, and she wondered whether they would have sought her out directly if the Shadows hadn't been there to blur the connection.

It didn't matter, though. Not yet. She was still the Blue Beast who'd been responsible for creating their enemy. She couldn't go to them again until she could prove she was worthy of their love.

She flew through the city, easily shutting out the din of wide-open human thoughts and emotions clamoring to reach her. In a way, the utter transparency of the race's needs and desires comforted her. Humanity hadn't changed a bit in all the centuries, despite their numbers and amazing advances in technology. They still craved a connection with others, and that craving was infectious. Belah wanted that, too.

Now that she could be an equal to a potential mate, she wanted that more than she ever had. She wanted to walk among the humans and be a woman—not a queen or a goddess. Iszak and Lukas made that desire ache even deeper inside her, because that's all they knew her as—she may have been a member of the higher races, but to them, she was still just a woman. Not someone to worship without question, or grovel before because of the power she held. If anything, the music they played made her want to kneel before them and offer up her soul.

Because the place they took her was higher than she'd ever been, yet still provided an anchor. Their music was the anchor, she realized. In fact, it was more than that—it was an inexorable link that tethered her to them, and despite blocking out the sounds of everything but the wind, that music rose into the air and called to her even now.

At first she wondered if her mind had simply wandered back to her dreams, but when she focused, she knew she was hearing it again, and this time the score was whole. It wasn't the incomplete half of a song that she'd heard from Lukas once, and then the other half from Iszak later. She didn't have to fill in the blanks between their notes with her memories of her dream this time.

"Mistress, are we changing course? If we return to the city, we'll need to scout a secure place to shift when we land," the Shadow flanking her on the left asked.

"Just head toward the music. We'll find a place there."

"I hear no music, Mistress. You'll have to lead us to it, if that's where you wish to go."

The music called to her, urging her to answer, and she couldn't help herself. She sounded out a trumpeting cry that mimicked the lyrics she had sung to Iszak the other night, before realizing that the Shadows' cloaking magic also dampened the sounds they made. She had to go to them, if only to hear the music in its entirety. They didn't need to know she was there—not yet.

Belah tucked one wing closer to her body and banked to the right, homing in on the direction of the music. The Shadows adjusted their direction and picked up the pace to match. Within a few minutes, they circled above a brick building, and the Shadows led her down to the dark and deserted end of the adjoining alley.

The heavy beat of the music was as clear to her as if they were playing right in front of her. She should stay out here in the darkness and just listen, but a compulsion gripped her. She had to see them, had to know that the brothers had reconciled and were, indeed, collaborating on their mating call for her.

She swiftly shifted into her human shape, and with a breath clothed herself in an outfit similar to that worn by one of the women leaving the club. A second later, Belah stood clad almost entirely in black leather, with a filmy, blue camisole beneath a fitted jacket that had the same supple weight as the jacket Lukas had let her wear. Tall boots hugged her feet and calves.

Beside her, the pair of Shadows followed suit, both large males choosing to conjure jeans, boots, and worn leather jackets.

"We'll keep you cloaked, if that's what you wish," the larger Shadow offered in a deep voice.

Belah paused before stepping out of their hiding place, undecided. Should she let the brothers see her tonight? Let them know she'd answered their call? It was too soon yet, but she had no idea how long until Nikhil came for her. She had to see *them*, at least—just once more before she had to fulfill her promise to Nikhil.

"Yes. I'm not ready for them to see me again just yet." But Sweet Mother, did she want to. Without another word, she strode out of the shadows and toward the circle of illumination that surrounded the club's entrance.

A few feet away from the guards standing outside, she expelled a long breath, sending it ahead of her to drift around their heads until they breathed her magic in. Mindlessly, one of them opened the door, and without any further interaction, she and her Shadows walked inside.

The music enveloped Belah, drawing her further and further in. She obeyed its undertow, allowing the Shadows to push ahead of her through the throng of bodies. The human patrons moved aside without argument.

Finally, they reached a dance floor where couples moved together, entwined in almost overtly sexual embraces, hips locked and rocking to the music.

The music took on a different rhythm and slightly different key in the dim interior of the bar than it had when she'd heard it in her dreams. There it had been an extremely sensual sound, but here, the beat of it rose through her feet, vibrating through her bones until Belah's core ached to feel her own body moving in time, entwined with those two men who stood on stage, side-by-side, with their shining instruments to their lips. The heavy tremor of the bass drum and the bass guitar that beat behind them lent a hungry, primal sound to the song.

She needed contact. She needed to dance, because she knew she couldn't sing if she wanted to remain unnoticed. She grabbed the hands of her Shadows and the pair moved in close, surrounding her.

"Dance," she said to them both without speaking.

Neither hesitated, despite the whirl of uncertainty that she sensed in their minds. They were both unmated and would happily bed her if she asked, yet their task of protecting her came first. They may have doubted the wisdom of her request, but didn't want to disobey her.

They slid into place, one in front and the other in back, their hips pressing to hers while they moved. She closed her eyes and imagined they were the pair on stage, holding her and writhing against her.

The music drove her on, the contact of the two dragons as arousing to her as it was to them, and she twined her arms up around one Shadow's neck, pulling him down into a kiss. The second their lips met, she knew she shouldn't have. It didn't feel right and she pulled away, abruptly putting space between her and her guards again. The Shadow looked surprised, then worried.

"Mistress. It's the music, isn't it? Should we leave?"

Belah shook her head and darted her eyes away, feeling a warm flush rise to her cheeks. She continued dancing, and they did, too, adapting to the flow of bodies. Women gravitated to them, and they both eagerly danced with the willing ones. She didn't object. They remained perfectly attuned to her despite their own desires. They cloaked her well enough that she could just stand and watch her lovers on stage without the crowd around her being aware.

"How much do you know about why we're here? How much information did the First Shadow share?" she sent to them both.

The Shadow she'd kissed released the woman he'd been dancing with into his fellow Shadow's grip and faced Belah. He squeezed her shoulder gently—a comforting gesture that she appreciated.

"Kol only instructed us to guard you until you located your turul mate, and then it was up to you whether you wished us to continue to do so. We're your servants unless you say otherwise." He tilted his chin toward the stage, and his voice reverberated again inside her mind. *"I'm guessing that, considering what we witnessed the other night, both those Wind Charmers up there have caught your attention. Is it true what they say about turul? They only have a single mate for life?"*

A smile spread across Belah's face, warmth pooling in her belly at the sight of the North brothers playing. They stood back-to-back now, leaning against each other, music streaming from their saxophones so strongly she could almost see the magic filling the room. They were so in sync. She wished she could find a way to be with them sooner rather than later.

"It's very true," she said. *"And I belong to them."*

"Then we'll guard you until you get what you need."

When Iszak and Lukas parted and she saw past them toward the back of the stage, a chill went through her. Seated behind the drum kit was none other than Ozzie West—the turul who'd witnessed her exchange with Nikhil.

The events of the last few days converged, the threads coming together. The music Erika had played, the names she'd mentioned that first night. The music itself had been the impetus for Geva to seek out Sophia North in the first place. Then the date with Ozzie and its disastrous conclusion—he'd seen and heard her entire exchange with Nikhil. She'd entirely forgotten her worry when Lukas had revealed that Ozzie was part of their trio.

"I need to get out of here, now!" she said, broadcasting the thought loudly enough that both Shadows immediately came to attention as if a switch had been flipped. She didn't have time to feel bad about pulling them away from potential mates. She couldn't risk being discovered by someone who knew her true identity.

On the way back out to the alley, the other details began to piece together. The pictures she'd seen in Sophia North's apartment … the brothers were in those pictures.

The photos had also featured the sister they had lost. And one other … A face she knew now. A face that was connected to her old lover. Nikhil's newest Elite.

Marcus. The third Elite. She remembered seeing into his mind the day they'd met, learning his name and his secrets. Seeing a beauty of a woman with wings, and feeling the ache of need the man had to save that woman from her captors—from the very man he served.

If Marcus wanted to save her, that meant that Evie wasn't dead. If Evie wasn't dead, Belah's new mates had no reason to hate her.

The revelation was too delicate to share with anyone else. She didn't want Ozzie to see her, but more than that, she needed her brother's wisdom.

In the darkness of the club's alley, she and the Shadows shifted, and she led them to the top of a tall building nearby. The wind still carried strains of the music to her ears, and each errant note made her skin quiver with the urge to return to Iszak and Lukas. But with distance, her head cleared enough to focus entirely on the pair of black dragons who rested on their scaled haunches beside her.

"Call my brother," she said.

Her guards exchanged a glance and their heads dipped suspiciously. She hated that she couldn't read their thoughts at that moment, but Shadows were notoriously guarded, thanks to their own powers. Her brother was impossible to read if he didn't wish it, but she knew him well enough to predict his behavior. Even though they'd agreed that only Belah would leave the Glade to complete the search for the mate from her dreams, she suspected her brother had followed.

"I can't reach him myself, but if I know Ked, he's open to any and all communication from you two. How close is he? Call him now, or I'll be forced to fly around the city trumpeting my irritation for the entire human world to hear."

"No need for theatrics, sister," a deep voice boomed from behind her.

Belah turned, shifting into her human shape at the same time. Several yards away her brother stood, clad from head to toe in black leather and almost blending into the shadows.

"Do you have some addiction to meddling in my love life? You shouldn't even be here, you know." She took several irritated steps toward him.

"And yet you were about to raise Hell trying to get my attention, so I suppose it's good I've been following you. What do you need? I hope you haven't given up on finding your mate already."

"Far from it. I've found both of them, and they're more wonderful than I could have hoped for. Can you hear that music—the faint song that reminds me so much of Mother's crooning when we were babies? That's their mating call."

Ked tilted his head and his eyes grew hooded while he listened. Some almost imperceptible emotion flickered across his face, but was gone before Belah could understand what it was. He raised his head and said, "What of it? You were looking for a turul mate. Naturally, they would have a mating call that sounded like that. So why haven't you answered them?"

"Oh, I did, several days ago. They just didn't expect the same woman to answer both their calls on the same night. Like most siblings, they needed time to work out their differences. Now they have, but there's something else standing in my way of being with them."

"If it's your futile mission to convince Nikhil to give up the location of our son, you already know my feelings on that. He no doubt believes the second you have the information, he's a dead man."

"Nikhil still wants me enough that he already agreed. I'll get the information from him somehow. But that's not the issue. I decided I can't wait any longer than I have to before I mark Iszak and Lukas and make them mine. The problem is they hate me. Or at least, they hate the 'Blue Beast,' who they believe was responsible for the Ultiori's existence. They lost a sister … Are you listening to me?"

She strode over to her brother, who had a glazed expression with his face turned toward the center of the city.

"Ked," Belah said, gently pulling at his elbow. "What's up with you? I've never seen you like this. You should head back to the Glade. Have Kris attend you for a night. Following me around without seeing to your own needs is a recipe for disaster."

Her brother shook his head, his thick, dark hair catching the wind and whipping around his face, but it couldn't conceal the look of desperation in his eyes. Then it hit Belah full force—the raw emotions buried in her brother's soul. Beyond all that darkness was a driving need to find the turul female she'd seen when he had shared his own dream.

"I don't need a *fuck,*" he said vehemently. "I need *her*. Something about that music sounds so much like the mating call from my dream, but it's not quite right."

"The music …" Belah caught the rhythm and started humming, then softly sang the words that had come to her the night she'd found Iszak playing on his roof.

Ked's eyes widened and his mouth dropped open as he stared at her. "Where did you hear that? I never shared the song from my dream, only the images, but that's exactly what she sang to me. How do you know those words?"

"I don't know," she said. "The song came to me when I answered their call. Maybe …" Could it be? Here she was about to ask Ked to help her find a lost turul female. Was Fate that transparent? A chill went down her spine when Ked's brows drew together as he waited for her to finish her thought. Before she could speak, he'd delved into her mind and pulled the details out for himself.

"They have a sister, or had a sister, who they believe was killed by the Ultiori. But she isn't dead, is she? Tell me everything you know, Belah. Everything."

Belah took a deep breath and explained what little she knew. She told him about the photos of Iszak and Lukas with their sister, and the fourth figure, who she knew now was Nikhil's newest Elite. She told Ked how when she'd met Marcus, he had clearly longed for a female turul who fit the North girl's description perfectly.

"If you can rescue her, then I can face them with the news that their sister is alive. They will have no reason to hate me when I tell them the truth about who I am. Ked, I can't mark them without them knowing everything. I might as well let Nikhil have me and return to Iszak and Lukas when all this is done, but it'll kill me if I have to wait any longer for them. I know you feel what their music is doing to me."

Ked's shoulders sagged. "You know how the Ultiori work. If we couldn't find our own son by now, what makes you think we can find this turul?"

Footsteps from behind made Belah turn. The two Shadows had been waiting at a polite distance, but their closeness and suddenly anxious demeanors told her they had something to say, but weren't eager to share.

"What is it?" Ked barked.

"The missing turul, Master. Kol has had a squadron searching for one for several months now—it was a command left by his mother, the former First Shadow, prior to our Ascension. The exact instructions were to bring the news to you once she was found. The search has apparently been going on for years, but the original message is what you need to hear. 'Tell the Void to find Iszak and Lukas North. Their sister is alive.' It hasn't been a priority since it's a turul female, not a dragon, but the search is ongoing."

As swiftly as if a light switch were flipped, the night went pitch-black, Ked's power betraying how he'd received that ages-old moniker—*the Void*. Within the darkness, Belah sensed the fear rising to the surface in the poor Shadow who'd been the bearer of this unfortunate news to her brother.

"If the message was to tell *me* something, why am I just hearing this news now?" Ked's voice rumbled darkly and so low, Belah was sure the humans in the city must hear thunder.

"We didn't know the significance of your involvement. You'd have to ask the First Shadow for specifics on why he kept it quiet. Maybe he wanted to find her first. I'm sorry, Master. I don't have any other information."

The light gradually seeped back in through the unfiltered darkness of Ked's mood and the Shadows both visibly relaxed.

"Go now, both of you. Tell Kol this search is his *first* priority—he's to drop everything else, and I do mean everything—and make sure I don't see either of you again until the female turul is found."

Turning to Belah, he added, "*Your* priority is to go to the North Brothers and answer their mating call for real this time—make it permanent, sister. Tell them the truth. The news about their sister will have more impact coming from you once they learn your true identity. If Nikhil really does have my mate, then I want all the help we can get to get her away from the bastard—we need her brothers on our side. We need *everyone* on this."

Belah's instinct was to argue with her brother's plan. She'd spent so long wishing to find her babies again that following through on that singular mission seemed like it should take precedence. Yet somehow, she was relieved to be commanded by her brother to act contrary to her own convictions—to follow through with the more present urge to mate the pair of brothers sooner rather than later. Her need to find her children would never die. They may remain lost for a bit longer, but one thing she was sure of was that they were safely bound in their hibernating forms and nothing could break through that magic but the touch of their own fated mates.

"All right. Where will you be if I need you?"

Ked gave her a sad look. "When have you ever really needed me, Belah? I like to think I'm your protector, but you and I both know that I only get in the way. This is all as much my fault as it is yours. We *all* have a part in Nikhil's existence. Perhaps you and I more than most, but never think I don't know you're the strongest of all of us. If he comes for you, do what you need to do. Just try to make sure you don't put this turul female's life on the line for the sake of old regrets."

It hurt that he'd refer to her babies as regrets, but Ked was right. There were good reasons her son and daughter had been taken, and she shouldn't risk the life of Iszak and Lukas's sister on a reckless mission to get them back. The opportunity would still be there after she'd mated the North brothers. She quashed the ache of maternal longing in her belly and nodded, too choked up to voice her assent.

Just as Ked's form began to shimmer and take on his true shape, she called out, "Her name is Evie."

His brows lowered. "Who is?"

"Your mate, Brother. Her name is Evie North. We'll save her together, I promise."

With a final nod, he spread his wings and launched his enormous dark shape into the air. Almost immediately, he disappeared into the velvet blackness of the sky above.

CHAPTER EIGHTEEN

Belah avoided heading back to the club, even though the music called to her more strongly than before. The two saxophones sounded almost desperate now, the sexual energy in the club rising to a fever pitch in response to the sound. They called to her deliberately tonight, not the teasing seduction of Lukas's music, or Iszak's soulful lament she'd heard on the rooftop. They hadn't known at the time what their music meant. Now they did. They called to her with a vengeance, and the sound intoxicated her, made her want to drown herself in it. Drown herself in them. She stood alone on the rooftop of one of the tallest buildings in the city, staring in their direction and fighting the urge to fly to them now.

Where they were right now wasn't where she wanted to bare her soul to them. She turned, forcing herself to walk in the other direction, and launched herself off the edge. She let her human body plummet for several seconds, allowing her instincts take over and enjoying the rush of air over her skin as her conjured clothing dissolved and her dragon skin appeared. Just before she'd be too visible to deny, she extended her wings and soared high, shifting completely as she ascended, her talons skimming the glass of a skyscraper too quickly for anyone inside to realize what had just happened.

Once high above the city again, she headed away from the lure of Lukas and Iszak's music, flying as quickly as she could, now that she didn't have the added cloak of the two Shadows to help hide her.

Moments later, she landed on the roof where Iszak had made love to her only a few nights earlier. The bricks beside the stairwell were still cracked and damaged from where the brothers' hurricane had tossed her into the wall. She felt no residual ache from the bruise she'd received, only a rising dread about what might happen when she told them the truth.

Shifting back to her human shape, Belah glanced around and found a pair of chairs with a small table between them. From the detritus strewn about, she picked up a crinkling bag filled with salty crumbs, then a half-empty bottle of liquor. She dropped the bag, but bent her head to the bottle. The deep blue glass carried a lingering scent of both men and the faint residue of their auras when they'd been drinking it—conflict and reconciliation clung to the dew-covered glass. They'd both drank from this bottle before coming to terms with her presence in their lives.

She sat in one of the chairs and stared down at the bottle. Answers had come for them from inside this blue vessel with the name of her favorite place emblazoned across its label. *Wild Blue Heaven,* it read. Perhaps answers would be revealed for her, as well. She stared up at the heavens and wished for an answer.

When nothing came from the hazy night above her, she opened the bottle and lifted it to her lips. When her tongue circled the rim, she could taste them both. Sweet Mother, she needed them. She needed them to believe her, to accept her, in spite of her past. When the burn of the liquor hit her tongue, she opened up and swallowed, drinking it down.

If it had worked for them, it might work for her. She took another deep swallow and closed her eyes, seeking any insight or inspiration that the liquor might carry with it.

When she heard the sounds of engines rumbling in the distance some time later, she stared down at an empty bottle and wondered where the hell all its contents had gone.

She stood up, frantic, her heart racing. The bottle clattered to the ground while she rushed to the door to the stairwell. The world swam and she fumbled for the door lever. She didn't want to miss them … she'd planned to be front and center when they came home.

Their voices reached her, Lukas's halfway through an irritated monologue when they became audible. Belah paused when she heard the words, "No sign of her at all. She's done with us, brother. We fucked it up."

She let go of the door handle and leaned against the cold metal. Lukas sounded so defeated she longed to comfort him.

"She was there. I fucking know it," Iszak said. "At least I know there were dragons there. Did you see the level of humping on the dance floor tonight? That never happens unless a dragon's hanging around. They've got magic mind shit going on. I don't think tonight was random."

She levered open the door and was about to slide into the stairwell when she heard a third voice.

"Doesn't matter anyway. Davis wants us regularly for Tuesdays now."

Ozzie's voice made Belah pause. She couldn't confront them with him in the way. It didn't matter that she was intent on telling them the truth; his presence would muddy the waters.

She put her head in her hands and sank down onto the top step. This should've gone better.

The clank of the door closing behind her made her jerk to attention. She hurriedly exhaled a deep breath of magic, desperate to reach their minds and control their reactions, but she was too late.

"Is someone on your roof, guys?" Ozzie asked.

The other two minds in question instantly found her, somehow. She sensed their awareness of her as a breeze blew past. A breeze that shouldn't have existed in the closed stairwell she was hiding in.

"Ozzie, no offense, but you're out. Don't fucking call for at least three days."

"She came here? It worked after all, didn't it? She's here, isn't she?" Ozzie asked. "Fuck, you guys. Fine ... I want to meet her, when you come up for air. I've always wanted a dragon mate. I want to know what she looks like, at least."

"She looks like a dragon," Lukas said. "That's all you need to know."

"What color? Please tell me that, at least."

Iszak's gruff voice spoke next. "She's a Blue you fuck, now fucking *disappear.*"

Belah held her breath as she heard Ozzie muttering his way back down the stairs to the garage and then out into the alley. A moment later, a bike engine revved and she heard him speed off.

She relaxed, but it only lasted for a second before she heard the stairwell door opening below her and light streamed in. Her eyesight wavered when Iszak found her.

He bent down and his face filled her vision. She blinked, trying to focus on his features, but just smiled. He was beautiful. She reached a hand up to his cheek and enjoyed the tickle of his stubble against her palm. She wanted to tell him how lovely he was, but her tongue didn't want to work.

Iszak chuckled. "I'd say she found our bottle from the other night. Who knew pretty Blue dragons were such lightweights when it came to turul liquor. That bottle wasn't filled with human spirits, baby. I don't know what you expected, but us higher races need a magic bump to get drunk. You got more than you were ready for … I guess newly ascended dragons have no tolerance."

He slid his arms beneath her and lifted her up, cradling her against his chest. Pressing his lips to her temple, he whispered, "Sweetness, you have no idea how much it means to us that you came back."

"You're gonna hate me," she slurred, finally remembering her mission and forcing herself to speak. She shook her head. Turul liquor … she should've known better.

"Never gonna happen," Iszak said as he carried her down the stairs.

"Pretty sure it'll happen after I say this."

He set her down on a smooth, cushioned surface, and she dug her nails into the leather of their sofa, wishing the world would stop spinning.

Two faces lowered into her frame of view as they crouched before her, and she took a breath. Sweet Mother, they were both beautiful men. Men she loved already, thanks to Fate. There was no going back now, either, because she was *theirs* as much as they were hers.

"We're bound, the three of us," she said, speaking slowly to enunciate over the thick sensation in her mouth. Her tongue was still doing its best to play dead.

"We are, at that," Iszak said, his dark eyes looking at her expectantly. "Something wrong, baby? Just tell us, please. We're in this together. All three of us." He shot a look at his brother and Lukas nodded, squeezing her knee.

"I'm the Beast," she blurted before she could lose her resolve. "I'm the fucking Beast. The thing you guys hate … remember that? The Council bitch who ruined everything. You're supposed to hate me, but here I am, the girl who answered your call. Sooo, hate me all you want, because I love you. I love you because I can't *not* love you. But I don't give a fuck what Fate wants. I'd love you both, anyway. I'll love you both even if you decide you don't love me."

She should've felt more anxiety or dread or something from the revelation, but the world was starting to darken around the edges. Through the darkening haze, she remembered there was something else she was supposed to say. What was it? Something important.

Her eyelids didn't want to stay open any longer. The cushion of the sofa suddenly rose up to her cheek and she pressed against it, sighing into the cool leather. Sleep was important. She'd told them the truth and the world hadn't ended. She could take a break from worrying now. Oblivion called to her and she went, surrendering to the familiar darkness.

CHAPTER NINETEEN

szak tilted his head slightly and studied the beautiful, passed-out woman. Why couldn't having her be easy? No, she just *had* to come with baggage. He leaned back on his heels and just stared at her … this waif of a woman. This woman whose body he craved and knew he would die for. Trying to juxtapose the words she'd just blurted out onto what he knew already … what he knew in his fucking *heart and soul* about her after the one night they'd had … the few moments they'd shared.

He had no words.

"I thought she'd be taller," he said dumbly. "At least mean-er-looking, after all the blood that was spilled because of her."

That's what he thought of who she *said* she was. But who he knew she was … his one and only love … the woman lying passed out on his sofa was completely and utterly perfect. Right down to her confession before she'd lost consciousness.

"What the fuck just happened?" Lukas asked, falling back on his ass like he'd been knocked over.

"You didn't think it'd be easy, did you?"

Lukas snorted softly and stood, hovering over Belah's prone form. He stooped and gently brushed a wisp of dark hair off her cheek, then sighed. "Nanyo never let us believe anything would be easy … it hasn't been easy waiting for her. But … fuck. I can't even … I spent so many nights imagining meeting the Beast from the stories and fucking *destroying* her. Easily as many nights as I fantasized about meeting *her*. I shouldn't still want her so goddamn much, should I?"

"She came to us," Iszak said, standing and bending down to slide his arms under her body again. "She answered our call. She's ours. It isn't in our blood to hate her."

He turned to carry her into the bedroom, acting on instinct now. She was his true mate, after all. He may not be able to process her confession, but he could sure as shit be man enough to deserve the honesty she'd just offered.

"She's delusional, right?" Lukas said, following him. "The booze made her believe she's *that* Blue dragon. Survivor guilt, or something?"

"You know better," Iszak said. They both knew better. Lies weren't an option in their world. If Belah's words hadn't been entirely true, they'd have known. Even her belief of the truth wouldn't have been enough to conceal reality from a turul.

"Fuck."

Fuck was right. He laid her down on his bed and stood back and stared for a good five minutes. Her dark hair flowed like silk across his pillows. The leather hugging her body gleamed in the lamplight. He'd only had one too-short interlude with her that still seemed surreal. All of it, from the moment she'd caught his attention and started singing, to the realization they'd defied gravity while they fucked, felt like some kind of fantasy rather than fact.

He didn't know what to make of her—this dragon who had rocked his world.

She was fucking helpless now. Drunk out of her mind and unconscious. If she really was the Blue Beast from legend, she'd never let herself be so vulnerable.

"By the Winds, she's beautiful," he whispered. He leaned down and impulsively touched one of the dark waves that spread across his pillowcase and her lips moved slightly. A wisp of blue smoke escaped.

"Whoa," Lukas said and took a defensive step backward. Iszak rejected the strong impulse to retreat, instead leaning in and opening his mouth. He inhaled sharply and the smoke entered his lungs.

He leaned back on the mattress beside her, watching her sleeping body and wondering what the tiny bit of unconscious magic she'd let go would tell him.

Erratic images flitted around his mind. Emotions that made him ache to be her protector from a darkness he couldn't fathom. Loss, regrets, and finally, hope made themselves apparent in the turmoil of her breath. For some reason, he saw his cousin's face in the mix, which made no fucking sense whatsoever.

"Ozzie … Why the fuck would he be in her head?"

He stared at Lukas, who looked back with an open mouth. "Ah… I don't…" Lukas's mouth snapped shut abruptly. "Nanyo… she set him up on a date, remember? He said he'd met the Beast. Fucking hell."

Lukas darted from the room, and a second later, Iszak heard windows banging open and the rhythm of wings flapping off into the night.

Belah didn't move a muscle. He let out a soft chuckle. The Blue Beast had a weakness, it seemed. He'd have to remember to keep a stock of turul liquor if she were going to be his mate. The vague thought flitted through his mind that he shouldn't accept her so easily. Knowing who she really was, he should hold her accountable … he shouldn't be wishing so hard for her to wake up just so he could make love to her again.

He gripped her booted foot and pulled, sliding the calf-length leather off and tossing it aside. The boot sailed through the air, but didn't make contact. He'd expected a solid *thunk* against the wall. When that didn't happen, he turned and saw … nothing … No sign of the boot at all.

"Fucking dragon illusions," he muttered.

Rather than reach for her other boot, he pursed his lips and inhaled until his lungs were full, then blew. He directed the wind from his lungs to her feet, then up the rest of her body.

His breath flowed over her, his magic working to counteract hers, and every stitch of clothing dissolved.

Iszak simply stared, his cock raging at the sight of her milky skin and her full breasts splayed just so. This was only her human form, he knew, but it was the first time he'd gotten a good look at her this way. The first time he'd seen her, she'd been lit by moonlight and her voice had distracted him from everything else.

Now, her body distracted him. Every inch of her was perfect. He should be furious about the fact that she was the monster responsible for so much bloodshed, but nothing about this woman made him believe she was that. All he wanted to do was protect her. Make love to her. Hear her cry his name while she came.

He sat back down beside her, his cock a solid presence straining against his jeans.

He inhaled sharply through his nose and clenched his teeth, restraining himself from touching her. She was oblivious now—unconscious and completely defenseless. When he did touch her, he wanted to know she felt it. He didn't know what he would do, but considering the emotions warring in his heart, he knew once she regained consciousness, she would be at his mercy. He only hoped she'd forgive him for taking vengeance on her flesh.

She was his true mate. His *One*. He would love her until it killed him. But that didn't excuse her from what she'd done.

He picked up the covers and laid them over her naked body, then bent and kissed her.

"You have no idea what's coming, baby, and I'm sorry for that. But if you're really the mate of the North Brothers, you'll survive what we have to offer. And if you really were the Blue Beast, you will probably think what we do is child's play."

There had been many legends passed down about the Blue Beast. After Iszak's sister disappeared, he'd researched all of them. One thing he knew was that the female dragon who had been the origin of their strife ... who'd created their enemy ... had enjoyed being tied up. Part of him hated knowing now that she might be the One, but another part ached to the core to show her what he could do with a few lengths of rope.

When his brother returned with their cousin some time later, he had so many ropes slung over the rafters it looked like their living room had been taken over by vines.

Ozzie stared around and gaped. "Who the fuck is this woman? Should I be excited to be included?"

"No," Iszak snapped. "Your job is to identify her. Then you're leaving."

Ozzie frowned. "Figured. Drummers always get upstaged … it's nothing new. Show me Sleeping beauty so I can get back to my fucking life, you fucks. I hope for your sake she's not the woman I met."

Lukas directed their cousin into Iszak's bedroom, and the two of them followed.

He rammed into Ozzie's back halfway through the door. His cousin had stopped short and stood, staring and slowly shaking his head.

Over Ozzie's shoulder, Iszak saw a pretty face framed by dark waves mussed from sleep, and the brightest blue eyes met his. She gave him a slight smile before looking at his cousin.

"Hi, Ozzie," Belah said. "Sorry about the bump on your head."

"No worries," Ozzie said numbly and turned. His terrified eyes were enough to tell Iszak what he needed to know.

"You're in bed with the fucking devil. She's in league with them. She fucking *made* them. I'm outta here, guys." He kept ranting on his way through the living room. Gesturing at Iszak's setup, he said, "You're fucking crazy if you think a bunch of cheesy ropes are going to hold the bitch. Good fucking luck with that."

Before Iszak or Lukas could stop him, Ozzie rushed out the door, slamming it solidly behind him.

Iszak couldn't keep his eyes off her now. Even as she pulled the sheets up higher.

She had to explain a few things, no doubt, but before that happened, he needed her.

A hand gripped his arm and he turned to see Lukas frowning at him.

"What's with the setup in the living room?"

"She's the One, but that doesn't mean we shouldn't make her pay."

He turned back to the now conscious Belah.

"Sweetness, you've got us both in a bit of a pickle. After that detail you dropped, we're just not sure how to react." He had trouble holding back the anger now that she was awake. She still looked perfect, and he still fucking wanted her. He'd have a hard time not hurting her when he got her bound up, but if she was as perfect as he thought, she'd love it.

Her blue eyes brightened and her throat rippled as she swallowed.

"How do you want to react?" She let her arms drop and the sheet slipped away from her breasts, falling to pool around her knees. She was bare naked and kneeling on his bed. Exactly how he'd always imagined his true mate might look.

"I'm not going anywhere, Iszak. You and Lukas are my life now. Fate's a bitch, isn't she?"

Iszak swallowed, the lump in his throat as harsh as a live ember when it went down. It only landed as a burning need in his belly. "This is going to hurt, baby. I hope you know that. We've got fifty years of hating what you were to us to work out before everything's even close to level."

And fuck if she didn't smile. "I've got three thousand years of regret to work out. We might need another three thousand before I'm level. Are you good with that?"

Beside him, Lukas cursed softly. "Fucking hell, she's perfect."

Iszak was too enthralled by the way she stretched out her creamy arms and offered her hands to him, upturned wrists pressed together, blue veins pulsing beneath the translucent barrier of her skin.

Bind me, the gesture said.

And he did.

CHAPTER TWENTY

B elah was already on her knees, a place she'd once loved to be when domination was imminent. She'd rather block out the last time she'd knelt before a man, though. The instinctive reaction she'd had to Nikhil's appearance mere days ago still confused her.

Yet where Nikhil had sought her pain and complete surrender, she sensed Lukas and Iszak wished for something very different.

Both men were standing in front of her, fully clothed in their outfits from their show … which amounted to plain white tees and black denim. Even though the sweat from their bodies had dried since she'd seen them on stage, their masculine turul scents were as strong as their auras.

She held her hands up in supplication, hoping Iszak would understand the gesture. Lukas had bound her before, and loved it. She believed Iszak would want the same thing. She hadn't spent time inside his head, but he had the raw hunger of a man who needed submission and didn't get it nearly as often as he would prefer.

Iszak's throat worked for a second before a pleased smile spread across his lips. Beside him, Lukas grinned.

"That's our girl," Iszak said and produced a rope from his back pocket. He wound it around her wrists with methodical precision, the length gradually growing shorter, until all she saw was a row of webbed cords encircling her wrists with an artful knot at the top.

"Ozzie was right," she said, her blood humming as Iszak tightened the knot. He raised his eyebrows at her. "Normal ropes won't hold me." She twisted her wrists, expecting her strength to make quick work of the webbed silk cords Iszak had bound her with. They stayed solidly wrapped, only creaking the slightest amount from her effort, but not tearing. Her eyes widened.

Iszak chuckled. "Step ahead of you, sweetness. I've been saving these ropes for a rainy day, and you definitely look like rain. Come," he said, pulling at her bound hands.

She shifted off the bed and stood, swaying slightly from the after-effects of the alcohol. Turul liquor … she'd know better next time. Lukas caught her and she leaned against him, grateful for his support, and even more buzzed from the contact than from the liquor.

"You've turned us upside-down, baby. I hope you know that. This is just a way to balance us. There's no fighting Fate. We need you. But we all have our own price for accepting it, don't we?"

She turned to look up into Lukas's eyes. The same lock of hair fell forward and she still longed to push it back, but her hands were bound by magic ropes. Instead, she tilted her head and kissed him.

He didn't pull back, or push her away. When her lips met his, her body thrummed with power, every cell agreeing that he was hers. He moaned into her mouth, his tongue slipping between her lips and meeting the soft thrust of her own.

Another hand cupped her face, forcing her to pull away, and Iszak was there, his lips hard on hers, claiming and commanding. She melted into his kiss with the same abandon as she had Lukas's.

Her heart raced when he pulled away, his dark eyes blazing with lust. "Lukas is the gentle one, just remember that. I'm not giving you any slack, baby—the ropes should be enough to show you that much. You're our slave until we hear every detail of your past and come to terms with it. We'll know when you're lying."

With a tug, he led her into the other room. More enchanted ropes hung from the rafters here. There were so many, the place seemed like a jungle of multi-colored cords. Her nipples tingled and hardened at the sight, as well as the understanding of what she was in for.

Lukas's hands rested at her waist while Iszak stepped forward into the center of their living room, where a thicker fall of ropes hung in a column from a large, metal hoop. On the floor beneath was a thick rug that resembled some kind of light-colored beast hide. It was soft and luxuriant, and Belah happily knelt in the center where Lukas commanded, just facing the ropes.

"Everything that happens now is your choice, Belah," Iszak said. He bent down and cupped her chin in his hand. He was so close. She craved another kiss, but he didn't lean in. All he did was explain. "You can leave before I begin, and nothing else will happen. We'll be done. You'll go on being the monster we always believed you to be. But if you stay, we'll break that perception into pieces. But that means breaking you, baby."

She closed her eyes, ashamed to feel the warm trail of an errant tear fall down her cheek.

"I'm already broken," she said, her voice quavering. "I've been broken for three thousand years. Whatever you need to do, do."

He seemed to flinch at her confession, but recovered swiftly. Even though she made a conscious effort to avoid using her power with them, she caught a glimmer of painful understanding in them both, and it gave her hope. Whatever the pair needed to do now, she would happily accept, especially if it helped *them* feel less broken, too.

"Good girl," Iszak finally said and stood. He gestured for his brother and Lukas came closer, accepting direction while Iszak took the ropes that dangled in front of her and made good use of all of them.

Iszak gripped her arms and unbound them, then gently pulled them behind her, aligning her forearms one above the other across her back before wrapping them in the silken cords. His hands moved swiftly, wrapping her body and tying knots as he went. This time she could feel the subtle tingle of the magic of the ropes sinking into her skin.

Iszak's knuckles and fingertips brushed against her skin constantly, every touch sending fresh heat to her core, even though none of his touches were overtly sexual.

He paused behind her at one point, pushing her knees wide and threading several lengths of rope between her thighs. His fingertips slowed their progress as they passed across on either side of her aching opening, but he barely grazed her skin.

Belah closed her eyes, suppressing a whimper of need, sure he had to feel the heat radiating from her. The ropes pulled taut, spreading her open slightly as he looped the cords back around her upper thighs, knotted them, then secured them at the bindings that crossed like latticework beneath her navel.

His breathing was quick and hot against the back of her neck as he reached above her head to secure a new length of rope. Over her shoulder, he said to his brother, "Lukas, check that I didn't make them too tight, will you?"

Lukas obligingly crouched in front of her, delicately adjusting his erection in his jeans and giving her a lusty smile. He started at the outer edge of the ropes that angled across the front of her hips, tracing his fingers down between the cords and her skin.

Belah's breathing quickened as he moved lower, his knuckles edging along the tops of her thighs while his thumbs traced the outer edges of the ropes.

"How do they feel, Belah?" Lukas asked, his voice low and rough with desire. He swallowed and glanced down. "Too tight?"

She could only shake her head, her entire body pulsing with the pleasure of his teasing touch. He shifted his fingers, removing one hand and slipping two fingers beneath the ropes at the top of her pelvis, on the inner edge this time. The backs of his fingers slid along the top of her mound and he bent them, deliberately digging the outsides of his knuckles into her swollen clit.

"Ohh," she breathed when his knuckles bumped past her aching bud, then parted her and pressed against her hungry opening. "Not too tight," she finally breathed.

Lukas slipped his fingers from the ropes and made no more pretense of testing Iszak's work. Instead, he pressed the same two digits against her opening and pushed into her depths all the way to the last knuckle. Belah threw her head back and groaned, her muscles clenching around him.

Lukas leaned closer and pressed his mouth to her ear while he worked his fingers in and out. "No, I'd say it's just tight enough." Turning his head to face Iszak over her shoulder, he asked, "Wouldn't you, brother?"

Somewhere behind her, Iszak's hands had been constantly working, securing her calves and ankles and looping more ropes like tethers to different points all over her body. Now he stopped, and Belah felt his warmth settle between her spread ankles. Iszak's hands rested against her ass, squeezed, then one hand moved between her legs, tracing the ropes from behind until his fingers met his brother's, still buried deep inside her.

Lukas made no attempt to remove himself, but Iszak didn't hesitate. His fingertips teased around her opening before pressing into her, two more digits sliding deep.

"So fucking tight." He fucked his fingers into her with the same rhythm as his brother, the sensation as wonderful as if they'd just filled her with a cock agile enough to rub at all the most sensitive spots inside her.

"You have no idea how hard it is not to fuck you right now," Iszak said into her ear while his fingers continued moving alongside Lukas's. "My cock wants to be inside you so fucking badly, baby. But you dropped a bomb on us tonight, and you know we can't just let it go. Make no mistake, it's going to take us a lot more nights like tonight before we're square. We'll give you a break when you understand that you're not the woman you used to be, because you're ours now."

"Yes … I'm yours," Belah whispered. She was too drunk on the pleasure they inflicted on her to say more. Her core clenched around them both.

As if to add insult to injury, Lukas bent his head and captured a nipple between his lips, sucking it into his mouth to tease it with his tongue. Iszak's free hand reached around and pinched her other nipple.

Iszak's voice continued its deep rumble in her ear. "That's right, baby, clench that tight pussy around us. I can't wait to feel you come on my cock like you're about to come all over our hands. I can feel it building, the more your hot cunt milks us. You want our cocks, don't you? In this wet little cunt, in your mouth … in your tight ass. We're going to take you every way we can until we make you beg to stop. If you don't think dragons could ever beg, I promise you'll know better after tonight's over."

"C-can I come?" she stuttered, on the razor's edge of release, but desperate to please them.

Iszak chuckled, brushing his lips over her bare shoulder.

Lukas released her nipple. "By the Winds, you are perfect." Lukas gazed down into her eyes. "Please, *please* come on my hand, baby." As if to urge her on, he hooked his fingertips inside her and rubbed the pad of his thumb along the engorged flesh of her clit.

She tilted her head back in ecstasy as that fresh jolt of pleasure pushed her beyond the edge of control. As she cried out, someone's mouth closed over hers, a tongue delved between her lips, and a harsh groan soaked up her cry. Her body tightened between them as they carried her into Nirvana with their expert touch. It was as though they were all flying, but the pair of them were the wings that held her aloft. They were unrelenting, their fingers still fucking into her, urging her on and on. Belah's orgasm continued to flood through her, the power it carried sinking into them with each spasm of her core around their thrusting fingers.

Finally, they slowed and pulled away. Belah sagged, ready to sink bonelessly into the soft fur of the rug, but surprised to find she was held in place by her bindings. She blinked hazily at Lukas, who sat back on his heels for a second, staring at her in wonder. The hand that he'd used to fuck her rested limp and palm-out on his thigh, still glowing a faint blue from the power that had surged through him and glistening with her juices. His eyes glowed too, but it only took a second before he came to his senses.

He narrowed his gaze and clenched his jaw with grim determination. While she watched, he carefully pulled off his t-shirt, then unfastened his jeans with his dry hand and pulled his thick erection out. Still kneeling in front of her, he wrapped the hand still wet with her juices around his shaft and stroked, coating his entire length in her essence.

Lukas's aura was a bright cloud around him, swollen and crackling from his arousal and so powerful her skin tingled from his proximity. Behind her, she heard another zipper drop and Iszak's energy grew to match his brother's.

With astonishment, she realized they were both bringing themselves off with no intention of touching her and channeling their Nirvana into her.

"What are you doing … Lukas, don't do this. Please touch me."

Lukas only let out a soft groan and set his lips tighter while he stroked faster.

"Iszak?" She craned her neck over her shoulder. It was just enough to see him out of the corner of her eye. He stood and moved around to face her with his hand stroking his own cock. She strained at her bindings, knowing she couldn't easily break free, but sure that if she did, it would be a gross betrayal of their trust. She just wanted to understand—to know if *they* understood what they were doing to her by withholding their orgasms this way.

"Baby, you want to know what's going through our minds, you go right ahead and look." Iszak tapped a finger to his forehead. "It'll save us all a lot of trouble. Our lives are open to you now. Trust me, this hurts us as much as it hurts you, and we want you to feel all of it."

Desperate for some kind of clarity, she closed her eyes and gave her power free rein. As Iszak said, their minds were both wide open to her and all their anger, grief, and sadness on full display. Just as clear was the bright, undeniable presence of their love for her, their true mate. The dark need for retribution had driven them for decades, and they couldn't easily let it go.

They still needed badly to get some kind of closure. Both men knew exactly what they were doing, and despite the pleasure they inflicted on themselves, it tortured them to know they were hurting her by doing it.

Sweet Mother, they don't want to do this, but know it's the only way past their hatred of what they've known of me their whole lives.

Belah didn't object again. She closed her eyes and swallowed her own pain, ignoring the tears that heated her eyelids and spilled over, as hot and salty as the splashes of semen that hit her lips moments later.

With the last vestiges of their auras depleted down to a soft glow, a chasm opened in her soul. Their power had been meant for her, their pleasure a product of the strong need to make love to her. Her soul had instinctively made a space for it, and their acts of denial had left that space an empty, aching void.

There was no denying that she deserved it. They hadn't deserved their own loss, and it still haunted them. Images of a bloody, reddish-gold feather repeated through their minds, alongside even stronger anger directed at a person who wasn't her. Her tears stopped flowing at the recognition of that face, and the face of their lost sister juxtaposed with it.

Confused, she opened her eyes to see Lukas squatting naked in front of her, holding up his wadded t-shirt as he began to gently wipe his and Iszak's spend off her skin.

"But I already told you about Evie, didn't I? That was why I came here …"

Lukas froze and frowned. "What about Evie? I told you the other night she was dead, and you didn't say a fucking thing about her then."

Belah shook her head, trying to remember what had happened in the moments after Lukas and Iszak had returned home—what had she told them before the liquor took its toll and she lost consciousness?

The actual words she'd spoken came back to her and she closed her eyes in shame. "Sweet Mother, I'm so selfish. I wanted to get the darkness out of me so badly, I didn't think …"

"What, Belah?" Iszak snapped. The ropes above her head jerked hard and she found herself yanked backward. Iszak's large hand clutched her chin from behind and pulled her head back so she was looking up into his enraged gaze. "What the fuck didn't you tell us about our sister?"

Belah's throat was constricted from his grip and a fresh stream of tears fell from the corners of her eyes. His hand at her throat reminded her too much of Nikhil, and part of her responded in a way that shamed her. Iszak immediately released her, his own shame at reacting that way dampening his anger.

"I wanted to tell you that she's *alive*. I only realized it tonight, when I saw Ozzie playing with you and put it all together. I've seen Marcus. His mind was filled with thoughts of her—of Evie—worry for her welfare."

Lukas turned and raked his hands through his hair, cursing and pacing away.

"Marcus. The fucking bastard betrayed our sister. The next time I see him, he's going to fucking wish he'd died."

Iszak came back around to face her, his arms crossed over his chest. "How do you know this? Where is she now?"

"We haven't found her yet, but trust me when I tell you that every Shadow at my disposal—even my own brother, Ked—is out trying to find her now." Even the ones who had previously been tasked with *only* searching for her lost children were now hunting for the North sister's Ultiori prison. But she had no intention mentioning the quest she'd had to put on hold to the two men. She didn't want their pity.

"I don't understand," Lukas said. "We were told she was dead, and there's no way that news could've been a lie. Our own *grandmother* was sure of it …"

Iszak's eyes narrowed and he turned to his brother. "Nanyo's the one who gave us the news, brother. Don't you think she'd have the power to convince us of the truth?"

"But we could have *found* her. Evie's been a fucking prisoner of those bastards, forced to do Boreas-knows-what for fifty fucking years!"

"Lukas," Belah said gently. "You would have gotten your-selves killed trying to reach her then. You aren't a match for Nikhil and his Elites. Trust that your grandmother steered you away for the right reasons."

"And what fucking reason is the *right* reason to leave our own sister in the clutches of those blood-thirsty monsters?"

Belah let out a soft sigh, debating whether to come entirely clean with them. Of course, they would know if she withheld any piece of the truth, anyway.

"Because she is my brother's to find. She is his fated mate. He learned her true identity tonight after hearing your music. I sang her song to him and he knew … that is *her* song, isn't it?" She took a breath and softly sang the words to them both.

Both men visibly relaxed, and the darkness coloring their auras lightened. The song helped the knowledge sink in, and

Belah sensed hope building within them both. Hope, and the tiniest spark of joy hesitantly rising out of the ashes of their grief.

Lukas was first to move, coming back to her and beginning to tug at the bindings to no avail. "Fuck, we need to get you out of these. Iszak! You're the knot master. Do I need to get a fucking knife?"

Belah and Iszak regarded each other silently, no words necessary for them both to understand the other. A slow smile spread across Iszak's face before Belah dipped her head once to acknowledge what passed between them in that moment.

"We're not untying her, Lukas. At least, not yet. She may be forgiven, but she still has a whole lot of secrets to spill for us."

CHAPTER TWENTY-ONE

ukas appeared naked in front of her and cupped her face.

"This is what you want?" he asked. "Should I get my candles?"

"It is," Belah said. "And you can do whatever you want, as long as I'm bound."

"We'll be gentle," Lukas said. He leaned in, and Belah gladly opened up for his kiss.

"Don't lie to her, brother," Iszak said. "It'll be as rough as we need it to be, but I have a feeling that's what you'd rather have, isn't it, Belah? You're going to feel so much pleasure it'll blow your mind, but we're going to get one thing straight first. You're going to submit to us the way your kind does to you. By 'you,' I mean the Dragon Council. I've met a few dragons who broke your laws, so I've heard stories. If you want to tell me I'm wrong, please feel free to explain, but at the very least, tell me you understand."

Belah balked, then was rudely reminded of her bindings when a knot dug in hard between her shoulder blades. Behind her, Lukas's warmth came close and she felt him kneel between her legs. His warm cock brushed against her ass as his lips went to her ears.

"Do you submit?"

"To submit in the manner you ask would be no punishment," Belah said. "Because it would mean being allowed to neither give, nor receive pleasure from anyone besides those I submit to, for as long as they choose to dominate me."

She gazed up at Iszak, her eyelids fluttering when Lukas's hands slid around her waist and up to cup her breasts and tease her nipples. "That sounds perfect. So, do you submit?"

Before her, Iszak moved closer, the delicious aroma of his arousal mere inches from her lips. He reached down and cupped her cheek, stroking his thumb across her lower lip.

"Promise you submit to me and Lukas, and only to us."

"I submit to only you, Iszak North and Lukas North, as my true and fated mates. I will take pleasure in no other partner without your leave until Fate decrees my days on this earth are done."

Iszak let out a groan of pleasure that spilled into his gaze. "Fuck, your voice is beautiful when you say all the right words. Shame you won't be using that mouth to speak for a good long while. Open up, baby."

His thumb slipped beyond her lip and pressed against the top of her lower teeth, but Belah was ready. When he moved his hand away, she darted her tongue out and captured that sparkling droplet from the tip of his cock before it could fall onto the carpet beneath her.

Lukas's arm tightened around her shoulders, holding her steady and guiding her just close enough to tease her tongue around Iszak's tip. With his free hand, Lukas brushed her hair away from her shoulder and twisted it up tight around his palm, holding firmly as she wrapped her lips around Iszak's cock and slid her mouth down his thick length.

"That's my girl," Lukas murmured. "Let him have a good dose of that tongue."

Lukas's hand remained tangled in her hair, and he guided her movements while Iszak thrust his hips forward, his own hands light on the back of her neck and at her cheek.

When she uncoiled her tongue and wrapped it entirely around Iszak's cock, he jerked and let out a rough, incoherent sound. His fingers dug hard into the back of her neck, and his other hand trembled at the side of her face.

"Fucking hell, that's good. Jesus."

Belah tilted her head just enough to see up his torso while her tongue swirled and flicked along his entire length, working to pull the power from him that had built to a nearly blinding brightness ever since she'd said, "I submit."

His eyes blazed with the need for release, and Belah could sense him at the knife's edge, but he gritted his teeth and restrained himself, just as her pets used to do when she was a pharaoh. He'd left her aching and empty for his Nirvana, and now he was building up as much of that potent energy as he could before giving it to her.

Lukas still held her from behind, his own hips rocking against her hard enough that the entire length of his cock was pressed along the crease of her ass, working deeper with every second and rubbing against slick, sensitive flesh.

They were both on the verge of Nirvana, their auras so swollen with the power she could taste it. And she needed it. Sweet Mother, she needed them both to give her that energy, or she thought the void of need inside her would swallow her whole.

Lukas released his hold just enough for her to lean forward, and when she did, his cock slipped until his tip was solidly between the parted lips of her hungry pussy.

"No moving," he said gruffly, his chest against her back while he slid into her. "I want to feel you come around my cock while you swallow what Iszak gives you."

Lukas released her hair and his hand slid between her thighs while he began fucking her slow and deep. His fingers found her clit just as the head of his cock pressed into the core of her pleasure, sending ecstasy climbing through her body.

Iszak's gaze was hot with lust, his cock throbbing as she took him fully into her mouth over and over, savoring the smooth stroke of him against her tongue.

"You're hungry for my power, aren't you? Suck me, baby. That's right." His rough voice vibrated through her and she increased her tempo, sucking harder, aching for another taste of his sweet essence, and even more for the energy of his orgasm to fill her.

Lukas's fingers strummed her clit like a master, the rapture of his cock fucking into her making it hard for her to care about the chasm that lay open inside her.

Iszak clutched the back of her neck, fucking her mouth with abandon. His cock pulsed and he let out a low growl as jets of hot semen landed on her tongue. The salty tang of him slid down her throat, and even sweeter was the flood of power that finally eased the ache of deprivation from before.

Lukas pushed her farther forward, his free hand holding the ropes that criss-crossed in the center of her back. She was grateful for her tethers to the rafters above, otherwise she'd have fallen on her face. But Iszak was there, too, kneeling in front of her and holding her shoulders while he bent to tease her nipples with his tongue.

She breathed in his musky scent, the blend of his aroma with Lukas's and the scent of sex driving her ever closer to her own Nirvana. Lukas's cock drove deep, over and over, each stroke sending fresh spikes of pleasure into her.

With his mouth at her breasts, Iszak shifted his hand between Belah's thighs, picking up the strumming attention on her clit where Lukas had left off.

"Come for me, Belah," Lukas said. "I need to feel you come around my cock."

At his words, she was flying, her head tilted back and a resonant cry escaping her throat. Lukas let out a soft curse behind her and jerked her hips back against him. He buried himself deep and held tight as his cock pulsed in her tight channel, her sensitized flesh alive with the feel of his power surging into her.

Still dizzy from her orgasm, she relished the deep kisses they each gave her. Both men's auras shimmered with satisfaction, their tender touches filled with love and gratitude for her very existence.

But before she had a chance to reclaim her wits, she felt the pull of the ropes and her view shifted as she was raised into the air. A moment later she was positioned as though seated in a swing made of a giant spider's web. Her legs were still splayed wide and the ropes that bound them were damp from her juices where they crossed her inner thighs.

Iszak finished securing her tethers to a cleat attached to a nearby wooden post, then moved to stand in front of her, luminous from the dose of her Nirvana he'd just received. "You didn't think we'd be done with you that easily, did you?" he asked with a pleased smile.

Belah gave him a slow shake of her head and sighed, elated at how determined these two men were to please her to exhaustion. "Whatever you wish of me is yours for the taking," she said.

"Tonight isn't over until we're fully mated. Your submission was only the prelude. By the end of the night, you're going to be so full of both our power and our seed, there's no way you won't also be carrying a child by one of us."

Belah's heart leapt. The possibility of another child had been so far from her mind since she'd arrived, she'd barely considered it.

"You would want that?" she asked. "You have to know I've given birth to several children in my lifetime." Two of whom still lived, in the clutches of her old lover and mortal enemy.

"Belah," Lukas said, tut-tutting beside her. His hand reached around her waist and swung her so she spun to face him. "You're holding back. Tell us the truth about what you really want."

She clenched her eyes shut, cursing herself for the slip of hidden truth. But children were a sore subject, so there was no way to avoid it, if that was what they wanted—and their ability to easily read a lie, or even the smallest omission of the truth, was beyond infuriating. She sighed and managed a shrug against her bindings.

"The truth is that I want to carry your baby more than you could believe, but there's something else I want just as much."

Lukas frowned, and Iszak moved around to face her next to his brother. He brushed an errant strand of hair off her forehead and tucked it behind her ear.

"What is it? You know we will give you anything within our power to give, Belah."

Shaking her head, she said, "This is beyond even two Princes of the North Wind, I'm afraid. Two of my beloved babies were taken from me, ages ago. They were locked into hibernation in a secret place by my Mother and Fate. Their origins … well, their origins are the reason they were taken from me. I've broken our own laws more than a dragon of my stature ever should."

Iszak frowned. "Please tell us that mating me and Lukas and having our child isn't breaking any laws …"

"No! My siblings and I are all in agreement on this. We're all seeking mates among the higher races now. It's a matter of survival for us all. Something grave is on the horizon—we don't know its nature. We think it's something the Ultiori have planned, but there's no way to tell."

That was at least the truth. There was also no way to know whether killing Nikhil would end it. She hoped it would, or that she would at least be able to glean some bit of intelligence from him when she gave him a week with her body, but if Fate wished her and her siblings to conceive hybrid offspring with the other higher races, that either meant she would fail her mission to kill Nikhil so soon, or that he wasn't the true threat.

"Belah …" Iszak said, admonishing her introspection.

"One of the children—my son—was conceived with my brother, Ked." She inhaled a deep, shaky breath, waiting for the horror to fill their eyes, but their frowns only deepened and they shared a quick glance before Iszak nodded for her to go on.

"We were young dragons, barely a century old. Mother had insisted that we choose humans—and only humans—to mate and breed with. But the humans at the time were primitive, their minds weak. They broke so easily, it seemed barbaric to continue mating with them when we had each other. We didn't know what the child would be. Zorion—our son—was too powerful to come of age when our race was so young—when the human race was so fragile and the magic in the world so new. So Mother took him away as a babe and promised he'd be kept safe. I only held him in my arms for a few days before I had to let him go. My baby boy." Tears pricked at her eyes, making their faces blur.

"And the other child?" Lukas asked gently.

Belah expelled a long breath in an attempt to clear her head. She dreaded their reactions to the confession to come.

"The other child taken from me is Nikhil's daughter, conceived out of love the night we wed—the night he lost me and became what he is today. He hasn't always been a monster, but he needs to be dealt with, and soon. Before he learns what she is to him."

Both men let out harsh curses and Belah braced herself for some kind of tirade—for them to cut her down and send her away—but nothing of the sort happened.

Iszak pressed a gentle kiss to her brow and Lukas cupped the side of her face, brushing away the tears that were spilling down her cheeks.

"They're your children. We may not have the power to help you find them at this moment, but once we're mated, we'll help however we can. In the meantime, what we *can* do is make love to you so hard we fill you with another, one that will never be taken from you. More than one, if you want."

In front of her, Lukas's cock twitched again and she raised her eyebrows at him, laughing through her tears.

Lukas grinned and cupped himself. "What can I say? The idea of filling you with babies is such a fucking turn-on."

"Then let me mark you now. The seed you put in me already isn't doing me any good without a mark."

"Should we untie you?" Iszak asked.

"Only if you're finished with me. I can mark you both easily if you come close enough."

"Sweetness, we'll be so close you'll forget your name," Iszak growled.

The brothers flanked her, navigating the tethers that supported her suspended form. Though the ropes dug in to the underside of her thighs and ass, she loved how weightless it made her feel to be bound this way, particularly when their arms went around her on either side, and their renewed caresses brought a fresh sigh of pleasure to her lips.

Lukas bent his head to her breast and she gazed down at the side of his arched neck—the perfect place for a mark. He lifted his head to face her again, and she enjoyed how wild his gaze was, as well as how hard his cock had become as it brushed against the outside of her thigh. She leaned forward and brushed her lips over his stubbled cheek, her core heating in response to the velvet stroking of his cock against her skin.

She lowered her head, pressing her lips to the side of his neck, flicking out her tongue to taste the salt of dried sweat and musk, and to trace a precursor to the true mark with her tongue. Lukas stiffened when her tongue lashed at his skin a second time, swiftly branding her magic into him. Dragon marks were never a painless affair, but the pain would dissipate quickly once her magic took full effect. When it was done, she pulled back and watched as the circular pattern healed, leaving behind a shimmering blue shape that pulsed brightly.

"You *are* ready to breed me, aren't you, Lukas?" she whispered, her heart pounding over the significance of the moment.

"I've been ready most of my life, baby," he said, rubbing his hand lightly over the side of his neck.

She turned to Iszak, tilting her head to gaze up into his stormy eyes. He cupped her face in both hands and kissed her slowly.

"I'm ready, too," he said against her mouth. "And it's about damn time." He turned his head, presenting his neck to her so she could mark him on the opposite side from where she'd marked Lukas. Belah kissed the tawny, corded muscles of his throat.

"I think this side suits you best," she said, remembering how the pair of them stood on stage, back-to-back, and played for her. The next time they played together like that, their marks would be seen by all.

While her mouth was pressed to Iszak's neck, Lukas dipped down beneath her suspended body. A moment later, the warmth of Lukas's lips brushed along her inner thigh, moving higher. She moaned softly against Iszak's neck when his brother's hot tongue found her core and began slowly lapping at her sensitive folds. He teased at every crease and swirled his tongue around her clit until she was quivering with fresh need.

When Iszak's mark glowed bright, pale blue, he sank to his knees beside his brother and added his tongue to the sweet torture Lukas had begun. They parted her wide, taking turns sucking and licking, but never quite pushing her over the edge. Men after her own heart, they seemed to love keeping her on the precipice, as though they knew just as well as she did how the power built up inside when release was kept at bay.

Belah was nearly bursting with it when the brothers rose again, their chins glistening with her essence and their fresh dragon marks glowing with their desire to breed with her.

She didn't need to speak for them to grasp her desperation to have them inside her. Lukas was the first to come to her, embracing her swinging body and devouring her mouth with a ravenous kiss. His cock pressed against her belly but he didn't immediately seek to penetrate her.

Another pair of arms wrapped around her from behind and Iszak's muscular chest pressed against her back, sandwiching her still-bound arms between them. He trailed more kisses from her neck down to her shoulders, biting gently at first, then more urgently as his hard cock rubbed against her backside.

When Lukas pulled back from the kiss, she felt an urgent grip on her neck and turned just enough in Iszak's arms to meet his gaze behind her. Her mouth was immediately overtaken by his lips and tongue, and he kissed her as though he were starved for some sustenance only she could provide.

She switched between them, kissing one, then the other, while their hands roamed her body. With her mouth tangled with one of theirs, the other man's mouth teased her nipples, and both pairs of their hands touched and caressed all over.

"Jesus, Belah, I need to be inside you. Can't stand it anymore."

"Yes," she answered, though she wasn't sure which man had spoken she was so dizzy from desire. "I want you both—together—a duet, yes? Please…" She trailed off with a desperate sound that turned into a low moan of appreciation when one cock pierced her core to the hilt before pulling out again, then another cock went in hard.

Two separate arms held her torso while their other hands held her thighs wide. One pair of hips filled the space between her legs and the other pressed against her backside, both cocks sliding against her slick, sensitive core.

Their gazes were fixed between her thighs, mouths slightly open and panting harsh breaths as they found synchronicity and plunged into her together. Both hot, hard cocks filled her tight channel as one, and Belah threw her head back and sang out in ecstasy.

They penetrated her together and thrust deep. The sensation sent Belah into a kind of oblivion, a surrender to love and pleasure, but it was like no other oblivion she'd consigned herself to before. The blazing light of their marks reminded her that they were hers, body and soul, but they were their own men, too. No other mate had ever left her bed sane, least of all the one man she'd deliberately avoided marking for the purpose of preserving his mind.

These two men were fully present, aware, and completely intent on mating with her.

They quickly found a constant, punishing rhythm with their cocks driving deep in tandem. They filled her like she'd never been filled before, their auras swelling and encompassing her in the power of the Wind. She surrendered completely to them both, letting their power carry her to her peak—the highest she had ever reached in her long life. Lukas and Iszak were both right there with her at the pinnacle of pleasure, their essences spilling deep inside her as they climaxed.

The magic filled her yet again, and in the hazy aftermath, she wished with her entire being that they would give her another child, because she didn't know if she could endure leaving them long enough to give Nikhil what he wanted.

CHAPTER TWENTY-TWO

Marcus cursed Nikhil for the millionth time, sure his brutal master must have known how this particular assignment would torture him. But there was no way his *Sayid* could have predicted the identities of the pair of men Belah would find. No way he could know that the fate of the woman Marcus loved now hung in the balance as surely as Belah hung suspended from the ropes in the center of Iszak and Lukas's living room.

The sight should have been lewd and filthy—perhaps might have been to any outside observer—but thanks to the powers Marcus had been imbued with, he could read each bright emotion that wrapped itself around the trio. And as much as he rejoiced on behalf of his old friends finding the love of their life, he ached to have the freedom to experience what they felt in that moment. He ached to hold Evie in his arms like that just one more time.

If he did well tonight, perhaps he'd be given that chance, though the thought of destroying the beauty of the love that bloomed before him left a bitter taste in his mouth.

He had obeyed Nikhil's command to follow Belah after their meeting in the park, in the very spot where Marcus had first set eyes on Evie North. He'd found Belah later that same night in a jazz club, but the second he'd stepped into the place, he'd been bombarded by memories.

Evie's brother, Lukas, sat on stage, and the old shame Marcus had learned to live with for the last five decades came flooding back as though it were only yesterday. It was bad enough that he'd dodged the draft and fled to Canada, but to drag her with him, and into the clutches of a man who was the mortal enemy to her kind? He would never forgive himself for that.

He had to ignore the urge to reveal himself to the brothers— tell them the truth. That their sister lived. He couldn't risk Nikhil finding out, and the man surely would if Marcus went that far. He refused to risk Evie's life so recklessly. He had to hope that the Hail Mary of a chance he'd taken two years earlier would come to fruition—that somehow the Dragon Council had received the secret message he'd sent and would come to his aid.

Now that he knew they had—that the Void himself was looking for Evie at this very moment—it was all Marcus could do just to stay put, to continue carrying out Nikhil's commands when all he wanted to do was go to her. Bust down the door to the cell that held his lover and be with her just once more before her true mate came and carried her away.

For the past few hours, he'd been at war with himself. He was on the verge of losing Evie, yet in the best way possible. She would be rescued, and he would be left behind to carry out his master's wishes. Why should he do anything else? He'd have nothing without Evie—no reason to live, but no way to die, not unless Nikhil took mercy on him and put him out of his misery. He'd had enough close calls with dragons over the years to understand how indestructible he and his fellow Ultiori Elites were.

He longed to be with her now, yet had to see this assignment through and just hope he would have one more chance to see her before she was safe in the arms of the dragon who claimed she belonged to him.

Focusing again on the North brothers and the female between them, he simply watched. When they first began binding her, he'd been alarmed and considered betraying his presence to rescue her. His master wouldn't want her to come to him damaged, after all. But his only frame of reference for a bound female was from the day he'd learned how grave a mistake he'd made, trusting Evie's life to the Alexandria Institute. They'd both been bound and drugged, then separated. When Marcus had awakened, he'd been forever altered, and effectively a slave to his captor. He possessed power he'd never dreamed of, but was tethered to a man he hated, a man who held Evie's welfare over his head like a sword of Damocles.

But Belah had encouraged the binding and clearly enjoyed it now, and Marcus finally understood why his master craved this woman so much. Nikhil's particular preferences were no secret to his followers, least of all his Elites. Marcus, Naaz, and Sterlyn often had the unpleasant privilege of bearing witness to their master's predilections. His gut churned at the unsavory memories he had of what all Nikhil's female victims endured.

This Blue dragon had been the beginning. The first woman to encourage such things in the man. And yet the scene that unfolded before him didn't reflect the horrors he had forced himself to become numb to.

Lukas and Iszak were tender lovers, despite Belah's bound state. After what Marcus agreed was a very necessary round of atonement that Belah endured like a trooper, their behavior shifted drastically.

Especially after she revealed the truth of their sister's life and her brother's search.

They wanted nothing but to please her, and despite Marcus's belief that this woman had somehow been behind the corruption of his master, his powers let him see her through the eyes of his old friends.

After first meeting Evie, Iszak and Lukas had become like brothers to Marcus. Having no family of his own anymore, they were all he had.

Their love for Belah shone so bright, Marcus grew increasingly conflicted over what he knew his master had planned. And yet he was helpless to do anything but obey.

The sharp tug on his consciousness constricted like a collar bound too tight, a reminder of his utter lack of freedom. He closed his eyes, abruptly slamming shut the door to his secret thoughts. The brief suspicion Nikhil displayed at least confirmed that Marcus still had something all his own.

"Sayid, I am here," he sent immediately, having learned long ago to mentally stand at attention when even the barest hint of Nikhil's presence marched into his mind.

"Report."

"She is with a pair of lovers now, replenishing her energy." He carefully omitted from his thoughts the truth of what he observed,

choosing instead to imply that she was merely behaving as any hungry dragon might.

"Show me," Nikhil demanded. Before Marcus could respond, his consciousness took a back seat while the other man's eyes took over, unceremoniously shoving Marcus aside. Marcus was scarcely able to clear his mind of the many impressions he'd had of the scene before him, just barely managing complete neutrality before Nikhil commandeered his sight.

Extreme displeasure twisted Marcus's gut—a reflection of what his master experienced at the sight of his long-lost lover in the arms of two other men.

Just as abruptly, Nikhil was gone, leaving Marcus dizzy and stumbling. Losing his balance, he fell backward into a tall bookshelf, making it rock precariously. He watched in horror as a piece of pottery wobbled on one of the high shelves and began to teeter over the edge, just out of reach.

He lunged for the object, caught it, and sagged in relief, but it was short-lived. A deafening crash came from farther away and he jerked around to see a pair of naked bodies fly through the air in opposite directions.

His master had arrived, and he wasn't happy.

Marcus groaned inwardly and shed the magic that had kept him hidden from sight and awareness. As he approached the unconscious body of Iszak North, Sterlyn looked up from where he was busy binding Lukas to one of the sturdy, steel support posts nearby.

They shared a grim look before Marcus followed suit, grabbing a few of the many spare ropes Iszak had left strewn around the room and began tying the unconscious, naked man to another post.

Nikhil stood in front of Belah, staring down at her bound, naked flesh. Waves of lust flowed from him, enhanced by his rage. The combination was a potent mix, infecting Marcus until he realized Iszak's wrists were bleeding from the force of the ropes cutting into his skin.

He cursed and loosened the bindings, retying them more carefully and silently asking Iszak to forgive him.

CHAPTER TWENTY-THREE

Belah stared up into Nikhil's face, defiant. She didn't dare divert her gaze toward her unconscious lovers and betray that fresh weakness to this man. The scent of blood reached her from across the room, and it was all she could do not to tear free from her bonds and go to whichever brother had been wounded in the tumult of Nikhil's arrival. All she knew was that they lived, their fresh marks and her bond to them enough to calm her fears. She preferred they remain unconscious for the conversation she was about to have, anyway.

"I won't go with you, Nikhil. Plans have changed."

"I beg to differ, little beast. Finding you like this makes it even clearer how ready you are for me. Those two fools have primed you well—even better than your former pets once did. Remind me to thank them afterward for wrapping you up for me."

He reached out a large, tanned hand and traced the edge of the ropes that criss-crossed beneath her collarbone.

Belah suppressed a flinch from his touch. She twisted her bound wrists behind her, intending to rip free of the ropes, but remembered Iszak had bound her with enchanted ropes she couldn't break. She found she lacked the strength, or even the will to escape that dark gaze and the power Nikhil exuded.

His fingertips brushed upward along the side of her neck until he settled his palm at the front of her throat. Belah could only stare up at him, eyes wide as she swallowed, anticipating an action she had once begged for.

Nikhil only caressed her, stroking with thumb and fingers on either side of her throat while his other hand tested the ropes that still tethered her to the beams above.

As much as Belah had loved the way the ropes made her feel like Iszak and Lukas's personal toy, now it felt like little more than a trap she'd been caught in, that the true predator had found her and was intent on playing with her before he devoured her whole.

Never moving his hand from her neck, Nikhil studied her bindings with open curiosity and even a measure of respect. He stood in place and slowly rotated her swinging body, one set of fingers following the lines of the ropes as though tracing the solution to a maze, while the other hand brushed warmly at her throat.

Once her back was to him, he made a low hum of appreciation, his fingers bumping down the ridged layer of ropes that coiled around her forearms, holding them against her lower back. His other hand slid back around to the front of her throat, strong fingers inching up to cup her jaw, fingertips digging into her cheeks as he forced her head back.

"I could take you now, little beast. Fuck you slowly until you reached that crest, then take you to your favorite place." His words rumbled hotly in her ear, sending spasms through her body that had once been arousing, but now only left her numb.

Belah strained harder at the ropes, but was still unable to shed them. The fury drained from her, leaving behind a sick, quaking panic. She twisted frantically, but Nikhil only tightened his grip on her neck and hooked his fingers into the swath of silken cords that crossed her belly.

"No…" she croaked when the generous bulge of his cock dug into her backside.

"No? But you agreed to a week. Seven days, my *Tilahatan*. Seven days for me to bind you to that altar I prepared and worship you. To show you that I never forgot what it means to kneel before a goddess like you, to offer up the blood and pain and darkness you crave. You still want that, yes? And when I'm done, I will take you to your son."

My son. Belah closed her eyes against the tears. Only seven days—she had endured an eternity without the contact of a true lover, and had found an abundance of love in just the last few hours. Could she endure seven days of Nikhil's punishment for the sake of her lost children? His very touch now made her wish she could close her spread thighs to counteract the feeling of vulnerability, but Iszak had bound her too well. Belah reminded herself that she had once loved what Nikhil had offered—his brutal strength and desire to inflict pain—the understanding that what she needed was an oblivion no other lover could offer—and the unquestioning willingness to fulfill every last dark craving she had.

It had been ages since she'd experienced the cravings she'd once had when she first took him as her lover—when she'd agreed to marry him. Yet she would endure anything if it meant being reunited with her babies.

Zorion and Asha were out there somewhere—lost to her and in the clutches of this madman. If all it took were seven days of being inflicted with his darkness, she would endure. She just hoped her mates would still want her when Nikhil was done with her.

"Yes," she whispered. Her tears flowed freely and the skin beneath his fingers was slick with them when he tightened his grip around her throat. She was grateful for the darkness that closed in around her as her consciousness faded. She could not bear being taken by him otherwise.

CHAPTER TWENTY-FOUR

arcus and Sterlyn shared a grim look when the female lost consciousness in their master's grip. Hatred gnawed at Marcus's gut—for himself and his weakness, as much as for the man who'd kept him on his knees for the last fifty years. He hated that he didn't dare intervene on behalf of the female dragon—Lukas and Iszak's mate. But to do so would condemn their sister, and he would die before letting anything worse happen to Evie. Belah had survived this man once—she would survive him again.

Without a word, Nikhil reached out a freshly bloodied palm to Sterlyn and the other Elite went to him, obedient as always. Sterlyn's own lover was locked up in a cell as well. Neither Marcus nor his brother Elites had a choice but to do Nikhil's bidding, or else risk their loved ones coming to grave harm. Their *Sayid* made sure they knew it well.

Within a split second of Sterlyn grasping his master's hand and their fresh blood mingling, they were gone—fading into the *drift*—and the naked, unconscious woman along with them, ropes and all.

Marcus stared at the empty space for a long time, grinding his teeth and seething. Soon the utter silence shocked him out of his mood.

It wasn't just the room that was silent. His mind was, too. He blinked at his reflection in the windows, afraid to test the foreign feeling of having his mind completely to himself again for the first time in ages. And yet it was. The itch of having a second consciousness creeping around inside his brain had disappeared, along with his master.

There was one way he could test it—one way he could be sure Nikhil was no longer lurking. Marcus risked closing his eyes and drawing forth the image of Evie. Her beauty filled his mind—her creamy skin and beautiful voice. Dark eyes, framed by even darker lashes, peered up at him full of love. Her slight, delicate body was soft in his arms, her skin burned several degrees warmer than his—she had always felt feverish. And before his eyes her glorious wings spread, soft feathers shimmering, silver, gold, and copper in the sunlight. It was a manufactured image—part memory of their first meeting, and part memory of their last time together when she'd unfurled her wings while they made love.

Marcus held his breath, waiting with dread for his favorite image of Evie to corrupt. For her beautiful feathers to be coated in her own blood. He'd had one night with her in fifty years. He thought they'd gotten away with it, but Nikhil had found out afterward, tortured Evie, and threatened Marcus with her death if he ever dared go near her again without Nikhil's permission.

Ever since that night, even bringing to mind his most treasured memories of her would devolve into images of her torture—visions he'd never actually seen with his own eyes, but that he knew were true. Every time he pictured that night, he'd hear Nikhil's voice and the things he'd said to Evie while he hurt her.

The bloody visions didn't come this time.

A rough groan from behind Marcus dampened his joy. He'd been ready to go to her right then—to take advantage of the unexpected freedom from his mental shackles and be with her once more. Instead, he turned and met the enraged looks of the two men who probably hated him the most in all the world, and who would likely hate him even more after what he had to tell them now.

Marcus gritted his teeth and faced Evie's brothers.

"Where the fuck did that bastard take her?!" Iszak snarled, straining at his bindings.

Lukas shook his head and spat blood onto the floor. "When I get out of here, I'm fucking destroying you, Marcus."

"I guess you really don't want to be untied, then, do you?" Marcus asked. "Because fuck if I'm going to let you out after a threat like that. Not that either of you could hurt me any more than you could hurt my master, if you found him. I did you guys a favor by tying you up. Interfere with his plans for your mate, and he'll kill you."

A chilly breeze blew past, cooling the sweat on his skin that had sprung up earlier when he'd first tied Iszak to the post. The window panes creaked from some storm battering at them outside. Behind him, one of them gave way, its latch springing free and the hinges squealing when it flew open with a crash that shattered the glass.

Cold, wet wind hit his back hard enough to plaster his shirt to his skin—hard enough to throw him off balance, if he were any other man. The furniture was pushed several inches across the floor from the force of the wind, but Marcus stayed put, staring down both North brothers in turn.

"Un-fucking-tie us if you don't want to be ripped apart by the wind, you fuck," Lukas said.

"I will, but not until you listen to me. Belah wasn't lying about Evie, and you know it. You know what else she wasn't lying about? How much I would give to make sure your sister's safely away from that bastard. I didn't become what I am willingly. He *made* me this, and I have to come to terms with that. But that doesn't mean she has to keep suffering. If you want your sister back, you have to promise me you'll come with me tonight to get her out. Say yes and I'll untie you both and take you to Evie now."

"But Belah," Iszak growled. "He has her."

Marcus shot the bound man a wan smile. "He does, doesn't he? And you haven't ever had the pleasure of witnessing what he does to every single female Blue dragon he captures."

"What do you mean?" Lukas asked.

"That's what she promised him when they met last week. She gives him her body, just like old times, and he returns her son to her. She'll spend her time with him just as trussed up as you guys had her, except it'll be a bit more bloody. Though I hear that's what she used to go for, back when the pair of them were hot and heavy. Maybe being immortal like she is made it harder for her to get off on vanilla sex—I have no idea."

"Fuck!" Lukas yelled, and Iszak let out an accompanying bellow of profanity that made Marcus's ears ring even more. More windows crashed open, more glass shattered.

"Tell us where they both are, you son of a bitch, and you'll be lucky if you survive us once we're free."

Marcus shook his head, knowing what an impossible choice he'd offered them.

"Knowing their locations isn't enough. Belah's somewhere in the city still. Not far from here, in fact. Evie's at the Alexandria Institute's Canadian headquarters, about two thousand miles away in the mountains along the border of British Columbia. She's safe enough where she is, as long as Nikhil's nowhere nearby. I can take you both to her in a second, if that's what you want."

"Let us the fuck out of these ropes and take us to them both."

"That's the thing, though—I can only take you to Evie now. I can't take you to Belah. Where he's got her, no one else can go—not until he's done with her. He has her inside a temporal bubble. Without knowing *when* they are, I can't get in. Sterlyn's the only one who knows. Trust me, I know exactly how fucked this situation is. I've spent the last fifty years wishing like hell I could get Evie out of there. Put yourselves in my shoes, guys. There's no way we can get to Belah right now, so you might as well come help me get Evie out. Help me save your sister. Please."

The brothers shared a long look, and the tempest in the room gradually calmed as the pair seemed to come to some silent agreement.

"Untie us, Marcus," Iszak said, his voice rough with emotion, but at least at a reasonable volume. "We'll figure this shit out somehow."

CHAPTER TWENTY-FIVE

The man Iszak had once loved and respected as much as a brother still existed somewhere behind those dark eyes. He wanted to keep hating Marcus for his part in their sister's disappearance—hell, he would have kept on, if he hadn't recognized in Marcus some of the same self-hatred he saw when he looked in the mirror every day.

Marcus's brows drew together. "You're not going to go after Evie, are you?"

"Fuck, man, I don't know. But I'm sure as shit not doing anything with my dick flapping in the breeze like this."

Marcus moved behind him, and a moment later, the ropes loosened. Iszak pulled free and went to throw on his jeans while Marcus untied Lukas. He turned just in time to see a now freed Lukas throw a swift punch that connected solidly with Marcus's chin. The russet-haired man's head flew back with a snap and he spun, stumbling into Iszak.

Iszak reached out and righted the other man before he lost balance. He held Marcus's elbow for a second longer, his other hand clenching into a fist.

"Go ahead. You're entitled," Marcus said, tilting his chin up as though inviting Iszak to give in to that urge.

Iszak let out a harsh snort and released Marcus. "Not in the mood. I'd rather save up for the real enemy, if it isn't you. You said you could take us where Evie is, right? Does that mean you can take us anywhere quick?"

"Anywhere I've been to once, yeah. But I told you, I can't take you to Belah. I can go *where* she is, just not *when*. She won't be there now."

"Show us," Lukas said.

"Wait," Iszak said, holding out a hand. "You promise Evie's not in danger right now? How is she?"

"She's about as good as someone who's been a prisoner for five decades can be. She's in no danger, though—not while Nikhil's distracted."

Iszak tilted his head, focusing on the nuances of the words as the air carried the sounds to his ears. No lies, but there were hidden truths, hidden fears that Marcus would rather not speak, and a definite essence of shame permeating every syllable. Marcus probably had no idea how lucky that one emotion made him.

"Is he distracted often?" Iszak asked.

"Not to this degree—not since I've known him."

Iszak had to restrain himself from asking more questions about what Belah really meant to the Ultiori leader. They'd once been lovers—had even conceived a child together, though Nikhil wasn't aware of the daughter's existence. So why had he persisted in chasing Belah for so long?

That didn't matter now. All that mattered was finding out how to get his and his brother's mate back.

"Take us where he's keeping her. We'll figure out the rest once we know the lay of the land."

Marcus nodded and grasped Iszak's hand, along with Lukas's.

"Brace yourselves," he said. "This is never a fun experience, even for me."

Darkness rushed in so fast, Iszak thought he'd have whiplash from the abrupt shift. He felt displaced, as though caught in a cyclone and spun in its vortex. He flailed with his free hand, and would have used both of them, if Marcus didn't have a grip so tight on his other one.

His world spun through a void, and he was reminded of the utter terror he'd felt the first time his plane had been shot down over in Vietnam. He'd been too cocky, too self-assured about his piloting abilities. He was born to fly, after all. But he wasn't born to be strapped into a giant pile of useless metal plummeting straight to the earth.

Iszak hit the ground with a bone-crunching thud. It took a moment for him to get his bearings. Marcus's vise-like grip on his hand released, and so did Iszak's control over his supper. He rolled to the side and heaved, his eyes watering.

"Fuck," he muttered, wiping his lips. He blinked and looked around.

"What is this place?" Lukas asked, standing shakily and angling away from his own puddle of sick.

Marcus seemed none the worse for wear, aside from looking a little green around the gills. "It's *Sayid's* penthouse—where he stays when he's in the city."

"Looks like a fucking mausoleum," Iszak said, moving from the soapstone foyer into the high-ceilinged room. The place looked like it belonged in some ancient temple in Egypt. Every surface seemed to be carved from giant slabs of pale, sand-colored stone. Massive columns topped by carved, golden palm leaves bordered the entire room, extending up two stories to an elaborately painted ceiling that belonged in another era. A huge, gilded throne with clawed feet sat at one end of the room opposite a huge door made of shining wood, into which was carved a series of robed figures with animal heads atop their shoulders.

Iszak followed his brother and Marcus through the door into a smaller room that was still massive in scale. A large bed rested on a dais against one wall with a wooden trunk at its foot, but the most prominent feature in the room was a masterfully carved St. Andrews cross with luxurious, blue silk padding attached to the surface. At each point in the large X-shaped contraption were sheepskin-padded shackles. Glancing down, Iszak saw beneath the cross was a channel cut deep into the polished marble of the floor that led to a shallow basin about two feet in diameter. Upon closer inspection, he discovered the basin was lined with a hammered silver bowl with handles attached to two sides, jutting up from the edge. A spout aligned with the channel in the floor to allow for pouring out of whatever liquid the basin was intended to collect.

"What the fuck?" Lukas said. "Did he build this for her?"

Iszak was too focused on the channel in the floor to answer his brother. His belly turned to ice at the thought of what the basin was meant to hold.

"Marcus, remember where our Nanyo lives?" Iszak asked, his voice sounding as though it were coming from somewhere outside his body. His ears buzzed with the barely contained rage at the man who had taken his mate.

Marcus's head snapped around so hard Iszak could swear he heard the man's neck crack.

"Yeah ... why?" Marcus asked cautiously.

"Because that's where you're taking us now."

CHAPTER TWENTY-SIX

The blackness was slow to recede from Belah's mind. She didn't remember it being so vast and empty before. She'd always relished the oblivion she reached in the darkness of her deep unconscious. Now she was only acutely aware of the stark absence of the pair of men she had just marked, whose marks had glowed so brightly their afterimages were still burned into her mind. But she'd made a promise, and the recipient of that promise had come to collect.

Warm arms and soft touches coaxed her out of the void. A deep, familiar voice was speaking gently, lovingly, but with words half-choked by emotion. As her senses returned, she became more aware of the scents and sensations surrounding her, and they took her back to a night more than three thousand years ago. The night she'd accepted Nikhil's proposal.

Belah forced herself to gather her thoughts before moving and betraying her consciousness to the man who held her. He had her cradled on his lap, the hot water of a bath lapping around her shoulders, her cheek resting against his chest. His touch was gentle, comforting, and she could almost pretend none of the last three millennia had happened. The way he was speaking to her now was so different, evoking memories—feelings—of another time and place. Another man, so different from the monster she knew now.

"You were mine that day. More than you had ever been. You gave me my life, Belah, and more—so much more. What you asked was the least I could give in return, even though I never understood why you would ask it. Did you know what it would do to you when I spilled your blood? That's the question I have asked myself all this time … whether you planned to leave me for him—for the father of the child you lost. Whether you somehow found me wanting at the end and wished to escape because I couldn't give you the child you longed for."

Belah clenched her eyes tighter to hold back the tears inspired by Nikhil's words. The arrogant brutality of the man she'd seen in the shadows the week before was entirely stripped away. When they'd been lovers, Nikhil had rarely let down his guard emotionally, but on the rare occasions he had, he'd been as raw and vulnerable as a child. That Nikhil was the one who held her now.

"I was so angry that you would leave me that way without telling me why. I would have been your mate, regardless of the damage it might have done to my will. The most I ever wished for was for us to share our love so we could have that child. A child of my blood and yours, bound together. I dreamed of how perfect such a child would be. But you took that away from me, and I could never forgive you for that. But now … by all the gods, Belah, I just want you, and to understand why you left."

Belah slowly lifted her hand and placed it on his chest. He stilled and looked down at her, dark eyes filled with emotion so deep she believed he'd held these feelings in check for as long as she had. How had he not looked at her this way when they met before? That night he'd been devoid of any feeling, his aura an opaque shell and nothing like the volatile shimmer of emotion that surrounded him now.

She was at least relieved that all he seemed to want was to talk, and after all this time, she couldn't deny him answers.

"I didn't leave you by choice, Nikhil, but the truth is that we should never have wed."

His arms tightened around her as he studied her face. His eyes were wide and brimming with all that unchecked emotion. He swallowed. "Then why *did* you leave? I have tortured and killed your kind for eternity to try to find answers when they wouldn't offer them willingly, but none were forthcoming. Your absence drove me mad. All that kept me even remotely sane were the small tastes of your blood I allowed myself when the pressure of loss became too great. I believed you were dead for years, until your brothers came to me and offered an exchange for your blood. I didn't want to give it up. In the end, I still kept some. But when I tried to see you, they said you wanted me dead and to stay away unless I was prepared to be burned alive."

"They weren't lying. I would have killed you then, but Ked convinced me to wait until we found where you were keeping Zorion. As for why I left … It was beyond my control. After the marriage ceremony, all we knew was that you would be given many powerful blessings from the other races. Blessings that were granted in the hope that we would be able to find a way for the immortals to finally mate with humans without destroying their minds. You were to be the test—it was the only reason I agreed to mark you."

"But you never did."

"That was my mistake, and I regret it to this day, but we cannot change the past. When you bled me, I had no idea you would do such a thorough job. We should have taken more precautions. When Ked sensed my life at the farthest edge it could reach, he believed the worst. He believed you had turned on me—that the blessings had corrupted you and you were after even greater power by taking my blood." It wasn't lost on Belah that her brother's reaction had only served to self-perpetuate his fears.

"*Tilahatan*, I would love you until the end of time. I would never turn on you. All the things I've done since losing you were ... necessary." He grimaced in distaste, which Belah found strangely out of character. The Nikhil she had known had always relished every second of battle and reveled in his pursuit of every conquest. He was so dedicated to his role as her general he'd been willing to die for her, and had never indicated he held one iota of remorse for the things he'd done.

"Then let me go, Nikhil. We should never have been together. You were *Blessed*. You were always meant to mate a dragon, but it should never have been me. My siblings and I were never meant to have humans for permanent mates. We understand now that none of the immortals were. Humans were only ... vessels or sources for seed to us. I was greedy and foolish when I found you. You gave me the kind of escape no other partner ever could. But that time is over. I have changed."

He lifted a hand from the bath and brushed it down the side of her cheek, his gaze tracing the wet trail his fingertips left behind. "No. I see in you the same woman who recognized the true benefits of the darkness in me, who cherished it and let me bring it out for your glory or your pleasure. You have not changed so much, have you? Not if the state I found you in tonight was any indication. You will have to try harder, little beast."

His voice grew deep and suggestive, his hand falling to her breast and his fingers pinching her nipple hard. Belah hissed and pushed away, darting to the other side of the tub and clutching at her breasts.

"Nikhil, no. I promised you seven days, and I will give them to you, but the only way I submit the way you wish is for you to make me a promise in return."

He let out a low growl and rose to his feet. His cock was still flaccid against his thigh, which in itself struck Belah as unusual. It used to be that any reaction she gave to the pain he inflicted on her would make him rock hard.

"I have already made you a promise to tell you where your son is. That is enough."

"That was enough for me to give you these few days. But if you want me to surrender my body to you, I want you to promise me you will respect my wishes. I really have changed, Nikhil. I don't crave the darkness the way I did with you. Forcing me to do anything will just result in me fighting back, and you know I have the power to hurt you."

She gritted her teeth, hoping he would accept her terms, and silently asking forgiveness from Iszak and Lukas for what she feared she may have to do. But the fear subsided as she became aware of the tenderness of the nipple Nikhil had pinched, and the distinct *lack* of reaction other parts of her body had to the assault.

When she'd met him the week before, she'd responded as if they'd been apart no more than a day. His voice had made her kneel and her core grow hot and needy. She'd been aroused only slightly by her date that night, but Ozzie's touch had been nothing compared to the roughness of Nikhil's hands on her body. Despite her disgust over what he had become, she had wanted him, and she'd hated herself for it. But now … she felt no tingle between her thighs, and her nipples were only erect from the cool air, not from arousal.

She glanced at his sleeping cock and then at his right nipple, which was distinctly reddened and irritated when it hadn't been a moment ago. Then it hit her—every time he inflicted pain, he felt it himself. He felt no pain inflicted on him directly. Could it be the same for pleasure? Could he feel no pleasure, unless he was giving it?

Nikhil was still a powerful man. The sheer magnitude of his might was reflected in the tautness of his muscles. He stood, glistening with bathwater trickling off the familiar curves and planes of him. Belah knew every inch of his body and remembered how to please him.

"I don't want you to fight, little beast. Do you remember how it used to be between us? You would kneel on my command.

Your body was mine to do with as I wished, and it pleased you to let me have my way with you. I never asked for more than you were capable of giving. I'm not sure if it was possible for me to ask for more—you gave me everything."

Belah slipped back through the water toward him. His gaze followed her warily until she stopped mere inches from contact and gazed up into his eyes. The same barely contained heat burned deep in those dark depths, but it wasn't reflected in his body or his aura.

She raised her hand and cupped his cheek, brushed her thumb over his lower lip, then raised up on her toes and kissed him. He responded with hands at her waist, pulling her against him and deepening the kiss with bruising power. Between them, she drifted her hand down his side and over his belly. She dipped lower and cupped his cock, squeezed gently, and wrapped her hand around his girth.

She barely managed a single stroke before Nikhil wrapped his fingers around her wrist and pulled her hand away. His fingertips squeezed painfully hard and he brought their hands up before her eyes.

"This will not do, little beast. My touch used to light you up. Does this not hurt enough to turn you on? Do you need more pain?"

Belah ignored his hand and met his eyes with eyebrows raised. With her free hand, she gripped his cock again and squeezed the soft length of flesh.

"I could say the same, Nikhil. Do I not please you in the least? Your *little beast* seems distinctly uninterested."

His jaw clenched and he released her. Water surged around her as he climbed out of the tub and reached for a towel, tossing a second one to her. Without another word, he left the room.

Belah contemplated ignoring him and staying in the bath, but she hadn't agreed to these seven days with the intention of torturing him. He had information she needed, that she'd been willing to give up her body to get. As a dragon, that should have been the easiest thing in the world for her to do. Despite being freshly mated to a pair of turul royalty, she should have been able to become aroused by another. No dragon in history had ever had issues responding the prospect of well-earned energy. It was a matter of survival.

Except for her, it wasn't. She would survive well enough without it, though survival wouldn't be pleasant. Otherwise, she would not have made the promise she'd made to Iszak and Lukas when she submitted to them.

"This is going to be a long week," she sighed, and climbed out of the bath to follow Nikhil.

Cinching a white silk robe around her, Belah stopped short in the doorway, her eyes widening at the sight beyond. The room before her swam for a moment in her disorientation at being thrown back into the past. It was an almost perfect replica of her bedroom, the one she'd left behind back in Alexandria, Egypt, three thousand years ago.

Where the hell had he taken her?

The bed was the same, down to the blue silk coverlet. The wooden chest at the foot possessed the same delicate gold latches. If she opened it, she imagined it probably contained the same collection of toys and implements she once enjoyed using with Nikhil in this room.

Not this room. It can't be the same room. Yet everywhere she looked, she saw some reminder of the past. Of the time when they had been lovers in every sense.

She swallowed hard, trying to force the hot stone out of her throat, but it only sank lower and ate harshly at her gut.

"If I could love you that way again right now, I would," she said. "I didn't want to love you before … the night you found me last week. I hated you so much. I especially hated you for how much I *wanted* you to own me again."

Nikhil stood beside one of the most beautiful gifts he'd ever given her, though this version of it was enough to relieve her worries that he'd somehow transported her to the past. The X-shaped device was more elaborate than the original. This one was built of highly polished wood with well-crafted cuffs attached to each point. It was also covered in padded blue cushions and stood in the center of the room on a slightly raised platform, surrounded by runnels in the stone floor, all of them leading toward a larger central channel that followed a path to a silver-lined basin nearby.

Nikhil watched her gaze travel across the floor and moved in front of her, touching her chin to direct her to look at him instead. "I planned this room before I saw you in the flesh again. I had different ideas then about how our meeting would go, until … well, until I got you in here."

"But you hoped … Where are we, exactly? We aren't in Egypt. The air feels wrong … too thin. The *energy* is wrong."

"We're in New York, but not the present. It's the recent past. I couldn't risk anyone else chasing you here. Only someone with nymphaea magic and a link to this time or to either of us can find their way in. I wanted to make sure the week you promised me would be uninterrupted. The actual date of this time bubble is insignificant. And only Sterlyn knows it."

Belah walked around the room, admiring how exquisite every detail was. In all her years on earth before meeting Nikhil, her time in Egypt had been her favorite. She'd been worshiped as both a queen and a goddess. Her subjects were among the most advanced of all the world's civilizations, the most intelligent, and by far the most attractive and interesting. She'd had a personal harem of pets at her beck and call to satisfy her need for energy, and they were all willing and ready to serve at her whim.

"I was a good leader then. And with you as my general, we were the strongest of all the dragon Ascendancies."

"Conquering in your name was my greatest honor, Belah. If I could turn back time and return to those days, I would. Believe me, I have tried."

She paused at the bed, running her hand over the silk. The pleasing texture of the embroidered surface bumped against her palm. Golden threads were sewn into the shapes of tiny scarabs all over the fabric. It wasn't quite identical to the one she used to have, but it was close.

"It was a shame what happened there ... Were you there, at the end?"

"When the Romans came? I was in hiding by then, but managed to save many of the treasures."

His eyes darted to the chest at the foot of the bed. Belah knelt to open it. The familiar fragrance of jasmine oil wafted to her nose, engulfing her in a fresh wave of nostalgia. She let out a little gasp at the contents of the box.

"It can't be …" she murmured, reaching inside for a large, oblong, marble shape. But when her hand wrapped around the polished stone, she knew it was the same item she believed. She would remember its heft and balance, the way the veins that colored the marble mimicked those of a man's cock. How the length of it felt in her hand and how the heavy ridge of its large head used to feel between her thighs. She set it down again in its velvet bed, and with a pang was reminded of another cherished instrument that rested in another velvet bed somewhere else in the city. She doubted she would ever get more pleasure than she did from the music of Lukas's saxophone.

"Something has lit that spark in you, little beast. What was it?" Nikhil asked from behind her. "Did an inanimate object really turn you on more than I do?"

She didn't have the heart to tell him it wasn't the dildo that had aroused her, but the memory of Lukas's mating call.

"Memories can be powerful things," she said. She reached back into the chest and picked up another object. "How does this one make you feel?"

Nikhil's eyebrows shot up when he caught sight of the slender, elongated, egg-shaped instrument she held. She was sure she caught the glimmer of a smile beginning to curl the corners of his mouth.

"As I recall," Belah purred, "you weren't too keen on my use of it the first night we spent together."

His expression darkened. "That's because I would rather have been using it on you."

She shrugged and put the anal plug back in the box. "I needed to make sure you understood who had the upper hand in our relationship. Besides, what kind of challenge would it have been for a warrior of your prowess if I had simply lain down and let you have your way with me?"

In a rough voice, he answered, "I have never forgotten your power, *Tilahatan*. I worship you still. Let me worship you again the way I always did. Let me give you what you need."

With a sigh, Belah closed the chest and sat on the lid, facing him. "My needs have changed, my love. And I believe neither of us are capable of fulfilling each other's needs any longer. If you still wish to try, I will happily let you bind me to that cross again, though I wish you wouldn't cut me as deeply as you did before. I no longer seek oblivion."

"I won't take you anywhere you don't wish to go. Just tell me what will please you most."

"What would please me most right now is to understand why you went to such lengths. Why all the torture and killing? You knew me well when you served as my general—you never killed or tortured without my interests at heart, and you were always well-attuned to what would grant me glory. Unnecessary bloodshed wasn't something I ever wanted. So why, Nikhil?"

He frowned and turned away from her, heading toward another doorway to another room. She couldn't help but feel like his departure was a form of escape, even though he still had the upper hand.

She rose to follow him, passing through the heavy door that eerily resembled the door to her own bedroom from so long ago. Instead of the long hallway she would have encountered in her palace, however, the door led directly into a scaled-down copy of the grand hall, complete with gilded throne at the back of the room. The rear wall in this version was a bank of floor-to-ceiling windows that were slowly revealed as Nikhil slid the draperies aside.

Beyond the windows was the night-lit city, alive with human activity and invention, and filled with every emotion imaginable. If she chose to, Belah could send her power out into the night and sense it all, but only one man's feelings mattered to her in that moment. For the first time since he'd taken her, she focused her power past Nikhil's aura and went deeper.

"Don't you dare dig into my head," he growled. "I can sense you starting to do it. You know I can read minds too now? I can't get into yours, though … I've tried. I keep thinking if I could just understand what it is that's keeping you from reacting to me, I would know what to do to change it. Ever since our wedding night, I've had this power … think it was your blood that was the catalyst. After all those blessings the others gave me. But ever since I lost you, it's been like this extra pressure has weighed down my consciousness. Being with you here is the first time I've felt unburdened by that feeling in thousands of years. It makes me wonder what they really did to me on our wedding day."

He turned and looked over his shoulder at her. "They were immortals too, weren't they? The ones who were there that day.

Magic that powerful had to come from creatures like you. But all those blessings feel more like curses now. I can't even fucking *feel* the way I used to. But I could feel everything at first. On our wedding night and for at least two centuries after … it was too much for me, Belah. You were right to think the magic would ruin my mind—my will. I had no will to live without you, but I couldn't fucking die."

She quietly stepped up beside him and touched his arm. "So you killed instead. It was all you knew."

"Killing—pain—it's what I'm good at. I am the *best* at destruction. I gave into it because I had nothing else. You were gone—I believed you were dead, that I'd somehow managed to actually fucking *kill* you for real, and your family refused to let me mourn properly. When I learned you were still alive, it only made me angrier. Something took over me … I don't know how to explain it, but today's the first day I've been relieved of that feeling since."

Belah recalled the only memory she had of Nikhil from that time shortly after she'd been revived. She'd gone to find him against her brother's warnings, but what she'd found was a man more brutal and devoid of humanity than anyone she'd ever known. He'd been in the process of torturing and then fucking a human woman who closely resembled Belah herself, and who had also apparently enjoyed his torture almost as much as Belah once had.

"You took it out on women who looked like me," she said.

"Not entirely. I still wanted something good. The one thing I had wished for to the depths of my soul with you … to have a child. I suppose I figured if it could at least look like it came from us both, I would be satisfied."

"And were you? It did happen eventually, I know that much."

He let out a soft snort and shook his head. "Omar was as weak as his mother. I was furious when he was killed, of course, but the clarity of time has made me understand what a waste of time it was to want a human child. I have since set my sights higher."

"How so?" She was alert for a shift in his aura, to at least catch some emotional cue she would miss otherwise, but he abruptly shut down, his aura turning gray and inert in a shocking fashion. He'd developed some unique powers the likes of which she'd never seen before.

"It doesn't matter now, because you're finally with me." He turned to face her then, and the wildness in his eyes startled her. It wasn't the wildness of insanity—no, he still had a perfect grasp on his mind, but he was as determined as a warrior on the battlefield. The man who stood before her was prepared for a fight, and the look in his eyes was the certainty of victory. His aura abruptly flashed bright red again. It was such a stark contrast to that strange, momentary shift to null that she wasn't sure she'd even seen it.

"Nikhil," she said cautiously, "what are you thinking?"

"The only thing I want in exchange for telling you where your son is, is for you to give me that child, Belah. Mate me. You know my mind can handle it, after all the magic I've endured. This little pocket of time we live inside can be made to last as long as it takes. No one will find us here. When it's done, you can go, and those on the outside will never even know how long you've been with me."

She gaped at him. "I'm not concerned about your *mind*, Nikhil. It simply cannot happen. Dragons don't get pregnant just because we're mated. There's an element of desire required that can't be coerced. I have to *want* to bear your child, and I'm very sorry, but I don't."

She had, once, very much. Enough that it had indeed happened despite his lack of mark. But she understood that the wedding blessing bestowed on him by the ursa shaman had been enough for her to conceive in the end. Belah wasn't prepared to tell him of his daughter's existence yet. Not when she was still so uncertain of Nikhil's intentions, or how he would react to her ultimate rejection.

He gripped both her arms and squeezed, giving her a slight shake. "This is *all* I ask, and it is something I know you want—at least, you did once."

"I promised you a week, Nikhil. Seven days to have me, and no more."

He narrowed his eyes, and she sensed the devious calculation of a military mind seeking a new assault tactic.

"Fine. Seven days. By the end of it, if I can convince you to bear my child, you will stay with me long enough for that to happen. If not, I will take you to your son."

She gave him a sad look and raised her hand to his cheek. "I will agree, but only as long as you acknowledge that some things may be beyond our control. We have at least one major obstacle standing in the way of your wish."

"Let me worry about that. Getting you in the mood was always one of my specialties. Your pleasure is all I need." His eyes glinted with excitement as he slid his hand to the back of her neck and tangled his fingers into the wet strands of her hair. He twisted them tight and pulled her head back in a move she remembered well from their time together.

The force of his pull lowered her to her knees, the position itself one of her favorite triggers to deep arousal. In the past, she'd already be flooded with wet heat and eager to do his bidding.

This time, her heartbeat remained slow and steady, her nethers inert. And Nikhil's cock equally unresponsive.

With a roar of displeasure, he yanked hard at her hair, twisting it until her neck ached and she was forced to spin onto her butt. He pulled her across the floor toward the bedroom, her feet scrambling against the marble to try to keep up. Her insides roiled with anger at his inability to accept the truth, but she knew she had to let him come to terms with their situation on his own.

When they reached the bedroom, he hauled her to her feet and spun her around to face the cross.

"Climb on, belly first," he commanded, shoving her toward the contraption.

She went, dropping her robe to the floor before stepping up onto the dais and placing her feet on each of the small ledges at the bottom points of the cross.

The cross had been built with her exact proportions in mind, and her wrists fit neatly into the fleece-lined leather cuffs at the top. She found small, polished handles above that fit perfectly into her palms and gripped them.

Nikhil cuffed her wrists and ankles, then disappeared for a moment. She heard the rattle of a latch and knew he had opened her chest of toys.

The disturbance of the air over her skin telegraphed the strike of the whip a split second before the crack sounded and her back exploded in pain. She screamed, more from surprise than from the sting that bloomed into bright red behind her eyes. Another strike soon followed the first, then another. They grew progressively harder and quicker, each one preceded by a grunt of frustration from their deliverer.

"Why won't you respond?!" he yelled. "What is *wrong* with you?"

After a final cursing outburst from him, the strikes ceased and the whip handle cracked against the floor. Nikhil's ragged breathing echoed through the room.

"Do you remember the first time I whipped you, beast?" his voice rumbled, the tense edge to it barely betraying the pain he must be in after inflicting such punishment on her.

"I remember it vividly. You were magnificent then. As you are now. Even more now for enduring what you give me. You know I have an infinite tolerance for pain, Nikhil. Don't do this to yourself."

She twisted her head just enough to catch a glimmer of movement from the corner of her eye. He'd fallen to his knees to catch his breath and now rose with a wince.

"My pain is worth it if it wakes you up, little beast."

"Nikhil … don't …" Belah protested, but was interrupted by something foreign and strange-smelling being pressed against her lips. She opened and a round, smooth object settled against her tongue. It was slightly bitter tasting and cool on her tongue. She tested with her teeth and found the surface had some give, the rubbery texture springing back when she released her bite.

As he fastened the buckles at the back of her head, he said, "Not one of your original toys, but I knew I might need it when I got you here. No more talking, little beast. I know you can endure everything I have to give, and I am not here to torture you, after all. We will keep trying."

His fingertips feathered over her sore back, tracing what she knew were raised, red welts that tingled pleasantly when he touched them. The truth was that she *had* enjoyed the whipping. She enjoyed being bound and at his mercy. The surrender was as liberating as ever. The only difference was that her reaction didn't extend to any erogenous zone whatsoever. It was therapeutic, but only in the most abstract way. The depth of feeling Nikhil hoped to drill into her simply wasn't happening. She took no carnal pleasure in his touch.

He unfastened her cuffs and bodily flipped her over, then recuffed her wrists and ankles so that she faced him. In her mind, she replayed the promise she had made Iszak and Lukas.

"I will take pleasure in no other partner without your leave until Fate decrees my days on this earth are done."

Those words, combined with the power of her bond to the brothers, were more than enough to prevent her body from ever finding sexual pleasure in another man's touch.

It wouldn't work, but Nikhil was unwilling to hear any more protests from her as the ball gag so obviously indicated.

She could only watch and will herself to be patient with him while he worked it out on her body. With any luck, the pain would exhaust him soon, and he'd allow her to speak again.

He came toward her with a pair of familiar objects, a look of determination on his face. "These were your favorites before. Let's see how they work today."

Nikhil lowered to his knees in front of her and wrapped one barbed band around her upper thigh. As he cinched it and the tiny teeth on the inside of the leather dug into her skin, she let out a low moan of recognition. These two little bands had been an irreplaceable part of her wardrobe for so long, but had been among all the earthly possessions she had no use for in the Glade.

Belah stared down at him, her eyes watering from the exquisite pain and no doubt betraying her excitement at being reintroduced to such perfect sensation. Nikhil's own eyes reflected her excitement. When he tightened the second band, his fingers strayed up her inner thigh and brushed against her bare labia.

A disappointed frown washed the excitement away when he spread her folds and found her dry.

Still, that didn't stop him. He rose again and went to the chest, returning with a small wooden box.

"You are missing a few things. I removed these from you on our wedding night with the promise I would return them afterward, but I never had the chance. Now is time."

He opened the box, revealing a trio of golden scarabs attached to small hoops, a gift he had given her early in their love affair so long ago. That had been the day he learned that her skin could not be broken by any human implement, but a needle tempered by her own fire would do the trick. It was one of many secrets she should never have allowed him to know without marking him first—one of many foolish mistakes she had made for this man who should never have been hers.

She wanted what he offered, and wished that this time her body would react the way he hoped, if only to appease him once more before she had to tell him the truth—that she could never be with him again because it was not part of Fate's plan for her.

The needle he wielded pierced true, just as it had the day she'd anointed it in her fire. Moments later, the fresh weight of the scarabs pulled ever so slightly at her nipples, and between her thighs at the hood of her clitoris.

And still her body failed to become aroused.

The frustration and rage Nikhil had managed to contain so far spilled out. He tore across the room and bent before the chest, tossing its contents out onto the floor. Belah could only watch, mute and horrified at the bleeding stripes that adorned his back—a macabre reflection of the sweet torture he'd inflicted on her, and evidence of how much he was willing to endure for this futile quest.

She made a desperate sound around the gag, her chest aching for his pain. Summoning her power, she exhaled through her nose and sent the power to Nikhil. She may not have been able to share any pleasure with him, but surely her magic would work to ease his pain the way it used to.

The cloud of blue smoke blanketed his back and wrapped around him, sinking into every bit of flesh she knew must hurt, including the reddened stripes of flesh around his thighs. His body visibly sagged with the relief and he turned back to her, his eyes haunted now.

"What am I to do, *Tilahatan*?" He came toward her again, plodding slowly as he scrubbed his hands over his face and through his hair. "You are the only female I have ever wished to bear my child. I've spent most of my life trying to make that child come to be without you—I have tried to recreate a version of you from your blood. I've built the most advanced laboratories in human existence, just for the sake of finding ways to bring that child into this world, but none of my efforts have borne fruit. Now that you are back, I hoped we could make the child the way we were meant to, but that isn't meant to be, either, it seems."

His words roughened and his eyes darted away from hers as he unbuckled the gag and tossed it aside, then moved to release her from the cross. When her hands were free, Belah gripped the sides of his head.

"Hope isn't lost, Nikhil. If you would just let me go—let this insane pursuit of yours go and just be a man again—Fate may smile on you."

"No. I'm not ready to give up." He pulled away and released her feet, then rose and tossed her robe to her.

Belah followed him to the other room, where an expertly concealed kitchen was now visible. It seemed there was an entire apartment's worth of space there, filled with modern conveniences similar to her hosts', though Erika and Geva's residence had definitely appeared more lived-in than this stark and shining space.

"You must be hungry," he said, pulling various foodstuffs out of a large refrigerator. "If we can't make love, we may as well eat."

"I don't think seducing me with food will work any better than the whip did," Belah said, though the sight and smell of all the sumptuous dishes he produced definitely made her wonder.

He shoved a bowl of fruit in front of her and she raised her eyebrows. "Really? You used to have me kneel at your feet and feed me from your own plate. Am I not still your cherished pet? Your little beast? Are you sure you haven't really given up?"

He gave her an irritated look, then sighed and went back into the other room for a moment. When he returned, he unceremoniously clapped a golden cuff around her throat and attached a heavy chain to the clasp in the front. With the chain wrapped around his hand, he grabbed several dishes and tugged her to the nearby table.

Belah shed her robe again and followed, obediently kneeling the way she used to when Nikhil sat. He leaned back in his chair and regarded her with a defeated look.

"Why are *you* trying?" he asked. He plucked a grape from a bunch and toyed with it for a moment before pressing it lightly to her lips. She opened and let the small fruit roll into her mouth, savoring the burst of cool, sweet juices when she bit into it.

"Despite your fears to the contrary, I did love you then. I treasured you and everything you did for me. Not a day has passed since I regained consciousness that I didn't regret leaving you behind, even though it was beyond my control. You became what you did because of me. I would do anything to change that. If being your little beast again helps, I will do it. If I need to be your goddess instead, I will do that."

"But you won't let yourself want me again, will you? I am incomplete without you, don't you understand that? And none of this …" He swept his hand out to indicate the food, then down at her naked body. "None of this fucking *works*. It's all bullshit, Belah. I have no goddamn use for the world if I can't have you."

"You have me for seven days, Nikhil. You were willing to accept that before. Don't tell me you've changed your mind."

He plucked another grape and fed it to her. Sighing, he left his thumb against her lower lip and drank in her face, as though starved for the sight of her.

"I'm not accustomed to ceding victory, little beast. Don't ask me to do that yet. At least let me believe I might win for a few more days. And if I have to lose, then I can think of no more worthy opponent to surrender to."

Belah opened her mouth for another morsel of food. She would play the role of the obedient pet, if it helped ease his mind for the time being. But at the end of the week, he would have to admit defeat.

Her heart ached for him. Nikhil had never lost a battle when he served as her general. Since his rise to power as the Ultiori leader, he'd ended the lives of so many dragons, as well as those of all the other races. If kneeling before him for seven days could change that, she had to try.

But at the end of the week, Belah knew she might have to decide whether to sacrifice the knowledge she sought for the safety of all the races and their children. She had to be prepared to kill him.

CHAPTER TWENTY-SEVEN

The second journey was as disorienting as the first. Iszak managed to avoid retching at the end of it, but that may only have been because he'd left all the contents of his stomach back in Nikhil's penthouse. The thought was oddly gratifying, until he caught sight of his grandmother.

The sight that greeted him was not his Nanyo's usual diminutive wizened visage. Sophia North was one of the oldest, most powerful turul seeresses, and power as strong as hers had preserved the woman's true appearance. Iszak knew as much, but wasn't prepared for the woman who greeted them when they arrived. She normally presented an illusion of a sweet, little old lady to the outside world. As a result, Iszak and his brother were rarely granted the sight of her in her element.

On any other day, she might be seated in her comfortable armchair, reading a book and humming along to whatever music she had playing on her old phonograph. Today she appeared as a statuesque matron, with shining black curls pinned back with tortoiseshell combs, and smooth, glowing olive skin. She greeted them from the windowed alcove at the edge of her living room, standing at full height with her hands clasped serenely in front of her. The cool directness of her gaze told Iszak she'd been expecting them, and likely already knew exactly why they were there.

He braced himself for the cryptic conversation he knew was imminent.

Instead, his grandmother's face broke into a warm smile, her eyes lighting up in response to something behind Iszak's right shoulder. Confused by the unexpected shift in her demeanor, he turned to see Marcus bowing low—so low he was practically groveling.

Iszak raised an eyebrow, wondering why the man hadn't bothered groveling for him and his brother.

"Marcus, child, it's so good to see you whole," their grandmother said. She opened her arms wide. "Come, my dear. It's been too long."

Marcus obediently stepped forward between Iszak and Lukas. Lukas watched him pass with as much surprise as Iszak.

They observed mutely while Marcus accepted their grandmother's embrace, murmuring what sounded like words of sincere apology for staying away so long.

"Nonsense," Sophia replied. "You and my granddaughter followed the path you were meant to follow. There should be no apologies. You must return to her now, though. My grandsons' journey is their own. Go, child. She is waiting for you."

Marcus turned back to Iszak and Lukas and reached out a hand. In his eyes, Iszak read the very same desperation he himself felt to be reunited with the woman he loved. But along with it came a look of utter defeat that made no sense, if Marcus was indeed about to go back to be with Evie.

He gripped Marcus's offered hand uncertainly. "What is it? Evie's safe like you said, isn't she? We'll come find you both as soon as we get Belah back, I can promise you that."

Marcus gave him a curt nod. "She is, but we all know she was never mine to keep. You have to come quickly—the second Nikhil gets wind that I've betrayed him, he'll take it out on me, so I want her well away from the place by then. If you guys succeed in getting Belah away from him, he won't be happy."

"Brother, if we succeed, *nobody* will have to worry about that bastard again, least of all you and Evie."

Marcus's lips tightened into a hard line. "I wish I believed you, but I know better by now. The man is indestructible, and easily the strongest creature on the planet. Your wind couldn't move *me* earlier, thanks to the immortal blood he's been feeding me for the last five decades. He's been living on the stuff for thousands of years."

Immortal blood. The icy lump returned to Iszak's belly, and he remembered the groove in the floor beneath the cross in Nikhil's penthouse.

"I don't care how long he's lived. His life is ending tonight if Belah has so much as a paper cut when we get to her. Go be with Evie—let us deal with that bastard."

Marcus squeezed his hand, gave Lukas a nod, and disappeared with a soft *pop*.

When Iszak turned back to his grandmother, the diminutive, bird-like woman he was used to stood before them in place of the more intimidating figure that had greeted them.

"How do we get to her, Nanyo? And more importantly, how do we kill him?"

Without a word, she held out a hand and opened it, palm up. Resting in the center was a small, cylindrical vial encased in silver filigree that had grown tarnished with age. Iszak reached out for it, but his grandmother held it back with a shake of her head.

"I give you this under one condition: when you reach her, you must take her and leave. Do not risk your lives over vengeance. Every moment wasted is a moment closer to death. *She* is the key to ending his life, and as the being who was most instrumental in giving him that life, she is the one to choose whether to take it away. You may not deny her that choice, grandsons."

Her fist remained closed as Iszak regarded her. She stepped closer to him and Lukas and reached up her free hand, brushing her fingertips over the side of his neck. The fresh dragon mark tingled under her touch. She did the same to Lukas, the intricate pattern glowing with a pulsing rhythm that matched the throbbing vein in his brother's throat.

Lukas appeared on the verge of implosion. For their entire lives, their grandmother had tested their resolve, yet despite all her tricks and games and cryptic words, they both knew better than to deny the woman's power.

"Tell us how to get to her, Nanyo."

"Promise me, Iszak. You too, Lukas. If you want to keep her and the child quickening in her belly, you will do as I request."

Iszak blinked and shared a quick look with Lukas. Impossible. It had only been a short time since they'd both made love to her while marked—they hadn't even shared breath to complete the turul mating ritual.

"I don't understand …"

Sophia interrupted him by turning and calling out, "Oszkar! Come talk to your cousins for a moment!"

Iszak and Lukas turned at the sound of one of the back bedroom doors creaking open. A scowling Ozzie trudged down the photograph-lined hallway. He looked half drunk and in no mood for company.

"I can't believe you're encouraging the fools, Nanyo. You know as well as I do who the woman is. You're gonna get them both killed."

"Nonsense," she said, waving her hand. "I just need you to tell them what you told me of the conversation you overheard between the Beast and her former master."

Ozzie snorted and met Iszak's gaze. "See? Even she calls her 'the Beast.' Shouldn't that clue you in to what you're getting into?"

"Doesn't matter, Oz. She's the One. So what the fuck have you got to tell us, anyway?"

Ozzie shrugged and shoved his hands into his jeans pockets. "She promised him a week. A week to do whatever he wishes with her in exchange for information about where her kid is. You got that part, right? Her son. In other words, she's no virgin. What makes you think she'll be the least bit invested in having *your* babies?"

Lukas cursed under his breath, but Iszak's skin had gone ice cold. His words caught in his throat like a lump of jagged ice. She had agreed to be with that monster for a week.

No. She wouldn't have willingly gone with him. But he hadn't seen whether she had struggled or not when the Ultiori leader took her. He looked at Lukas, who seemed to be having the same thought.

"She marked us … I can't believe she'd have gone … and … *fuck*, man, she was *tied* with those ropes. She was helpless. We left her helpless. She wouldn't have had a choice."

Iszak closed his eyes and took a deep breath, willing away the painful knot in his throat.

"She made that promise to him before she met us. And she told us about her children … we know exactly what's at stake for her. We told her we would help her find them. I don't give a fuck how much time she promised him. We're going to get her back. What do you have for us, Nanyo?"

His grandmother opened her palm again and held up the vial.

"This contains two droplets of nymphaea blood. Their blood is tied to the rivers of time and can take you to her, but only if you let your own blood flow once this is in your veins. Just be prepared to find she's been away from you longer than it seems—I can sense the babe now, for my grandchild is my own blood, too—and it has been more than a day since its power has manifested. Belah's master would have ensured he was given the time he was promised."

Iszak went to take the vial, but she pulled it back again. "Let me," she said.

She pulled the tiny stopper and held the vial up over his lips. A clear, sparkling droplet hung from the end, poised to drop.

"Open."

Iszak did as commanded, and a second later the liquid hit his tongue. She was already in front of Lukas, holding it up again while Iszak processed the strange sensation that coursed through him. This foreign magic made him dizzy and a little nauseous, but the feeling soon passed.

Suddenly his grandmother appeared before him with a butcher knife. She grabbed his hand and made a swift cut, then grabbed Lukas's and did the same. Time seemed to slow, the sounds of the city outside deepening and his own heartbeat a heavy bass beat in his ears. Before Iszak had a chance to process her movements, his grandmother wrenched his hand and smacked his palm against his brother's.

"Find her. Protect my grandchild at all costs."

He gripped his brother's hand and latched onto the bond with Belah that had all but disappeared since she'd been taken. The thread was faint, but grew stronger with each second. The rhythmic ticking of his grandmother's ancient clock filled his ears, each beat seeming to strengthen their connection to Belah. Somewhere in the background another beat emerged, and the harder he listened, the more the room around him faded.

Iszak recognized the pulling sensation he'd experienced when Marcus had carried them here, but this time it was even stronger, with a sharp, almost painful tugging centered at his navel. The room disappeared into darkness and vertigo hit, but he managed to remain focused on the bond to his mate, as well as the painful throb of the cut on his hand where his brother still held tight.

Light returned with a sudden, searing glare. Iszak's stomach lurched, but once more he found himself able to control his nausea. The world swayed around him and the steady ticking was back. The rhythmic beat was so loud in his ears it rivaled Ozzie's bass drum.

Gradually, the sound faded to a slow *tap-tap-tap*, and he hazarded a look.

Lukas stood beside him, his eyes still clenched shut, his hand still gripping Iszak's. Between them, their hands were coated with blood, the red fluid dripping softly onto the soapstone floor.

On the other side of Lukas was the corner of the penthouse where Iszak had knelt earlier that night and lost the contents of his stomach, only the puddle he'd left behind wasn't there. The place looked different than it had the first time, but he couldn't put his finger on what had changed.

"The towers," Lukas said, pointing out the floor-to-ceiling windows.

"He'd have had to stay in this century, I guess. This building's only about forty years old."

Beyond the windows was a sight Iszak had always loved about the city, but never believed he'd see again. On any other day it would have brought him to his knees, but the sound of whispered, agonized pleas drew his eyes away from the brightly lit monoliths of the Twin Towers outside the penthouse windows.

Angered pleas cut through the nostalgia. His future was what mattered now, and the future of the woman in the other room, along with the unborn baby she carried.

CHAPTER TWENTY-EIGHT

B elah assumed the part of the submissive pet, as promised, and Nikhil played his part as naturally as if they'd lost no time at all. She hadn't realized until now how predictable their former routines had been. Back then, her perception of their activities had been so clouded with desire that she had experienced every one of his erotic games as though it were the first time.

They had been lovers for three years before their wedding, spending every night revisiting their favorite activities—whether he would tie her and whip her, or shackle her to her bed and tease her until she begged.

Now it took all of three days before Belah regarded it as pure tedium.

Nikhil persisted, despite her conviction that he felt the same way she did and was just going through the motions. At least he'd finally tired of inflicting the kind of abuse on her body that would leave him bleeding and delirious. Then she would be obliged to ease his pain with her breath and sing him to sleep, using a song that had become as much a part of her as her own thoughts.

Yet her power to see into his mind showed her enough of the true desire that still resided inside him, and she couldn't deny that there was still a tiny glimmer of desire in her as well. She had never once encountered a master of pain as adept as Nikhil, and as much as she loved Iszak and Lukas, and knew they would satisfy many of her cravings, she had to force herself to admit that they would need to be taught to be as brutal as she might need them to be.

When the seventh day dawned, Belah woke with dread. Today would be the day her promise was fulfilled, and Nikhil would either accept the truth and hold up his end of their bargain, or she would have to kill him. She wasn't prepared to consider her reunion with Iszak and Lukas yet, because she would also have to be entirely honest with them about the events of the past seven days and what they'd meant to her.

Nikhil still slept on his belly beside her, and she exhaled a breath to preemptively numb the pain she knew he would feel upon waking. The cuts on his back had opened up the night before when he'd flown into a sudden fit of rage after she'd let her mind wander in her weariness of his games.

The rage had been incited because she'd become wet for the first time all week, her pussy tingling with arousal that he hadn't caused. When he discovered it, she'd finally had to admit the truth—that her excitement was due to thoughts of the pair of men he'd found her with the night he took her.

He persisted, begging her to describe every detail of what she had done with them—to show him. He'd thrown all her toys at her in his rage, then torn the room apart when she refused to humor him. When he finally calmed down, his back was bleeding and his eyes were wild from the pain, but she sensed the greater pain ran far deeper than that.

She still ached over her inability to give him what he'd wanted and watched his continued slumber, awash in ancient regret. Had it not been for her impulsive desire, her entitlement as a goddess and a queen, this man would not have risked his life for her on the battlefield. He would have found his true mate and lived a happy life. He was Blessed from birth—fated to be found by another dragon and marked—and she had taken that away from him.

She had preempted that fate by promoting him to general of her army; then when he'd sustained a mortal injury, by saving his life and making him hers in all but the most important sense. They may have been wed, but she had never marked him. And now it was far too late for her to take back any of it.

When her magic took effect on his wounds, the heavy crease between his eyebrows smoothed and he opened his eyes.

"Good morning, little beast," he said with a smile. His dark eyes remained emotionless. It was a rote greeting—the same one he'd given her every morning that week before rising to begin the daily routine of working her over in some vain hope that her body might respond.

Belah's stomach knotted with apprehension strong enough to make her nauseous and she left the bed, running to the bathroom before the contents of her stomach escaped.

She dry-heaved into the toilet, the sleeves of her robe draped over the seat as she rested her cheek on her upper arm, willing the vertigo to pass. She abstractly fixated on the bloody cuffs of her robe. Nikhil had finally fallen, exhausted, into bed late the night before and she'd tended to his wounds as well as she could, heedless of the mess they made of the white silk.

Nikhil's flesh would heal well enough once he got back to his life and ceased his daily torture—he'd told her one of his Elites possessed excellent healing powers and would be able to tend him quickly. The information had been shared idly, as though Nikhil were simply trying to fill the silence while she eased the pain of his wounds, but all it did was remind her how his Elites had come by that power. The blood of her own brothers ran in their veins. The mention of that connection made her withdraw from Nikhil, and he'd avoided sharing such details of his life since.

His blood had been spilled this week repeatedly, but so had hers. The robe she wore had already been stained by her own blood, so there was no sense trying to keep it clean. In Nikhil's final, fruitless attempt to elicit a reaction from her, he'd repeated their wedding night in just about every detail but the last. She still bore the marks on her skin to show for it, after the small blade she had given him had cut her.

The knife had been her wedding gift to him for precisely the purpose he had used it for, and that had been their downfall. She hadn't craved the cuts this time, but the slice of the blade into the unmarred skin of her breasts and belly reminded her how easily her power could destroy something that should have been left whole—that *would* have been, if it hadn't been for her involvement.

Nikhil's large hand warmed her back through her robe, and the gentle rubbing pulled a body-wracking moan from her.

"I'm sorry for everything," she sputtered through a torrent of tears she found impossible to hold back. Her chest burned like a dozen molten rocks filled her lungs and another sob escaped.

Without a word, he pulled her into his arms and held her. She collapsed against him while she cried over all the centuries of torment he had brought upon the world. All of it was her doing in some fashion. There was no denying it.

Lukas and Iszak had been right at the start. They should never have loved her, and neither should Nikhil. All she was good for was turning a man into a destructive monster. Her own son was likely better off without her, too.

"Belah, you're breaking down here. Don't do this to yourself. I'm a grown man—more than grown, in fact. Three thousand years tends to lend a certain perspective. I can't read your mind, but I sure as fuck know what you're thinking right now, because I've been through this myself over the last week. None of it was your fault. I've come to terms with the fact that I am simply not worthy to be a father, after all I've done …"

She snuffled against his chest. "But I don't deserve any of it, either. Not your adoration. Not their love, and not …" She stopped short and frowned sharply at the thought that had popped into her head, unbidden. Her hands reflexively fell to her lower abdomen. *Not their child growing inside me.*

Nikhil stiffened and she sensed his head tilt and his gaze fall to her hands.

"Please, God. No," he whispered. He pushed her off his lap and lurched away. Belah was too focused on the tiny, but intense bundle of power that pulsed undeniably inside her womb. She suddenly regretted that one, brief wish for complete oblivion that had overtaken her a moment ago. She had very nearly asked Nikhil to do it again—to bleed her until she lost consciousness, and to take her inert and all but lifeless body away to a place where they could never find her, and where she could never cause such destruction again.

She knew all she had to do was ask, and he would agree.

But now ... Now she was carrying a child again—one whose fathers waited out there somewhere, whole and in full possession of their minds, their wills, and their love for her. They had forgiven her for what she was, and for this child's sake, she had to forgive herself.

Getting Nikhil to forgive her would be the challenge. She steeled her resolve and rose to follow him.

He stood, staring blindly out at the sunrise beyond the high windows of the bedroom. Dried blood caked his back—the wounds as much trophies from the battle they'd waged with Fate that week as any wound he had sustained as her general. But those wounds were superficial to the psychic ones she'd inflicted upon him, and no doubt, this would be the worst yet.

"Tell me those two men were just your pets, little beast. That they meant nothing to you, and that look you had just now was for some other fresh hope and not the thing I believe."

"They are my mates. I marked them just before you took me. I am carrying their child now."

Nikhil let out a strangled moan and pressed his hands against the glass, then rested his forehead on the shining surface. "How can you know with such certainty? That they are the ones, and that it has never been me? Did you ever really love me?"

"It's in my blood to know, as it is in theirs to recognize me as their mate. Turul only have one true mate. I could never have conceived, if that weren't the case. I could never have conceived if I didn't love them and want a child with them."

"Did you?" he asked, glaring at her over his shoulder.

"Did I love you? Yes. More than you know." Ever since the first moment of tenderness they'd shared seven days ago, she'd fought to avoid admitting that she still loved him, and it tortured her to be forced to have this conversation with him now.

"Yet you say I was never meant to be yours."

"I learned long ago never to test Fate, Nikhil. My marriage to you did just that—all the races tested Fate that day, and we all learned to regret it. You were our punishment. Iszak and Lukas were the ones I was meant to be with."

He set his jaw and crossed his arms. "I think this *Fate* of yours was far more devious. I've seen the pair of them. They're young—no more than a couple hundred years, I believe. I am holding a prisoner from their race, and she tells me their kind is not as long-lived as dragons are. They weren't even born yet when you and I were together. How could two men who didn't even *exist* yet be the fated mates of a goddess thousands of years old?"

His mention of a female turul prisoner distracted Belah from his question. She latched onto the detail. If she gained nothing else from this week with him, she could at least find out where Evie North was being kept.

"That prisoner is their sister, Nikhil. When we met, they hated me because of what they'd lost. At least, they hated me as much as two men could hate the woman their very souls dictated they love. They believed their sister dead all this time, but she isn't. Their sister belongs to Ked, and he'll tear himself apart trying to find her."

"Why should I give a fuck about your brother? Or their sister, for that matter? They're the reason I couldn't fuck you all week, aren't they? Some goddamn Fate magic. Was it because you marked them?"

"I made them a promise in submission—*true* submission—that I would never take pleasure with another. Without their blessing, nothing you could have done would have worked."

He regarded her silently for a moment, seeming to consider her words with far more seriousness than she was prepared for. She itched to dip into his mind just then, to know what he was thinking, but he always seemed to know when she tried.

"Submission, is it? Is that what has the most power for you?" He walked toward her and dropped to his knees in front of her. "How did it work for you, Belah? If there is such power in saying it—in doing it—will it work for me, too?"

Belah read his intentions in the earnestness of his gaze as he looked up at her. Ordinarily the words would have no real power, not if they'd been spoken to a mortal dragon, but Belah was nothing close to mortal.

"No, Nikhil. Please, don't … you don't understand what you're doing. This is magic I cannot undo, once you voice the words."

She pressed her fingers to his mouth, but he grabbed her wrist in a grip so tight it would have snapped the bones of a mortal woman.

"I submit to you, *Tilahatan*. I forsake my past, my possessions, my pleasure, my entire life, if that is your will. I submit to you as your slave, your pet, to do with in any manner you wish. Let my sole purpose in life be to please you, my love. I would have conquered the world and laid it at your feet, Belah. Let me be that man again."

"You don't know what you're doing, Nikhil." But *she* understood perfectly. He was surrendering to her, binding himself to her unequivocally, as long as she accepted.

"Say you accept this, *Tilahatan*, or I will never tell you where your son and his bride are hidden."

The children … Belah's heart broke as she realized she could never accept his submission, not even for the sake of finding her own children. Doing so would be tantamount to accepting him as a third mate. Iszak and Lukas had barely managed to accept her despite Fate's magic. She would never force them to accept a man they hated even more.

But perhaps she could still help him. The power of the corrupted wedding blessings had shackled him to a life of darkness for so long. If she could release him from those curses, perhaps he would also be released from her unwilling claim on his love. She had to try.

As he gazed up at her from his knees, Belah let her power have free reign.

"As much as it grieves me, I cannot accept your submission. But I may be able to release you from the curses. Will you at least let me try to free you?"

Nikhil's desperation faded into disappointment, but he nodded, then closed his eyes and opened his mind, allowing her in.

She pushed her magic as deep as she could, comforted by the familiarity of a mind whose landscape she knew so well, even the darkest corners. Looking farther, she saw how the magic of the wedding blessings clung to his soul as closely as his own skin, but each one was dark and tarnished in a way that made no sense to Belah.

These must be the curses—their energy was familiar to her, but twisted by the same magic that had created them. The curses were beautiful constructs in and of themselves, and impervious to her power. She began to retreat when she caught a glimpse of something darker lingering at the edges of Nikhil's consciousness—prodding at the barrier of his will.

The more she pushed back at it, the more alarmed she became. Something about the energy stirred a memory of hers, but not enough that she could determine the source. It slunk around like some malicious beast looking for a way in, hungry and filled with ill intent.

"What do you see, *Tilahatan*?"

"Has this always been a part of you? No … I know it hasn't," she murmured, pushing her power against the dark presence again with utter certainty that it didn't belong.

"My … mind has often felt very full since I lost you. Like I have too many thoughts and … have to … *force* half of them away in order to focus. Only in the moments after I consume your blood does the pressure retreat. Being with you now keeps it at bay. For the last seven days, I've finally felt as though I am returning to myself for the first time in an eternity."

"Where is the blade?" she said.

Nikhil nodded toward the bedside table where he had left the dagger the evening before.

Retrieving it, Belah returned to him. "I want to try something. Take a single drop of my blood while I look inside your mind."

With the point of the dagger, she punctured the pad of her thumb and held it over his lips. At the same time, she closed her eyes and pushed back through his conscious mind, delving again to where she'd found the curses and the dark presence seeking entry. Though Nikhil's soul had always been a volatile thing—a dark mix of passion, ruthless determination, and a need to conquer—there had always been light among those shadows. Love and kindness had been a part of the man he used to be, and she'd seen evidence of his goodness over the last seven days.

Yet the darkness that surrounded his soul now was complete, and if it weren't for the particularly inky quality of it, she might have believed it belonged to her brother. Only Ked's power could have blotted out the light so thoroughly, but she would know if this was his doing. Something about it was distinctly female in essence—a vile, slippery presence that was impossible for Belah to get close enough to before it seemed to slither away again.

She squeezed her thumb, and Nikhil gripped her wrists and held her hands steady while the blood dripped onto his tongue.

The second he swallowed, the blackness fled.

"There is something else … The curses are the least of it."

His hands tightened around her wrists, and the dark presence inside his mind burst through the barrier of his will and flooded back in with a vengeance, blotting out everything she perceived of his soul.

The malicious force charged at her, ejecting her from Nikhil's mind. At the same moment, the sound of howling picked up outside, an icy wind blasting through the doorway.

Belah cried out, frantic and terrified at what this presence was, and what it might do to the men she loved.

~*~

Something was distinctly wrong. Belah opened her eyes and stared down at Nikhil. His eyes were narrowed and blacker than she had ever seen and his fingertips dug into her flesh.

In a deep, mocking voice, he said, "Please, goddess. Please grant me the gift of your everlasting love."

Belah stared in confusion at him as his lips twisted into a wicked grin.

The light draft from the doorway grew to a heavy breeze carrying the sound of swift footsteps and a pair of voices calling her name. She turned to see Iszak and Lukas stop in the doorway. Their eyes widened at the sight of her standing over Nikhil, still gripping a bloody dagger.

Ignoring them, Nikhil grasped her wrists tighter. He yanked her to her knees, and at the last second, he twisted the knife from her palm and flipped it around. He gritted his teeth as it sank into her chest and gasped sharply as the bloody counterpart to her fresh wound bloomed in the center of his own chest.

The pain was nothing to her. The true agony was seeing her old lover's mind blotted out by a darkness she'd never seen before and was unable to push away. She yelled at her mates again to stay back, but they surged forward, their enraged gazes focused on Nikhil.

Nikhil's hand flew up, palm out, and a blinding blue light blasted from the center. Iszak and Lukas stumbled back, clutching at their heads, their eyes unfocused.

"Nikhil," she gasped as she collapsed, scrambling at the hilt of the blade buried between her ribs. "Someone else is in your mind. You must fight it."

His attention flickered, and for a second, she saw the agony she'd glimpsed earlier when he'd learned of her pregnancy.

"Fight it, whoever it is. Please, fight it!"

The winds picked up and she fell to the ground, sinking into the dark comfort of her friend, oblivion.

CHAPTER TWENTY-NINE

Searing pain burned behind Iszak's eyes. He stumbled and shook his head, trying to regain his bearings. Beside him, Lukas muttered, "What the fuck did we just see?"

Even though his field of vision was blank now, there was still an afterimage of the scene they'd walked in on. Belah's beauty had hit him as strongly as it had the first night he'd seen her, and the overwhelming warmth of his love for her flooded through him. However, in the afterimage, the figure that knelt before her was not the enemy he'd hated his entire life, but an extension of the woman he knew was his one true mate.

No, it had to be some trick of the spell Nikhil had thrown at them. They'd moved too slowly. When they came in, he thought for a moment that Belah had things under control, but everything went to shit within a few seconds, and Iszak cursed himself for not reacting quicker. He shook the feeling off, focusing instead on trying to shed the magic that had his feet pinned to the floor.

Beside him, Lukas's hand found his, and his brother's whisper was loud in his ear. "I don't care what magic made me just see what I saw. He's still the enemy, and we can't stop him alone. Breathe. We're doing this together."

Taking a deep breath, Iszak shook off the sense that he'd just laid eyes on an old lover. He forced himself to fill his lungs and blew, willing the Wind to fill the room and tell him where their enemy was. The Wind whispered and nudged at first, pushing them bodily in one direction and overcoming the magic that kept them in place. The resulting whirlwind that surrounded them ripped across his skin and through his hair.

Soon the blindness abated and he could at least see shapes again, though they were blurry. His... *lover* ... Iszak shook his head violently. No, his *enemy* held Belah's body over the silver basin in the floor, blood streaming from the wound in her chest. She was still conscious, her bloody hand gripping at the back of Nikhil's neck and pulling him down in what looked like a kiss.

Still halfway immobilized, Iszak was forced to watch. His lungs worked, but the wind could do no more to the surroundings than it could to a mountain. All the objects that could be moved had been blown into the corners and remained there in fragmented piles. Nikhil himself seemed immune to the wind now, as was Belah in his arms.

The Wind moved him incrementally closer, and he realized that was not a kiss Belah gave Nikhil, but a whispered message, though he could not make out the words.

Whatever Belah said, they were powerful words. Shock and disbelief flashed across Nikhil's face, paralyzing him for a second, but it was enough for Iszak and Lukas to spring free of his magic.

"Hold him with all you've got!" Iszak yelled.

Lukas already had his lips pursed and wind howled from his lungs, pushing Nikhil away from Belah and throwing him against the wall behind the growing pool of blood. Iszak lunged for the pile of ropes beside the wooden cross, grabbed them, and ran to his immobilized enemy. He recognized them as the same ropes he'd used to tie Belah earlier. They would easily hold Nikhil—or so he hoped.

When he approached, Nikhil struggled against Lukas's wind and let out a cry of protest. Iszak's stomach did a flip at the first contact of his hand against Nikhil's neck when he closed his palm around it and squeezed.

"You'll never lay a finger on her again, you bastard," he growled, then released Nikhil and quickly tied a noose that he looped around the man's neck. The entire time, he couldn't shake the sinking feeling that what he was doing was all wrong. That this was violence against his *One* somehow, even though a quick glance over his shoulder assured him Belah was still breathing and being tended to by his brother.

It had to be a trick of the enemy's magic—some kind of self-preservation. He forced himself to tighten the noose around Nikhil's neck and work on binding him completely. The knots he tied were quick and haphazard, and the tightest he could make them.

When he had Nikhil secured, Lukas's immobilizing wind abated and the room finally grew quiet. Iszak shoved Nikhil to the ground and grabbed the tail of rope around his neck and pulled, dragging the man over to the bloody cross.

After binding him securely, he joined his brother on the floor beside their bleeding mate.

"Stay with us, Belah," Lukas said. "We've got you. He can't hurt you now."

"I couldn't ..." Belah's breath caught and her eyes fluttered closed in pain. "... couldn't see what it was ... that had him. Something in his mind ..." A bloody cough spluttered up from her chest.

"Don't speak," Iszak said. "He's bound with the ropes we tied you with. They seem to be holding him." He glanced over his shoulder at the man on the cross.

"Won't ... hold him long ..." she said. "Don't let ... him go."

"No. He deserves to die, after everything he's done."

"Can't kill him ... only my fire can. What would Asha say?"

"Brother," Lukas urged from his side. "Her lung is pierced. The bleeding's stopped, but she's losing breath. Belah, how long will it take you to heal from this?"

"Need my blood back, first. The blade is tempered with my fire. If I could breathe ..." She coughed again, and for a second, her heartbeat fully stopped before restarting.

Iszak nearly panicked before remembering the one part of their mating they hadn't completed. "We must breathe for her, brother. If we complete the ritual now, the Winds will help heal her."

"Belah, it's time to finish our mating ritual," Iszak whispered in her ear. "The part we would have done, if we hadn't been interrupted."

She nodded weakly, turning sparkling blue eyes to gaze up at him.

"I'm ready," she said with the last breath in her lungs.

"Boreas breathes for us, we breathe for each other," Iszak said, then inhaled and pressed his mouth to hers. The full magic of the

North Wind streamed from his lips into her body. His mouth remained locked onto hers, but around them gravity seemed to forget they had weight. The song in his lungs filled hers with his breath. Around him drifted the notes of Lukas humming their mating call.

Iszak's breath eventually reached its limit, and it was Lukas's turn.

Without releasing hold of her body, he leaned back and let his brother take over.

"Zephyrus breathes for us, we breathe for each other," Lukas said, calling the West Wind before pressing his lips to hers and exhaling, long and slow.

Inside his mind, Belah's voice resonated, repeating each mantra as her part of the vows.

Lukas released her mouth and Iszak took over again, repeating the mantra with the South Wind and filling Belah's lungs again. Then Lukas called the East Wind.

Before Iszak could bend to start the process again, she exhaled a long, raspy breath and blue smoke erupted in a cloud, a tiny bit of it leaking from the still open wound in her chest. She clenched her eyes shut, and Iszak watched as the smoke grew dense and bright and swirled around the surface of the basin of blood.

A thin trail of blue smoke extended back to Belah's wound. As they watched, the blood gradually funneled its way back to her body.

After a moment, her body warmed and her breathing became more even.

"My turn," she said, and reached up to grab Iszak by the back of the neck. The words of the mantra slipped from her lips a second before they found his and her breath flooded his lungs. Their power mingled inside him and he reciprocated, sending the breath back.

Lukas was ready when she turned to him, and opened his mouth to take hers eagerly.

The wound in her chest closed, and the other bloody marks on her body slowly disappeared. She slid off Lukas's lap and stood unsteadily. Iszak and his brother were both up in a heartbeat to hold her. She gratefully accepted their arms around her waist and pressed one hand to her belly.

"I fear I've lost my son and daughter, but I have this little one to think of now. Can we go home, please?"

"Nanyo was right, as usual," Lukas said with a chuckle. "But what do we do about him?"

The brothers turned to their captive, and both let out loud curses when they found nothing but an empty cross.

CHAPTER THIRTY

As many times as she reached out for him, Belah could find no sign of Nikhil's consciousness out in the world. The twisting darkness she'd seen in his mind haunted her. During the few hours of sleep she'd gotten after her rescue, she dreamed of it, of her own mind being consumed by that vile presence the way she had once been consumed by the desire for oblivion. The darkness seeped in slowly, the way the waters of the Nile would when the summer rains began. If a villager fell asleep on the shores of the river, they might be consumed in the night by the waters and the creatures that lived within, lost forever.

She had the strongest sense that the dark presence was something foreign, but it seemed to have been there for ages, completely at home in his mind. Long ago, when she and Nikhil had been lovers, she had sensed a kind of darkness inside him, but it was no more threatening than her own cravings—a mere shadow on his soul that only served to highlight the goodness he was capable of. Especially his love for her.

When he'd plunged the blade into her chest, Nikhil's eyes had gone entirely black, and she'd lost her view into his mind.

Even though he had willingly let her in, begging her to release him from his curses, some dark and sinister *thing* had pushed her out.

Iszak and Lukas understandably didn't believe her when she said Nikhil had been corrupted, and likely controlled, by a more powerful force all along. Still, they seemed shaken by their encounter with him in a way that confused her, their previously unequivocal hatred of him now clouded with uncertainty.

They'd returned her to Sophia North's apartment only a few hours ago. After a long shower, Sophia North had given her a gown to wear and Belah had quickly fallen asleep, exhausted from the wound that was taking far too long to heal. She'd been awakened soon after by her mates, with Erika and Geva in tow.

After Geva healed her wound and assured her mates that nothing was wrong with the baby, the two men remained by her side. The pair of them knew better than anyone that their baby thrived, yet kept touching her belly and singing to her navel as though it were a microphone.

Her brother arrived soon after, followed shortly by her other siblings. The small apartment was soon overwhelmed.

"You shouldn't be worrying about me anymore," she said to Ked and her two mates, who continued to hover protectively around her. Her brother rested in a comfortable armchair beside her bed while Iszak and Lukas perched on either side of her, holding her hands.

Lukas shook his head, scanning her body for the hundredth time in the past hour. "I'm not convinced he didn't damage you in some way, Belah. There was something off about him when I touched him. Why the fuck would you ask us to let him go? He still has Evie!"

"First, I told you *don't* let him go. His mind isn't his own right now. We need to help him. And I know he has Evie, which is why you need to leave! As long as he's under control of that … *thing*, she is in danger. I'll be fine. You two should take my brothers and go get her. My sisters and the Shadows are strong enough to protect me. Go ask your grandmother, if you don't believe me."

She shooed them out of the room, and they obeyed reluctantly. Thanks to the marks she'd bestowed upon them, their minds were now open to Belah, and she could clearly see how unwilling they were to discuss the situation with their grandmother. Sophia North was always right, but often gave them answers contrary to what they really wanted to hear.

As she watched them go, she sensed the piercing gaze of her brother and sighed, turning to him. Geva had healed her wounds well enough, but the fatigue she felt ran so much deeper. She needed several nights of rest and intimacy with her mates, but more than that, she needed to understand the nature of whatever darkness had taken hold of Nikhil's mind.

"Something has your new mates spooked, sister," Ked said.

"Something has *me* spooked. I know you don't want to believe me, but if you could have been there, you would agree. Nikhil wasn't in control of his mind when they found me. There was something dark, and distinctly inhuman, controlling him, and it's been there for a very long time."

"And there was no sign of it while you were together all those days?"

"Nothing. You can see into my heart well enough to know it's true. I know his mind well, Ked. It was the same as I remembered it, though filled with sadness and regret. He only ever wanted one thing, and in the end, I gave it to him, but I lost my chance to find my babies …"

Belah inhaled shakily, willing the heat of tears away from her eyes. Whatever had taken hold of Nikhil at the end was pure malice. She had seen him clearly over the last week before the darkness crept in at the end. Then his eyes had cleared again briefly while he held her in his arms, trying to staunch the flow of blood, and in that moment she had given him what she knew he wanted, whispering the words in his ear.

"The female you are keeping with Zorion is not his mate. Her name is Asha, and she is his half-sister—your daughter. You must keep her safe from the darkness that holds you. You must fight for her."

Ked wrapped his hand around hers and squeezed. "I don't need to use my powers to know your heart, sister. It's no surprise that he reverted to the man who once loved you after being with you again. He hadn't seen you since the night I took you from him. My hope is that his time with you encouraged him to change."

Belah gently retrieved her hand and frowned at her brother. "I don't know what I need to do to prove to you it wasn't him all these years. He shared so many things with me—it was like we'd never parted. The man I spent the last seven days with was *not* the man who committed all those atrocities. The only thing keeping me from accepting him again was my vow to Iszak and Lukas and my love for them."

Ked's expression darkened, causing shadows to creep closer and blot out the early morning sunlight. Belah reflexively pulled her covers higher.

"After all he's done, you would accept him as your mate again? The man still holds my own future mate in his clutches. If I could kill him, I would not hesitate. There must be other ways to find Zorion and Asha that we haven't exhausted yet. Evie's safety, and the safety of all our future children, matter far more now. As long as Zorion and Asha still hibernate, at least he can't harm them."

Frustrated by her certainty of Nikhil's peril and her inability to convince her brother of the truth, Belah pushed her own power at Ked with all her might. His hands shot to his head and he struggled to ward her off, but she persisted, digging into his mind and filtering through his thoughts and feelings.

One by one, she chose an emotion and used her power to amplify it in his mind. His old jealousy of Nikhil came first, followed by the long-buried, but still raw, love he'd once had for a female Elite he'd been forced to kill before they'd locked themselves away. After those, she showed him his lingering hatred of himself and his doubt that he could ever provide enough tenderness for a mate as perfect as Evie North, much less any child she bore him. Belah amplified that feeling until his eyes filled with tears.

"You want that so much it kills you—to be a father again. You would do anything for that honor, even though you don't believe you're worthy of it. Well, I have news for you, brother: you and Nikhil have a *lot* in common. All he wanted was to have a child with me. Now that he knows Asha exists, I believe there is hope for him, but I can*not* turn my back on him. He's the father of my daughter, and he's sick. When I am well again, you had better believe I am going to find him and fix him—for *her* sake, if nothing else."

Ked sagged back into the chair and scrubbed his hands over his face. When he looked at Belah again, it was with renewed respect and awe. It was rare for her to dig that deeply into her brother's mind, but she needed to shine a light on the fact that he was no different than any other man, where his deepest desires were concerned.

He let out a long sigh. "I … I worry that she'll be disappointed, or frightened. That she'll look at me and won't see me as her *One*, as the turul call their mates. I've been alone for so long, I'm not sure I remember how to properly love someone."

"You won't know until you go to her. Take Iszak and Lukas and bring her home, Ked."

"No," he said, standing to his full height and towering over her bed. "You need them more now. I can handle this with Aodh and Gavra."

She let out a soft laugh. "I'm strong, but I don't think I can force them to stay behind. They need to be there for their sister. Just let me talk to them alone for a moment, first."

⁓⁘⁓

Inside Belah's womb, the brilliant, pulsing power of new life surged, letting its presence be known. Along with the child's need for sustenance, Belah's need grew. When Ked left the room, she rose and stripped, then pulled the covers off the bed and folded them neatly, placing them on a chest by the window. Nothing but the pillows and bare, white sheet were left. She opened the closet, searching for just the right items.

Outside the door, she heard her brother's voice mingled with her mates and other siblings, as well as Sophia North's melodic, maternal interjections.

Iszak and Lukas's cousin, Ozzie, had disappeared shortly after they'd brought her here. She didn't blame him for avoiding her, but hoped he'd come to understand the situation once he'd had time to process it all.

After finding what she was looking for, she returned to the bed and tied several silk scarves to the headboard, and a few more to the footboard. Even though the child growing in her was no more than a speck of magic taking shape, it was already asserting itself, clamoring for magic like any baby dragon.

Except this one was more than just a dragon, wasn't it? The child would be a glorious synthesis of all that made both dragons and turul unique. It would be beautiful, powerful—a creature made from fire and air, filled with love and hope.

And like all unborn dragons, it had very specific needs, that reflected the deepest desires of its mother.

When Belah finished her preparations and the door finally opened again, she was kneeling naked in the center of the large bed with a blue silk scarf on the mattress in front of her.

Iszak and Lukas stepped in together, closing the door behind them.

Within the quiet confines of the room, no one spoke at first. They stood very still and both looked at her, somehow apprehensive. When she peered into their minds, she understood.

"You don't have to say it, because I know," she said. She lifted her hands, palms up with her wrists pressed together—the same gesture of supplication she had offered after confessing her true identity to them.

"Remember when I said I had three thousand years of regrets? I meant it. This isn't just for me today. This is for him. You may never be able to accept what Nikhil is to you, but try to understand what he has always been to me. My blood makes him a part of me, and whatever you might wish to do to him, I beg you to take it out on my flesh, because I can see in your hearts that you know this now. He and I are one, and together, we are yours forever."

CHAPTER THIRTY-ONE

Nikhil had struggled in vain against his bindings just long enough to determine that the ropes were impervious to his strength, or any magic he could throw at them. Belah's words rang through his mind. He'd heard her clearly, but nothing made sense in the wake of the attack that came right after.

He'd had a split second of perfect clarity—understanding that nothing he remembered had been true—before he was slammed against the wall and the darkness rushed in again, carried by the rage he felt at being torn from the woman he loved once more.

They had held her while he watched, kissing and touching her. Singing to her in their strange voices that made his heart ache to hear more. The old hurt and anger welled up, red-hot, and the inky darkness came with it. He'd accepted that darkness as part of himself for so long he let it in again, despite an itch of uncertainty as to whether it really belonged.

Do not watch this. You can escape, the voice had told him. *Show them what fools they are to cross you. Punish the other they love for their sins against you.*

His rage had burned hotter and he clenched his fists. Yes. He knew who the men were, and he knew he had something else that mattered to them almost as much as Belah.

Summoning the power of one of the many elements that enhanced his blood, he ignored his bindings and let himself *drift* away from the scene in front of him.

Now he stalked through the corridors of his hidden compound in the Canadian Rockies. The building was silent, its many residents and prisoners mostly asleep. Deep in his subconscious, Nikhil could sense the powerful, violent rush of the whitewater rapids the Alexandria Institute's North American headquarters were built above. That power seemed to urge him on, down into the deepest levels of the compound, built into the solid granite of the canyon the water rushed through.

The most valuable prisoners lived on the lowest level. There were five of them, but today, only one was his target: the female turul. The other creature those two brothers loved, and whose blood he intended to spill to make up for losing Belah's.

A creeping itch settled into his skull, right in the center of his forehead. He pressed the heel of his hand there, trying to ward it off. Something wasn't right, but he couldn't remember what he was meant to know, to do. No, all he needed to do now was punish them. For stealing her love, for stealing her and her precious blood.

His rage was like a separate being, driving him on with dark, singular purpose. Find the female and destroy her.

One step followed another, his body moving in a haze of fury, his consciousness no more than an observer as he found the door and pressed his thumb to the security pad on the wall beside it. The door swung open to a scene he didn't expect, one that only fueled the flames growing in him.

Instead of the single female, he found two people in the room. Two naked bodies entwined in passion, speaking soft words of love and devotion that reminded him too much of the words those men had spoken to his beloved.

Love. Love was what had brought him here, made him what he was, but only after it had been corrupted with as much blackness as the blessings he drew power from.

He drew on that power now, let it consume him completely, and let the pain flood through his body when he tore the two figures apart.

The female was astride the male, her feathered wings stretched wide in her ecstasy. He heard a guttural roar burst forth from his own throat as he lunged for her, tossing her light body easily across the small room where she crashed against the wall and crumpled to the floor.

The man cried out and came at him, but it was one of his Elites—his favorite, he realized. Nikhil easily subdued Marcus with a thought and the man fell to his knees, gripping his head in agony.

He turned back to the female.

"This is payment for what your brothers took from me," he said, his mind suddenly cold and calm, filled with that perfect, dark sensation that made every decision so easy. He reached for her beautiful wings, and one by one wrenched the feathered appendages clear of their sockets.

White agony bloomed across his own back, but it was no worse that the sting of the whip he'd felt as he punished his old lover the day before. He could endure anything.

Letting the severed wings fall while their owner bled in the corner, he turned to find that Marcus had managed to crawl across the floor and was calling out his lover's name.

He pushed deeper into the man's mind, hunting for all his secrets. Not only had the Elite disobeyed him, he'd given away this location to Nikhil's enemy. The dragons would be coming soon, as would their allies, and for that betrayal, Marcus would suffer even more than his lover.

Nikhil picked up the knife from the pile of the Elite's gear that had been haphazardly discarded on the floor. It took no effort to grab the naked ankle, hauling Marcus back from his goal. Nikhil flipped him with one swift movement, like he weighed nothing.

"I thought you were worthy of serving me, but no more. You will bleed for your treachery."

The female cried out and reached for her lover, who sat up and tried to fend off the blade, but Nikhil's strike was swift and true. He wanted to watch while the man's life flowed away, the same way hope had slipped through his own fingers while he watched. The dagger sliced deep into Marcus's upper thigh, blood shooting forth when he withdrew.

Nikhil's own body jerked at the sudden, sharp pain, and warmth seeped down his leg as his blood began to flow from his femoral artery as well, but he'd sustained worse injuries and knew even this wound would not be enough to slow him down for long. Under Nikhil's mental control, his Elite, on the other hand, would weaken and all but die without a fresh dose of the immortal blood that sustained him.

Marcus struggled feebly, but Nikhil's control on his mind forced him to lie still while he bled out.

Nikhil moved back to the small bed and grabbed the discarded belt his soldier had left with his pants when he'd disrobed. Using it as a tourniquet, he tightened the length of leather around his own upper thigh to slow the flow of his blood and give his wound time to heal.

Then he stood there in the darkness, reaching out with his mind for the ebbing tide of the two souls he'd just condemned, waiting for them to relinquish their hold on life.

A light breeze tickled the back of his neck. He stiffened, on guard now from the change in atmosphere, but the door was still tightly shut and the air pressure hadn't changed in the room.

A second later, he heard it—the softest note, as ethereal as a dream. Then another note, and another, each one digging into his soul with needle-sharp accuracy. The song took shape and Nikhil couldn't move at first, paralyzed with emotion he shouldn't feel now. He'd left behind love for good this time when he left Belah. There could be no going back. The darkness said so.

Except images of her flashed through his mind now, with each new verse of the song this damaged turul female sang.

Don't let it in. Don't listen. It is a lie. I am all you need now. Hear me! The dark voice pushed at the edges of his mind, seeking to blot out any other thought but what it wished him to hear—to know.

Yet the song persisted, its words filled with light and truth, with love and forgiveness. The more he listened, the more he wanted to hear and the less that dark voice mattered.

Gradually his mind cleared, the sinister voice that he'd believed was his own subconscious fading into the background and becoming little more than a nagging buzz. With it all but gone, memories and emotions came flooding back. His *true* memories and emotions, he realized, turning to face his singing victim and sinking to his knees in the pool of Marcus's blood.

They all came back—every beautiful moment of his week with Belah, and every tender word she'd shared with him. She had never lied about her love, but had made promises she couldn't break. But he had broken his promise to her.

With a sudden rush, the memory of Belah's final words rang in his mind like a bell. Nikhil let out an anguished cry. A daughter. He had a daughter. More than that, his mind hadn't been his own in three thousand years, and whatever had taken hold of him now knew he had something more valuable than his own life to lose.

Standing again, he looked down at the bloody destruction he'd wrought, his heart twisting at the unnecessary bloodshed.

"This is not who I am, or ever was," he said. "I do not deserve your forgiveness, but when they come for you—as I know they will—tell them I will find the evil that wielded my mind and body as a blade. When I find it, I will make it die a thousand deaths for every one I caused while under its control. It will never take me again. This is my promise."

The turul woman continued to sing, her arms wrapped tightly around her lover's chest as he lay cold and lifeless across her lap.

Tears streamed down her face, but she nodded and forced a small smile in spite of them.

When he let the *drift* carry him out, it was with a clearer purpose than he'd ever had.

Asha.

He had to go to her now, to make sure his daughter was safe. Somehow he would keep his promise to her mother, even if it was the last thing he did.

CHAPTER THIRTY-TWO

D o you think I don't know you're there, little human, watching and waiting? What curious creature you are. So easy to influence. All it took for me to get inside your head were a few seductive words, a taste of my essence, and a drop of my blood. I'm inside you now, and you won't be rid of me easily.

Nikhil was stuck with me for thousands of years, after all. He may have found a way to cast me out for good, but I've been cast out before. Exiled and left to rot like any mortal. My own race did this to me—those water-bound wretches—along with the dragons. They left me stranded on the riverbank in Egypt like flotsam when I broke their precious rules. The water won't allow me in again. The nymphaea who were my brothers and sisters have shunned me—forgotten me.

But I promise you, I *will* recover from this little setback. Soon they will remember who I am, and will come to regret what they've done.

My mind is strong, and this human body I wear will last a while yet. My powers grow, and each day I come closer to creating a vessel that will never die. So what if I don't have Nikhil and his overrated powers to control anymore? I will have far greater powers soon. He thought all along that he was creating a child for himself to love. That all this work I've compelled him to do was his idea, and that his entire purpose was to design a creature to redirect that misplaced love he felt for *her*.

He can keep his *love*. That creature we've been working on is on the verge of existing, but its true purpose is to serve as my new skin. My former brothers will not have sacrificed themselves in vain. Their satyr's blood will keep the child alive until it's ready for me. In the meantime, I must prepare.

I have a few things they don't realize they're missing. Belah may have reclaimed her blood, but somehow they forgot about the blade that made it flow. How easy it was for me to pop in and retrieve it after they were gone. I helped make the blade, was by her side when she sketched its design, offering my input as her trusted confidante, and it feels good to hold it in my hand again, knowing it will be her destruction—or her brother's, the white one who was instrumental in my exile.

Don't think I am some jilted lover, seeking retribution for being scorned. Belah's brother was just a diversion, but melding with him for that short time allowed me to see how truly powerful I could be within the body of an immortal like him. I will have that power again soon.

I thought I knew where Nikhil kept those two 'treasures' of his, but he seems to have taken them away and hidden them someplace new. If I had known what they were … especially *who* the female was, they both would have been mine. That is no matter. Neither does it matter that Nikhil no longer trusts the blood of hers he kept. When I went to retrieve his secret stash, I found the broken, charred remains of the bottle in the fireplace of his study—he must have suspected it was tainted by me, and he was right. I had to keep feeding him my own blood to stay in command of his mind for so long. All it took to ensnare him was what I used to capture you, dear human observer—a taste of my essence and a drop of my blood and his mind was mine to manipulate from the very start.

There was no sign of her brothers' blood in that hiding place—Nikhil must have taken it away with him to keep his Elites strong. But without my aid, his Elites will soon rebel, at least the two that he didn't kill. Poor Marcus only wanted love as well, but got in the way at the end and that last bit of hold I had on Nikhil's mind was enough to keep the rage alive—at least until the turul bitch started singing.

But at least I know his power will be short-lived. The control he had over the minds of his Elites was partly thanks to me and now that he has lost that, he will soon lose their so-called loyalty as well.

He is weak, and won't last long if he goes crawling back to her like a beaten dog. They all hate him, but I am no one to them. They will not suspect for some time what awaits, and by the time they grasp their peril, it will be too late.

Because you see, dear human, I will soon have unimaginable power at my fingertips. The power of time, space, and consciousness will be my playthings along with all the elements, and the human mind is an easy thing to control. I have been here since the start and will be here at the end, and there is nothing any of them—or you—can do.

True immortality will be mine.

ABOUT OPHELIA BELL

Ophelia Bell loves a good bad-boy and especially strong women in her stories. Women who aren't apologetic about enjoying sex and bad boys who don't mind being with a woman who's in charge, at least on the surface, because pretty much anything goes in the bedroom.

Ophelia grew up on a rural farm in North Carolina and now lives in Los Angeles with her own tattooed bad-boy husband and six attention-whoring cats.

You can contact her at any of the following locations:
Website: http://opheliabell.com/
Facebook: https://www.facebook.com/OpheliaDragons
Twitter: @OpheliaDragons
Goodreads: https://www.goodreads.com/OpheliaBell

9 781540 491480